M000196083

THE

DEMON

SEEKERS

BOOK THREE

JOHN
SHORS

INTERNATIONALLY BESTSELLING AUTHOR OF *UNBOUND*

Published by Blackfin Books.

Cover design: Caroline Johnson

Interior formatting:
Mark Thomas / Coverness.com

THE

DEMON

SEEKERS

BOOK THREE

CHAPTER 1

Osaka, Japan
May 5, 2171

The submarine arrived at the port city of Osaka just before midnight. The moon, low on the horizon, joined the starlight and distant fires to faintly illuminate an eerie, surreal landscape. Most striking was the sight of vast container ships that lay on their sides, partially sunken and marooned. One vessel had settled straight down to the bottom, and its exposed top deck held hundreds of once-new cars, which stretched out in tidy lines. Beyond the ships, massive cranes rose skyward, frozen in time like the broken, skeletal fingers of a steel giant. Across the bay, a towering Ferris wheel tilted toward the water, as if eager to spin one final time. The city's buildings, set farther inland, served as mausoleums—each marking the resting place of the men and women who had once labored within them.

While she stood on the sub's conning tower, Tasia studied the sights before her, trying to ignore the dull ache of her wounded leg and burnt hands. She gripped her silver staff, her gaze rising to the sky and then falling to the city. Jerico stood next to her, with Rex at his side. He also held a staff, as did everyone else on the conning tower—Aki, Valeriya, and Trax. The companions stood in silence, aware that the darkness cloaked many dangers.

Trax lifted a two-way radio to his mouth and whispered orders to his second-in-command. The sub changed course, its speed slowing. At one point, a series of smaller ships had been moored to a nearby pier. But rising waters and the passage of a century had flooded the pier and sunk the boats. A red-beamed searchlight flickered to life in Trax's grasp and he appraised potential landing places. Clucking his tongue, he glanced to his left, then right, swinging the red beam to and fro.

"I radioed ahead," he said quietly, "and I do believe they'll be waiting for us. Just keep looking, my esteemed companions."

The submarine continued on its path, which ran parallel to the pier. Something metallic scraped the bottom of the sub and Trax winced, as if he'd cut his chin while shaving. The screech was loud and long. The sub's captain muttered to himself about the dangers of damaged propellers but made no course correction. He shined the red light into the water, swinging it back and forth, asking no one in particular why there wasn't a better place to land.

"There," Valeriya said, pointing her staff toward a distant group of horses. The red light swung to them, revealing about a dozen men and women on horseback, with at least as many mounts unencumbered by riders. All of the horses stood in water nearly up to their knees. A small man waved.

Trax whispered more commands into his two-way radio. The sub drifted toward the submerged pier, bumped into something, and then slowed to a stop. Crew members threw loops of rope over the few posts that stuck out above the water, pulling tight to secure the vessel. A narrow metal walkway appeared from belowdecks, carried by crew members. They swung it to the shore, its end resting a few inches underwater. Trax patted the steel of the conning tower, then rubbed his hand over it, as if caressing a lover. He gestured for Tasia to go ashore first, which she did, shuffling along the walkway into the water.

To her surprise, she recognized Ishaam, the scientist who had accompanied Draven from the Arctic Stronghold to Kyoto. Ishaam sat astride a grey stallion and shifted in his saddle. Though his rifle was slung over his shoulder, its barrel had swung downward, so that it pointed at the stallion's belly. Tasia hoped the gun's safety was switched on.

Nodding to Ishaam, Tasia waited for Aki, Valeriya, Jerico, and Rex to come ashore. Once they had, muted greetings were exchanged with their welcoming party. The companions each climbed atop a horse, settling into their saddles. Tasia had never ridden a horse and didn't know what to do with the reins that someone handed to her. Feeling vulnerable, she glanced at the sky, searching for demons. The moon was falling below the horizon and the darkness thickened.

Several riders turned on red-beamed flashlights. The horses began to head away from the sub, and Tasia was thrust back in her saddle when her mount decided to join the procession. She tried to catch Jerico's gaze, but he was busy calling to Rex, who whimpered repeatedly while wading forward in water that rose above his chest.

Moving ahead in the darkness, through black, debris-laden water was unsettling. Tasia was reminded of Manhattan—of when her family had rushed into the flooded city, trying to escape the demon that then killed her father. Though he had died only a few weeks earlier, that night seemed like a lifetime ago. She'd watched him slip away from her, then dropped from Stronghold to Stronghold, fallen in love, been captured, and finally escaped. Her journey was so convoluted, so full of highs and lows, that she was uncertain what to think of it. Reminding herself of the highs, she glanced again at Jerico, thought about the staffs they carried, and then took a slow, deep breath of salt-laden air. With a vast amount of luck and strength, the War for Earth would be won by the people around her.

The convoy of horses proceeded from the submerged pier to what might have been a road between several buildings. The land was still flooded, and the splashes of more than a hundred hooves sent a chill down Tasia's spine. If a demon were nearby, it would find them. And though their staffs would drive it away or kill it, someone would die first.

Rex was struggling in the deep water, and without a word, Jerico looked at Tasia, gave her his staff, and climbed down from his saddle. He whispered reassuringly to Rex before picking him up. As Rex licked his face, Jerico handed him to a mounted stranger, climbed up his own horse, and then the man passed Rex back over. Nodding, Jerico positioned Rex so that he lay draped over the saddle. Tasia then returned the staff to Jerico as he moved backward, going as far to the rear of the saddle as possible. Rex licked his free hand.

"He's worried about being left behind," Jerico said quietly. He scratched Rex's ears and rocked forward and backward until his snorting, unsettled horse lurched ahead. The rest of the group had continued on, and his mount, along with Tasia's, was a stone's throw behind.

"Maybe he misses the sub," Tasia replied.

Jerico nodded, then smiled. "I called him Captain Rex a few times. He seemed to like it."

"Well, he has that sort of … distinguished look about him. Just like Trax."

"Except Trax doesn't whimper in the dark."

"Or chase mice."

"Or growl at his own shadow."

Smiling, Tasia glanced at the sky. "The next time we're on a boat, let's just keep going. We'll find an empty beach and not even bother looking up. Because the demons will be gone."

Jerico started to respond but then stopped, as if he'd changed his mind about something.

Tasia wondered what he was going to say. She thought about asking him but didn't want to be intrusive. Maybe he didn't believe such a future could exist. Maybe he was thinking about losing her, about how the hate in the world seemed to outweigh the love.

"We'll find our beach," she finally added.

"I know," he replied, absently petting Rex. "I wasn't thinking about that. Actually, I was wondering if you were okay, if your smile was … real. You were alone for so long and you—"

"I'm fine. Don't worry."

"I hated imagining you alone with all those demons. That must have been terrible. You must have felt so helpless."

She thought about K'ail, then Ur'sol. "There were just two of them who … hurt me. One's dead. The other's probably close by. Somewhere out there."

Jerico's horse stumbled over an unseen obstacle and he nearly fell from his saddle. He winced, shifting Rex forward. "I never imagined vengeance would be something I thought about so much. But it is. I want to hurt them. Because they hurt you."

"I'm fine, Jerico. Really. Don't worry about me."

"I was so afraid I'd never see you again."

A horse neighed in the distance. The smell of rotting seaweed lingered in the still air—musty and pungent. Ahead, the red beams of flashlights swayed in different directions, as if playing some strange game of tag.

"I used to want revenge," Tasia said, still speaking quietly.

"Even a week ago. But when I was in that cell, something changed in me. And now I don't want to kill to avenge people. I want to kill to honor them, to try and make the world into the place they hoped it would be."

Jerico twisted in his saddle, looking at her. "That's a better way to see things."

"The demons hate us." She glanced up again, searching the sky, seeing the light of the stars and wondering how many millions of years it had taken to reach her eye. "But I don't want to be like them. I don't think we can win by being like them."

"So how do we fight them?"

"We fight for the people we love, not for the hate inside us."

Once again Jerico pulled Rex closer to him. "To be honest, it seems like you used to fight for the hate."

"I still hate the demons. I always will. But when I was imprisoned, and K'ail told me all about his hate for us, I saw how it blinded him to certain things. He couldn't see our strengths, couldn't understand how we thought or what we were trying to do. And I don't want to be like that. Because if I don't understand their strengths, I won't live long enough to help beat them."

A shooting star darted across the sky, born and dead within a single heartbeat.

"I never met your father," Jerico said, "but you told me how he looked for beauty in the world, and I think you're becoming more and more like him."

"Well, you've helped me look. You've reminded me what's out there."

"There's still so much more to see. And I want to see it with you."

Relaxing in her saddle, Tasia glanced again at the sky, searching the darkness for their foes. "Don't worry about me being gone for so long. You did something amazing. Something indescribable. You came from the other side of the world to save me, just like I knew you would. And even though they tried to hurt me, I think I had to be there—that I was meant to be there."

"Why?"

"Because I know how to destroy them now. Once and for all."

"But doesn't that make you a target? Won't they come for you?"

She gazed at the stars, thinking about K'ail. "He'll come. So we have to be ready. We have to always be ready."

"And we will be."

"He's one of the biggest demons I've ever seen. And he only has one eye. Fareed took his other."

"Fareed?"

"K'ail killed Fareed. Back by the train. But Fareed took his eye, and when he did that, he saved me. Because that's how I knew K'ail wasn't my friend, like he pretended, but the worst kind of enemy."

Jerico turned in his saddle, looking behind them. "Does he know about me? About us?"

"He knows I care about you. So when you see him, just run. Or hide. Because he understands that the cruelest thing he could do to me is to hurt you, so that's exactly what he'll try to do."

CHAPTER 2

K'ail had flown for most of the night. After reaching Japan, he'd rested for a short time atop an ancient temple. Hating the cool air, he had taken flight again, drifting over dead cities and overgrown rice fields. He'd seen several of his fellow gods, including a big female whom he hadn't encountered for years. Word had spread that the humans were about to place all the staffs together, summoning the gods' ship. And every god wanted to be present for its descent, for the final battle in the War for Earth.

K'ail had resisted most of the conversations that his fellow kind sought, though he'd entertained enough questions to realize that Tasia hadn't told any of the other gods that she had tricked him. Her decision pleased him, as he would have suffered endless humiliation if the gods knew how events had unfolded.

Now, as he neared Kyoto, K'ail was more aware than

ever that he'd need to forever silence Tasia, and he flew with determination. At one point he plunged from the sky toward a pair of humans who were planting seeds by candlelight in a somewhat hidden field. After feasting on them, K'ail continued onward, empowered by the taste of their blood and the memory of their screams. He hadn't let them die quickly.

Long ago, K'ail had concluded that humans experienced pain much more acutely than gods did. While K'ail could feel the strike of enemy, to him it was like a dull ache. To humans, a fresh wound was a terrible experience, often overwhelming them with agony, neutralizing any strength or courage they might have possessed.

Only Tasia had been different. And while K'ail had never torn her apart, had never listened to her screams, he was convinced that even pain wouldn't completely break her. She would somehow use agony to her advantage, hardening herself, just as she'd done with Ur'sol's torments. Tasia, K'ail believed, was a foe worth fighting—a mortal of course, but one who was beginning to understand the origins and extents of her power.

The big demon flew higher, wanting a good vantage point of Kyoto. The darkness didn't cloak the landscape from his keen eye. In the dim light present just before dawn, he saw a series of low green mountains that seemed to protect the wide valley beneath him. Then came a river that bisected a sprawling, dead city. Nondescript buildings dominated much of Kyoto's skyline, though a soot-covered tower pierced a collection of low clouds. Most of the city's once-revered temples had toppled over, and many looked to have burned down to the giant granite blocks that marked their ancient foundations. And yet several tiered temples and shrines still rose skyward, as if determined to resist the passage of time, thereby honoring the brilliance of their makers.

K'ail recalled the vast, legendary monuments of his home planet. He pitied the humans and their insignificant sanctuaries. They prayed to gods that they couldn't see or hear, prayed to imaginary beings that didn't even exist. K'ail's civilization had once been the same—so petty and trite. But then his kind had explored much of the universe and realized that they were the dominant species. At some point thereafter they began to think of themselves as gods because they ruled every other species—conquering some, enslaving others. Many were simply ignored.

Closing his good eye, K'ail projected his thoughts toward Tasia. *When you cross the universe, when you are the strongest of billions of species, you become a god. You acquire the right to decide the fate of countless civilizations.*

Tasia offered no reply.

Earth is wounded, Tasia. Yet soon your frail planet will be forever rid of the plague known as humanity. And after a hundred centuries have come and gone, very little shall remain to hint of your existence. What have you touched that will endure the cold passage of time? A stone? A shoreline? Because once you fall, your love will vanish. The love you hold so dear. That you claim gives you strength.

Once again, Tasia remained silent.

K'ail shrieked, then spotted a dark and distant train station and adjusted his course. Flapping his powerful wings, he sped up, wanting to present as difficult a target as possible in case a human sniper was below. Buildings blurred around him. The stale, cool air rushed past—a river of sound. With the grace of a hawk, K'ail landed on the train platform, memories flooding back into him. He recalled attacking the group of humans and charging toward them. The bearded man had surprised him with the sword, managing to take his eye. Yet even as the ache of the wound had spread within him, K'ail had realized his good fortune that the blade hadn't cut deeper, hadn't ended his life. Craving revenge, he'd then feasted on the mortal, ripping his flesh from his bones while he still lived.

The human's remains were where K'ail expected. Rodents must have picked his bones clean, because they were already somewhat bleached by the sun. K'ail walked over to them, remembering the man's face, as well as his screams. Wishing that he could have prolonged the mortal's suffering even more, K'ail stepped on his bones, snapping several.

Tasia had cared for the man. She had said as much. K'ail knew humans usually buried their dead and believed Tasia would want to honor his bones. And yet K'ail would possess them. He would use them to lure her into a trap of his making.

K'ail studied the train platform, looking for something with which to carry the bones. He spotted a stainless-steel bin next to an escalator, flew to it, ripped it from its moorings, and returned to the bones. With disdain he collected the small and shattered remnants of the man who had hurt him, dropping them into the bin. Soon only the mortal's skull remained on the ground. K'ail picked it up, studied it, held it over the bin, and crushed it between his talons. The skull shattered, pieces falling. K'ail opened his fist, releasing more fragments of bone, which fell like white grains of rice. The smallest bits were lifted up and borne away by the wind.

Extending his massive wings and gripping the bin against his chest, K'ail leapt from the ground, taking flight.

Soon he was once again high over the city. And as dawn broke, flooding the sky and land with tendrils of red and amber light, K'ail was reminded of his home planet. The memory pleased him. Soon he would be in the stars again, soaring through the universe where he belonged.

Kyoto drifted beneath him. Still thinking of the heat of his world, K'ail searched for the place where he would spring his trap, the spot of land where Tasia would scream, bleed, and then kneel before him.

CHAPTER 3

Midmorning had arrived by the time the companions reached the Stronghold of Kyoto. Though tired after their long journey, they dismounted from their horses and hurried underground. Aki and Valeriya left the group to visit Aki's family. Ishaam, so weary that he stumbled forward more than walked, led Tasia, Jerico, Trax, and Rex through the Stronghold, informing them that they'd been asked to attend a Council of Thirty-Three meeting. Though Tasia recalled Ishaam to be talkative, he seemed strangely withdrawn, as if something deep within him had broken.

While Tasia kept pace with Ishaam, she remembered what her parents had taught her about the Council of Thirty-Three. The group had been created almost a century earlier, after the power of the thirty-three staffs had been discovered. The council members numbered thirty-three, and governed the Strongholds as well as orchestrated all military strategy against the demons. Tasia had never been to a council meeting before. She didn't know what to expect but was certain they would ask about her imprisonment and her ideas for how to defeat the demons.

Jerico walked beside her, but even as Tasia spoke with him, her thoughts lingered on the Council. She needed to persuade its members to attack the demons in the manner that she wanted. Though he hadn't intended to, K'ail had shown her how to win. He'd told her too much because of his overconfidence. Yet Tasia worried that the men and women of the Council would be skeptical of her plans. They'd question her age and judgment. Worse, they might be timid when they needed to be strong.

Word must have spread throughout the Stronghold about Tasia's return with the staffs. Groups of people clapped and whistled as she walked past. Children stopped what they were doing to acknowledge her, running over to tug on her free hand, to jump up and down beside her. Tasia had rarely experienced the feeling of pride, but the deeper they moved into the Stronghold, the more boisterous the celebration became. She couldn't help but smile. For most of her life she'd tried to contribute to the fight against the demons, but she had failed more often than not. She hadn't been able to protect Calix or her father or Fareed, and she blamed herself for their deaths. But now, when she least expected it, people were cheering for her. Their enthusiasm was infectious, and she took Jerico's hand within her own, squeezing it tight.

Ishaam led them into a part of the Stronghold that she

hadn't visited. They walked past a series of glass offices, then approached four armed guards. The two men and two women stood in front of a pair of double doors. Tasia remembered then that the Council met in what had once been an underground movie theater. A century earlier, people had come here to watch stories unfold on giant, wide screens. Tasia had wondered about movies, never really understanding what they might entail. She found it hard to imagine sitting in a chair and watching people pretend to be heroes and villains and lovers. How could anyone in the audience believe them? Were they so good at imagining?

The doors were opened by the guards, and Ishaam led the group forward. The theater contained about forty rows of seats. A stage had been erected before the seats, and a large group of people sat around a diamond-shaped table that dominated the stage. As soon as Tasia entered the room, everyone went silent.

There was a pause, and then the members of the Council began to applaud. They stood up, facing the new arrivals, clapping enthusiastically.

Unsure what to do, Tasia nodded, holding her staff vertically with both hands.

An unusually tall, light-skinned man stood out among the council members. He had long white hair that seemed to merge into a beard of similar composition. Raising his right fist, he locked eyes with Tasia and gestured for her to come forward. She glanced at Jerico, squeezed his hand once again, and stepped toward the stage. A stairway led up to it, and she ascended toward the Council.

The tall man then asked Tasia to stand before them, pointing to a gap in the diamond-shaped table. At first she didn't understand what he wanted, but then realized that she was expected to move to the hollow center of the table. Stepping through the gap, she tried to slow her speeding heart. She didn't want to appear nervous, but was suddenly panicked by the thought of speaking to so many important people. Biting her lower lip, she tried to gather herself, to remember the pride she'd felt just moments earlier.

"Once I was a Guardian of the Staffs," the tall man told her, "so I understand the burden of what you carry—of all those heavens and hells. They call me Zeus."

Tasia nodded to him, curious as to why he was dressed in white pants and a white button-down shirt. She noticed that his left forearm was twisted awkwardly upwards. His wrist was bent downward, so that his left hand pressed against his shoulder. Thin and frail, his hand wasn't much more than a collection of bones wrapped in age-spotted skin.

"I'm Tasia," she finally replied, wondering if he had been wounded or born with the disfigurement.

"Speak up, child," he answered. "So that my old ears might better hear you."

She repeated her name and then looked at the men and women who encircled her. Though they seemed to represent every culture and background, most were far along in their years. Their faces were weathered and often scarred.

Zeus cleared his throat. "They let me do most of the talking," he said, smiling. "Not that I'm particularly skilled at it, but because I'm the oldest among us. You see—we honor the old here. We honor wisdom."

Suddenly self-conscious of her youth, Tasia nodded. "Then maybe I should just listen."

"They say, child, that you have quite a story to tell," Zeus replied. "We've been waiting to hear it."

"But it's so long. Where should I begin?"

"At the beginning, of course. Where else?"

Tasia glanced at Jerico, who sat next to Trax and Ishaam in the first row of the theater's chairs. Rex lay at Jerico's feet, oblivious to the proceedings. Nodding, Jerico encouraged her.

Tasia's gaze then drifted back to Zeus. She tried to forget about the other council members and pretended as if she were only speaking to him.

Still unsure of where to start, Tasia told the story of her capture and imprisonment. She spoke at length about her conversations with K'ail, of what he had revealed, as well as her own ideas for how to defeat the demons. Occasionally members of the Council asked questions, which she answered patiently. As she spoke her nervousness dissipated somewhat, though she felt increasingly weary.

"And you believed this ... K'ail," Zeus asked, "when it said that all the staffs, put together, would create an Orb? And that this Orb would summon the demons' ship?"

"I did."

"And maybe you were right to. And maybe not. Still, tell

us everything that damn demon said. It's far better for you to speak too much than too little."

She glanced from Zeus to Jerico to the other faces around her. "I believed K'ail then and I still do. Because the demons have been trying to collect all the staffs. But when that didn't work, or when it was too slow, K'ail wanted to trick me into bringing him here, so that he could get ours. Then he'd have put them all together and called his ship."

A bald, dark-skinned woman shook her head. "You spoke before about your desire to call their ship. But why would we bring it here? It would only destroy us."

"Because—"

"What you say doesn't make any sense," the woman interrupted.

Zeus held out his good hand. "Please, let the child continue. A bunch of fossils like us should know better than to be impatient."

Tasia looked from one face to the next, detecting both admiration and mistrust. She started to doubt her thoughts and plans, but then remembered her father's dying words about how she should embrace herself.

"What I said makes sense," she finally replied. "K'ail said I can drop from one Orb to whatever one I choose. He said I had that power. We've always thought the drops were random. But what if we could control them? Everything would change."

"How?" Zeus asked.

"Because we could unite all the staffs next to the Orb that's already in Kyoto. We could call their ship. And when it arrived, we could take the staffs and step into the other Orb. We'd drop where I wanted us to, and I could lead us into their ship because I'm sure it has an Orb in it. And then we could destroy it from the inside."

"She's insane," a heavyset man replied. "Utterly insane."

"But I could—"

"You have no idea what you could or couldn't do," the man interrupted. "And worse, maybe this demon corrupted your mind. Maybe it turned you against us."

"He didn't turn me against—"

"Maybe it wants you to call its ship in exactly the way you just described!"

Tasia took a half step toward the man. "No, that's not right."

"You have no idea what's right!"

"But I—"

The man slammed the palm of his hand against the table. "You simple child! You'd be doing its work for it! That demon lied to you about burning the Earth, about turning our planet into some kind of star. All it was trying to do was scare you into bringing the staffs together!"

Tasia again started to reply but stopped, biting her lower lip instead. Suddenly she was tired of standing in front of the Council. Her burnt fingers ached. She could feel the wound deep in her hand, where Ur'sol had hurt her. She had come so far, endured so much. Yet here she stood, being judged by people who knew nothing of her.

"I'm young," she finally answered. "But I haven't been corrupted. And I'm not insane. What choice do we really have? On the morning after the full moon, the demons will set fire to the world. They'll turn Earth into a star. And when that happens their ship will come. So why wouldn't we call it? Why wouldn't we want to control where it arrived?"

Zeus smiled again. "Spoken like a true Guardian, a true fighter. You sound like we once did—before the passing of too many damn years stole our nerve. But Tasia, can you really control the destination of your drops? And how do you know for certain that an Orb exists within their ship? If an Orb doesn't exist in it, we'd have nothing to drop into, even if you could control our path. We'd summon their ship and drop into some city halfway around the world. And none of us would be here to fight those devils."

Tasia gripped her staff more firmly, remembering how it felt to fire the weapon again and again, how strength replaced fear within her. "Tomorrow morning I'll step into the Orb and go to Angkor. I'll see my family. If I return tomorrow night, with a stone from the temple in my hand, you'll know that I was able to control my path. And if I don't come back … you'll know that I couldn't control anything. I dropped somewhere I didn't want to."

"You'll drop twice in one day?" Zeus asked. "That hasn't been done for many years. And when it was, it wasn't done well. Seekers died."

Glancing at Jerico, Tasia nodded. "I understand it's a risk.

And that's why I'll make the two drops as far apart as possible on the same day. But I have to know what I can and can't do. Can I drop where I want to? Can I do it twice in a day? I've seen the demons do that. We all have. And I'm connected to them in so many ways. I think I can do it too."

"But what of the Orb on their ship?" Zeus wondered. "Why must they have one there?"

"Because they think they're gods. They're not going to fly up to their ship and climb into some hole. I'm sure an Orb will be on it. At least one and probably a lot more."

Zeus eyed his fellow council members. "Are there further questions for her? If not, she should rest. And we have much to discuss. The demons, damn them to eternal hellfire, have left us little time."

No one replied. Zeus thanked Tasia and said that she was free to go.

"If you don't mind, there's one other thing," she said, her pulse once again quickening.

"And what, child, is that?"

She took a deep breath, trying to stand still, to resist the doubts that seemed to eat away at her beliefs, as if termites in dying trees. "There are still hundreds of demons on Earth," she said, nodding to herself. "I think we should kill them before their ship arrives. If we don't, they'll just drop into it when we do. And we'll have to fight them inside it. And we won't be able to blow anything up if we're busy fighting them."

Zeus glanced up, as if searching the sky for demons. He

sighed deeply, nodding. "You've pondered these things, I see. So, how might we defeat them on Earth before their ship arrives? Remember, if you're right, we only have a few more days. Time is not our friend."

"I thought a lot in that cell," she answered, ignoring the twitch near her left eye. "Thinking kept me alive. And it seems to me that we can pretend to gather somewhere with the staffs. The demons couldn't resist such a fight."

"Why not?"

"Because gods don't run from mortals."

Zeus nodded once again. "Go on."

"My friend, Aki, told me about a huge castle near here. What if we filled it with some of our people? What if we created a trap? Aki said the castle is surrounded by tall buildings. We could put our best snipers in them, and then, when the demons flew to the castle, the snipers could knock them down from every direction."

"And Guardians could fight them from the castle?"

Tasia shook her head. "No. Because we can't risk losing a single staff. Without them all, we can't call their ship. But we could use silver paint to make fake staffs. And then the demons would come. They'd find us and attack us. But our snipers would shoot them from the sky."

"Painted staffs," a gray-haired woman said, laughing to herself. "Traps. Snipers. Castles. Gods and mortals. She's got a wonderful imagination, Zeus. I'll admit to a bit of envy there. But this child's imagination isn't going to help us do anything other than pass the time. She's obviously not equipped to—"

"I've spoken to the demons," Tasia interrupted, again tightening her grip on her staff, tired of trying to remain patient. "Have you? Because I know what they're planning, and the only way to defeat them is to bring their ship here and destroy it from the inside. But we can't do that if every demon on Earth is dropping into it along with us. And when their ship arrives, that's exactly what they'll do. So we have to kill the demons here first. At least some of them. And if you don't want to even consider what I have to say, then I think you've been underground for too long."

"You have no right to speak—"

"Maybe not. But maybe you've forgotten what it's like to fight."

Zeus was about to reply when Trax stood up. "I do believe Miss Tasia is correct on all counts," he said. "You'd be wise to listen to her. I saw her face those demons, and I tell you—she beat them away like flies. If Miss Tasia says her plan is the best way to win, well, that's more than good enough for me."

"We can't hide any longer," Jerico added, standing up. "Hiding hasn't gotten us anywhere. Tasia taught me that. She showed me how to fight. So don't talk about her imagination, and don't call her a girl or a child. She's a Guardian now. And she's seen and done things that none of us ever have."

Tasia bit her bottom lip, grateful that Trax and Jerico had defended her, that they believed in her. Suddenly it didn't matter what the council members thought. She had come to them wanting to impress them, to further redeem herself. But maybe the opinions of strangers didn't matter at all. What mattered were the thoughts of her companions.

"I'm going to Angkor tomorrow morning," she said, looking at Zeus. "I'll be back by night. And if you have a better idea than the castle, that's fine. Actually, that'd be great. Do whatever you think you should. But we need to kill some of the demons before we call their ship. We just can't drop into it with hundreds of them right behind us."

Zeus nodded, shaking the raised, clenched fist of his good arm. "Thank you, Tasia. Thank you for stirring up our blood a bit. We could use that. I hope you make it to Angkor tomorrow. I hope you're right."

"Thank you."

"When you return, we'll find you. And by then we'll have discussed your plan and others."

Tasia started to reply, but stopped, instead eying the council members. "It was an honor to meet all of you," she finally added. "And I'm sorry if I seem a bit … difficult. But I'm tired and I've thought about these things a lot."

Zeus stood up as she left the center of the table. Her eyes met his and she thanked him again. Then she stepped away from the Council, moving toward the man who knew her better than anyone, whom she trusted more than herself.

Jerico took her hand in his and they left the room together.

CHAPTER 4

Several hours later, in defiance of almost every rule she'd ever been taught, Tasia led Jerico and Rex on a walk along the exposed and unprotected bank of the Kamogawa River. She was angry, as the Council of Thirty-Three had voted to reclaim all of the staffs she'd brought them with the exception of hers. The staffs were to be given to various Guardians and Seekers. Although Tasia had been allowed to keep her staff, she was irate that Jerico, Aki, Valeriya, and Trax were forced to hand over their weapons. She believed since they'd rescued her, as well as the staffs, that they each should be able to wield one. The staffs would have protected them in the days ahead. Instead they'd be forced to fight, once again, with only rifles.

The river was shallow and wide. A century earlier it must have been beautiful, but storms had blown trash into it, and its verdant shoreline was littered with countless plastic bags, bottles, and other litter. Gray cranes stepped gingerly over the debris, hunting for minnows. The cement pathway that ran along the waterway had been split open by the roots of nearby trees. Human skeletons lay here and there, often still somewhat astride fallen, rusting bicycles. Though the trees offered Tasia and Jerico some protection, the companions remained vulnerable to an attack from above, and both often paused to study the sky.

"They don't trust us," Tasia said, stepping over a fallen branch. "Because if they did, we'd still have those staffs."

Jerico scanned the sky, squinting. He leaned down and broke off a part of the branch, throwing it ahead for Rex to fetch. Tail wagging, the young dog bounded forward, unaware of the dangers around him.

"They let you keep yours," Jerico countered. "And for the most part, they listened to you. So I wouldn't say they don't trust us. They just want the staffs for their own people."

"The people who lost them in the first place."

"They didn't lose them, Tasia. Demons ripped the staffs away from them. Just like they did to my father." Pausing, Jerico leaned down to take the stick from Rex's jaws, tossing it ahead once again. "You know, I hate to say it, but you sound like Draven."

Tasia winced, remembering Draven's leap, his sacrifice. She had left him alone and in pain. If she survived the war, she'd share his story with as many people as possible.

"Draven knew what needed to be done," she finally replied. "If we had more fighters like him, the war would be over already."

Several birds took flight from a tree behind them, and Jerico pivoted, aiming his rifle toward the sky. He peered through its scope, swinging the weapon from north to south, then east to west. Tasia also pointed her staff toward a large, low-hanging cloud, wondering if a demon might descend from it.

Jerico lowered his rifle, but still held it ready. Rex had returned with the stick, and Jerico bent down and threw it ahead. "We're still young in their eyes," he said. "And though they need us, they don't really believe in us."

Tasia swung her staff from left to right, still searching for demons, still trying to sense them. "Zeus seemed fine," she replied quietly. "He believed in us. He trusted us. But most of them have spent too much time in that theater. They've forgotten what it's like to fight. They think we're reckless and naïve and foolish. But what they don't understand is that we've been fighting all our lives. We're tired. We're ready for it all to be over—one way or the other. And we have a chance to be free, to win. Of course that's going to require taking risks. And if they just want to sit in that room and talk, then they should hand over all the staffs and let us get going."

Smiling, Jerico shook his head. "I don't remember you … being impatient. You were working so carefully on that scarf, trying not to rush it."

"Maybe if I'd rushed it, I would have finished it. Maybe it wouldn't be at the bottom of the ocean."

"Maybe Aki's rubbed off on you. She's as patient as a forest fire."

A rifle shot sounded far to the west, prompting more birds to take flight from a nearby tree. But no distant demon rose into the sky. Nor did the weapon fire again.

"I was nervous talking in front of them," Tasia said, thinking about the woman who had called her a child. "And I'm not wise or experienced or part of a famous group. But I know things they don't. And it makes me mad when they treat us like children, like their sacrifices were more important than ours."

"They're afraid, just like us."

"And they've done their part. But we're doing ours. And I want them to trust us."

Rex dropped the stick at Jerico's feet, and he tossed it once again. "They listened to you."

"Only because of Zeus. And they still took your staff. And Aki's. And Valeriya's. They took things that didn't belong to them. They made a decision that affects you, and you didn't even get a say in the matter. And that's not right. Everyone should have a say."

"You're just tired, Tasia. You'll feel better tomorrow."

"I'd give you my staff. You'd be safer with it and I'd let you have it. But … but I need it. K'ail will come for me. For us. And when he comes, I have to be ready."

Jerico lifted up his rifle and pretended to aim at an imaginary target in the sky. "I can still shoot straight. And I don't need anything more than what I've got right here. If I had a staff, I'd probably just light something on fire. Probably myself."

In the nearby water, a moss-covered turtle struggled to

climb up a partially submerged boulder. Tasia watched the reptile scratch and claw its way out of the river until it was able to rest in the sun.

Rex came bounding back to them and dropped the wet, gnawed stick at her feet. Bending down, she rubbed the young dog's head, and then picked up his prize. She smiled at his wagging tail. Twisting, she tossed the stick ahead. He rushed after it as if she'd thrown him a piece of perfectly cooked meat.

"When we're older," she asked, "do you think we'll remember what it was like to be young? Or will everything change? Will we change?"

"I don't know," he answered, shrugging. "But if we win, everything will be different. We won't have to fight anymore. So maybe we will change."

"But what if there had never been a war? What if the world had never changed? Would we be different when we're old?"

Jerico glanced at the sky, and then back at her face. "I read a book once."

"You? Really?"

He pushed her playfully. "It was called … *Lonesome Dove*. And it was about these two old cowboys who rode their horses halfway across America. They had all sorts of adventures, and were funny and sassy and I think they hadn't changed much from when they were younger. One of them even still liked to chase buffalo on his horse. Not to shoot them or anything, but just to remember what it was like to ride after them."

Tasia nodded, then bent down and threw the stick once again. "What'll we want to remember?"

"I don't know. It'll be different. Because that old cowboy, he got to do the best things when he was young. Like chasing the buffalo. So he wanted to relive those memories. But we haven't gotten to do the best things yet, because we've always been fighting. So maybe it will be even better for us, when we're old. Because we'll get to do so many things for the first time. We'll sort of live our lives in the opposite way that the old cowboy did."

Tasia thought about how Jerico's words reminded her of something her father might have said. "I want to walk on a beach," she said quietly, "without looking up."

"Then we'll walk on a beach. And whoever looks up first will get tossed into the water."

"That'll be me."

"Perfect."

She smiled. "And what about you? What do you want to do?"

"So many things. I wouldn't even know where to start."

"Start with one."

He took her hand. "I want to be with you."

"But you're with me now. Tell me something you want to do that's totally different from what we could do today."

Glancing at the sky, he looked for demons, then turned again to her. "Well, it sounds kind of silly, but when I'm old, I'd like to help build something."

"Like what?"

"A place that's kind of a museum and kind of a library—something that can hold thousands of books and paintings. Maybe in an old church, with stained-glass windows and stone walls."

"That sounds like something you'd do. It sounds amazing."

He bent closer to her, kissing her. "Everything's amazing now, because you're here now. With me. And I really missed you. It's like ... time moves so fast with you. And so slow without you."

"I know. It hurt to be away from you."

"Time has a whole new meaning for me."

Pulling him tighter against her, she leaned forward, and their lips met again. "I'm excited to drop into Angkor tomorrow and introduce you to my mother and brother. I think they'll be there. And you're going to like them."

"I'm sure I will."

"I can't wait to see them. It's been too long."

A distant rifle shot emerged, followed by two more.

Jerico turned to stare in the direction of the gunfire. "We should go back and help them plan. They listen to you more than you think."

Scanning the sky, Tasia ignored Rex and the wet stick that he gnawed by her knee. "I'll try to be more patient with them. I could work on that. Maybe Aki has rubbed off on me."

"Just don't start calling me names."

"I don't have her talent for that."

"Lucky me."

Smiling, Tasia turned back toward the Stronghold, and then threw the stick ahead for Rex. She eyed the river, imagining families picnicking alongside it, children splashing in its shallows. She longed to hear echoes of their voices, of their laughter. But only the sound of water moving over rocks filled her ears. The land around her appeared so very empty.

And yet, Tasia didn't feel alone. Jerico was beside her, and his presence seemed to fill the voids of the world with color and warmth and promise. And while she feared the coming days, she also believed that the two of them might live to experience so many wonders together. Like Jerico had said, if they survived, the tomorrows of their lives would be so much better than the yesterdays.

"We need to live," she said. "All of us need to live. Then we can grow old and chase whatever kinds of buffalo we want."

CHAPTER 5

Valeriya thought the bamboo forest was one of the stranger places she'd ever been. The forty-foot-tall green stalks were as wide as her thighs and rose skyward, often growing in clumps. Stalks rubbed together in the breeze, creating low groaning sounds that could have come from predatory animals. The stalks swayed from side to side, constantly moving. Though sunlight filtered down through the bamboo, the forest was ruled by shadows. Aki had told her that she came here often as a child, that it would be a safe place for them to fish.

They'd spent the rest of the morning with Aki's family, and while Valeriya had enjoyed meeting her companion's parents and siblings, she felt claustrophobic within the concrete bowels of the Stronghold. In her homeland of Russia, she'd been raised mostly outside. Within deep woods her grandfather had taught her how to thrive in the wilderness—how to fish, hunt, navigate, grow vegetables, collect rainwater, and avoid both humans and demons.

Because Valeriya and her grandfather were rarely underground, they'd stayed safe by blending into the landscape around them. Whatever bushes and grasses were nearby had been woven into their hair and clothes. Whatever dirt was beneath their feet had been brushed onto their faces.

In all those years only once had Valeriya been caught off-guard by men who sought to harm her. Two of them had surprised her when she returned from visiting a friend. They'd bloodied her lip and pinned her to the ground by the time her grandfather arrived, and she hadn't felt bad that he shot them. Afterwards, as he'd held her, the sounds of the forest had returned—crickets chirping, birds taking flight, deer crashing through the underbrush. Nature and her grandfather had comforted her in their own ways. She loved them both.

Because she'd grown up outside, Valeriya had never liked the Strongholds. For months after the deaths of her grandparents, she'd felt broken, and had been lucky to stumble upon Neverland. Beside the beautiful lake she'd slowly healed, making friends and learning to trust certain men, even fishing with several. In Neverland she grew to appreciate the strength of a community, of good people who shared common beliefs. Twice groups of bandits had endangered that community, and on each occasion Valeriya had fought alongside the men and women of Neverland—bleeding with them, sharing victories with them.

Only one time that year had a demon dropped from the sky. It killed six of Neverland's protectors before someone shot it down, and Valeriya had thought about her grandparents as it sunk into deep, clear waters. Maybe it had been the same demon that had killed them. Maybe they'd been avenged.

Somehow Neverland had thawed the freeze in Valeriya's heart. Perhaps that warming came from the nearly constant laughter of children who played by the lake. After all, the whole premise of Neverland was to encourage children to be children, to celebrate their lives until they were fifteen. And when Valeriya wasn't fishing or on guard duty, she'd watched boys and girls play, enjoying their joy, feeling younger and more optimistic in their presence.

After leaving Neverland, Valeriya hadn't expected to fall in love, but she had come to understand that her feelings for Aki were real, not a product of curiosity or loneliness. Aki's personality lit a fire within her that warmed her insides. That fire made her glad to be alive, as well as grateful to her grandparents, and to the parents who she couldn't remember.

"I feel like I'm an ant on a giant green dog's back," Aki said, pointing her rifle at a clump of nearby bamboo. "I hope he doesn't scratch himself."

Valeriya smiled. "Where is this lake, anyway? I thought it was close."

"You thought wrong. But that shouldn't surprise anyone."

"It would have been faster to just walk back to Russia."

"And you still could. But there's an ocean, remember? You'd

have to do a bit of swimming too. And you don't look like much of a swimmer."

"And how would you know what a swimmer looks like?"

Aki stopped, her gaze sweeping up and down Valeriya's body. "Nope. Not you. You were made to catch fish, to trap squirrels. Not to swim across seas. Your shoulders and hips aren't big enough. The waves would push you wherever they wanted."

"So, you're an expert on—"

"Everything. Most of all you. And I can tell that my parents liked you. So did my brothers and sisters. They were happy when I said that I'd decided to keep you."

Valeriya started walking again, holding her fishing pole in one hand and her rifle in the other. "To keep me?"

"That's right. And I am keeping you, by the way."

"And what about your girlfriend back in Beijing? What'll you tell her?"

Aki looked to her left and then right. "The truth," she replied, her words slowing, her tone more serious. "I'll tell her I'm sorry, but I've fallen for someone else. I've been kidnapped by some forest girl from Russia."

A body of water appeared ahead. It wasn't large enough to be considered a lake and was more like a big pond. Yet Valeriya believed it would contain fish. Her pace quickened. She wondered what kind of bait might work best, finally deciding that a silver lure would do nicely. After moving to the water's edge, she propped her rifle against a clump of bamboo, then opened a small tackle box. Before long, she had her fishing pole ready and stepped forward, casting the lure with ease and grace. It splashed into the water and she reeled it in slowly.

"I saw a big turtle in here once," Aki said, standing nearby. "Maybe you'll catch it."

"With a worm and a hook I could," Valeriya answered. "But not with a spoon."

"A spoon? What do you mean? I thought spoons were for eating."

"They are. But they're also the name of a certain kind of lure. The kind I'm using."

"Why don't you call it a fork?"

"Because it looks like a spoon."

"Are you seeing straight?" Aki asked. "Because that thing doesn't look like a spoon to me."

"I'm seeing—"

"What do I look like to you? A mountain goat?"

Valeriya laughed, casting again. A fish immediately struck but wasn't hooked. "I might have to switch to something smaller," she said, still reeling.

"A smaller spoon?"

"Maybe. Or a quieter mountain goat."

Aki sighed. "You know, if I didn't really care about you, I wouldn't be here. I'm not particularly interested in things with gills."

About to respond, Valeriya felt a strike and pulled her rod back, setting the hook. A hand-sized fish leapt out of the water.

Valeriya lowered her rod, reeling steadily, trying to keep her line away from a fallen, half-submerged branch. Before long the fish, a smallmouth bass, was in Valeriya's hands. She removed the lure from its mouth, set it back in the water, and watched it swim away.

"You're not going to keep it?" Aki asked.

Valeriya washed her hands in the water, rubbing them together. "No, not today."

"Why not?"

Her smile vanishing, Valeriya thought about the coming fight. "Because I don't know if I'll fish again. I might not come back. So I'd rather just catch a few and let them go. I don't want the last fish I catch to die in my hands."

Aki didn't respond and Valeriya continued to cast. The bamboo forest groaned around them as if some sort of magical string orchestra. More fish were caught and released. Even Aki tried a few casts, clapping when she pulled in the largest bass of the afternoon.

Finally, as the sun dropped into the forest, Valeriya reeled in her pole for the last time. She leaned it against her rifle, then thoroughly washed her hands. Aki was sitting nearby on a smooth boulder, and Valeriya settled down beside her. "You enjoy fishing more than you pretend to," she said, then kissed Aki's cheek.

"Well, I did catch the biggest one. That helped."

Somewhere in the distance, the crack of a rifle sounded. Valeriya looked up, trying to peer between the bamboo stalks.

Another shot echoed. And then another. Somewhere people were shooting at a demon.

Valeriya closed her eyes, wishing that she didn't have to hear such sounds, that whoever was shooting at the demon was safe. "Why do you fight?" she asked, turning to Aki.

"So my family doesn't have to."

"It's that simple?"

"I don't want my brothers and sisters to do what we do."

"You're good to them. Really good."

"And why do you fight? Why didn't you stay in Neverland? You could have caught fish forever there."

Valeriya started to respond, then stopped. "My grandfather once told me that our story hadn't yet been told. He didn't think we were finished. So I guess I fight for something a lot bigger than me. I don't want us to be finished either."

Leaning slightly sideways, Aki kissed her, and Valeriya felt the warmth and softness of her lips. Her pulse quickened. Suddenly she forgot about the fish and the war and the future. She longed for Aki's touch, to feel the warmth and comfort of her. Their lips met again. Whispers were exchanged. Valeriya started to unbutton Aki's shirt, moving slowly, kissing her neck, then the tops of her breasts. Aki moaned quietly, her voice nearly lost within the groans of the bamboo.

Valeriya stared into Aki's dark eyes, then kissed her once more, moving faster now, empowered by the overwhelming ache of shared intimacy. Their lips met again and again.

"I don't feel small … when I'm with you," Valeriya whispered.

"Everything ... is so big."

Aki nodded. For once, words seemed to have left her. And so, instead of speaking, she shifted even closer to Valeriya, wrapping her arms around her, holding her tight. The two companions embraced, rocking slowly back and forth. Then they started to kiss again, their bodies moving together like the swaying stalks of bamboo around them, pressured by unseen winds and forces.

Deep within the forest, Aki and Valeriya celebrated their togetherness, soon drifting into an extraordinary, magical realm that neither could have entered alone.

And as they touched and kissed, this world protected them, keeping them safe from so many dangers—both real and imagined, distant and near.

CHAPTER 6

L ater that night, Tasia lay awake in bed. Jerico slept on his side next to her, his long hair covering part of a pillow, his arm across her chest. She studied his face, noting the tiny imperfections of his skin, including a pair of half-healed cuts on his forehead. The faintest of age lines intersected with the cuts, and also appeared at the corners of his eyes. In time, she knew, these lines would deepen—but she hoped from laughter and not worry, from joy and not fear. She was increasingly anxious that he would die young, that he'd never experience all life had to offer. He deserved to see and do everything he wanted. As someone who cared for others, who tried to fix a broken world, he'd earned that simple right.

More than ever, Tasia also longed to live for many more years. Hope had always sustained her, and she believed in a better, more beautiful future. Unlike many of her peers or elders, it wasn't difficult for her to imagine a life without the demons. A victory for humanity wasn't impossible. Her loved ones might know peace and quiet. They might walk on empty beaches, pray in open places, and laugh without fear, as people once did.

Her father had taught her about the power of optimism, and Tasia was grateful for his perspective. He'd seen signs of victory in every defeat. He'd talked about light when others saw only dark. And he'd been the one who first told her that she was different, that she should embrace her uniqueness rather than run from it. For many years she heard him say such words, but she'd never really listened to them. It had been easier to think that she was like everyone else, that she could best survive by blending into her surroundings rather than standing apart from them.

As a child it was risky to be different because other children often ridiculed what they didn't understand. And so Tasia had never spoken with her friends about how she was able to sense the presence of demons, how she'd felt connected to them, even at a young age. She'd buried those feelings deep within her, only sharing them with her father when she was older. But now that she'd put her childhood firmly behind her, she finally understood that being different was good. As her father had once told her, if humanity contained only a single kind of person, if everyone looked and acted the same, it would be like staring into a jungle with only one kind of tree. The jungle would still be there, but its magic, beauty, and soul would be gone.

Shifting her attention back to Jerico, Tasia carefully lifted his arm from where it lay across her chest. She lightly kissed a faint age-line on his forehead and then crept out of bed. She had lain awake for too long and was hungry. Unsure what she might find to eat, she tightened her robe, picked up her staff, and tiptoed toward the door. Rex, who rested near the end of the bed, whimpered until she returned to stroke his forehead and whisper into his ear. After slipping on her sandals, she moved toward the door. But as soon as she touched the cool steel of its handle, K'ail's words drifted to her. She thought about ignoring him once again, but decided to unlock her mind, to let him communicate with her.

How are your hands?

She opened the door and stepped into a dimly illuminated hallway. "My hands?" she whispered. "What do you mean?"

You burnt them on the beach. And Ur'sol almost took one from you.

Tasia's grip tightened on her staff, causing her palms to ache. "Ur'sol didn't take anything from me," she said quietly.

Because I saved you.

"Because my friends saved me."

Somewhere in the distance, a man coughed. The scent of roasting garlic lingered in the air. Tasia glanced up and down the hallway, wondering how far K'ail was from her.

I am told there are fires in Osaka Castle. It seems that your scouts inspect its walls and roof. But why? You must know that such an old, ruined fortress cannot be defended. Not from gods, in any case.

"We have all the staffs, remember? We can defend whatever we want."

You shall summon our ship to that tired place?

"Maybe."

And you shall drop into our ship? Leading as many mortals as you can gather?

Tasia started walking down the hallway. "They don't tell me everything," she whispered, noticing a guard who leaned against a faraway wall. "I don't know much about the castle. I've never seen it."

The Council of Thirty-Three Fools. This is the name we have bestowed to your esteemed group. A council of weaklings, of cowards. They hide deep in the ground and call themselves leaders. But what do they know of wisdom? Of the world above them?

"They don't—"

There is one bright mind among them. He is called Zeus— named after one of your false gods. I fought him once. Even with that crippled hand, he knew how to wield a staff. After I feast on you, I shall look for him.

"Why are you bothering me?" she asked, turning around and walking away from the guard. "Do gods get lonely?"

Gods get whatever they want.

"Then why don't you have me? Why didn't you win this war a long time ago?"

Do you miss your friend? The one who took my eye?

Tasia stopped. Tired, she leaned against a wall. "I'm not interested in what you have to say."

I have his bones. Did you know that? I can even see where I bit them.

K'ail's words seemed to pierce Tasia's mind, then body. She slumped against the wall, sliding down until she sat on the floor. "Why … why do you care about his bones?"

If you wish to honor him, to bury him, you will come and claim him.

"No," she answered, shaking her head.

Then I shall scratch my backside with him until he is no more than dust. I shall set his skull on a field of waste and let the rats feast on him.

"Please don't."

You threatened me once. You said you would tell other gods that you tricked me.

"I haven't told anyone."

I know. But there is an unfinished fight between us, a storm that has not yet arrived. I wish to silence you forever. You wish to bury him.

Tasia thought about Jerico. "That's not enough," she whispered. "Fareed wouldn't want me to risk—"

You say love empowers you. Prove it.

"What do you mean?"

The boy who came for you. I know of him. I have seen him. And I could put a bounty on his head. As sure as gods can fly I could have him killed.

"He's safe here. You can't—"

I can have him killed beyond your Stronghold or within it.

She bit her lower lip, shaking her head. The skin at the back of her neck tingled. "What do you mean? How could you have him killed here?"

Come fight me. If you win, you may have the bones. And Jerico will live. If I win … the memory of you will vanish from my mind.

"I'll hide him," she whispered, looking around, suddenly feeling small. "Somewhere you'll never find."

You lie. Because if he loves you … if love is as strong as you claim, he will be by your side in the days ahead, and in the coming fight. Yet I can change his fate. I can call for his execution this very day. By a god or by a mortal.

"No one here would hurt him."

Wrong. So very wrong.

"But why? He helps people. He cares about people."

Do not be naïve, Tasia. Do not make me prove my point. Do not mistake Jerico's kindness for invulnerability. Only if I am dead shall he remain anonymous, like the light of a star too distant to see.

Tasia closed her eyes, suddenly fearful, as if K'ail had reached out and touched her. "He wouldn't want me to fight you," she replied quietly. "Not alone, at least."

You have today to do as you wish. Straighten what is twisted in your world. Say your goodbyes. And then meet me tomorrow. A golden temple rises on the northern edge of the city. If you wish, bring your staff. But come alone, as I will. Our war is between us. The bones will be there.

"Please don't—"

Deny me this fight and I shall take everything from him. How will he fare, Tasia, without his senses? Will his pain be worse or better if he cannot hear himself scream? And what of his dog? Shall I make him watch that animal suffer?

"Stop," she whispered, trembling now, her skin damp with sweat. "You don't need to say any more. I'll come. I'll be there."

I will look for you in—

"He didn't do anything to you. He likes to read, to help children."

A noble weakling. How touching.

She clenched her fists, again feeling the ache of Ur'sol's strike. "You call yourself a god, but to me you're a demon and you'll never know what it's like to be one of us."

Would an ocean wish to know what it felt like to be a stream?

"A stream feeds an ocean."

A stream trickles. An ocean rages. The same difference as you and I.

"Do you know what? I'm going home today. To see people I love. Then I'll come back here. I'll find that golden temple. And I'll fight you, and even if you win, you'll never take some things from me—the best things."

Come alone. And die alone. I shall claim your staff for a moment, but then return it to your kind. You see, I want them to call my ship. I need every staff to be reunited.

In the distance, the guard coughed.

Tasia took a deep breath. Though she trembled, she stood

up, tightly gripping her staff. "I'm going to bury Fareed. And protect Jerico. And I wonder if you'll think of yourself as a god when I knock you out of the sky, when you see me standing over you and you know I won."

A dream. No more.

"And dreams come true. Every day."

Sleep as you wish. Dream as you wish. But face me or that benevolent boy shall forever disappear from your life.

CHAPTER 7

D awn had come and gone by the time Tasia, Jerico, Rex, Aki, and Valeriya approached Kyoto's Orb. As she had many days earlier, Tasia crept through the dormant bullet train, avoiding broken glass. From time to time she glanced at the nearby cement platform, looking for Fareed's bones. At first, she saw no remnant of him, but finally, where she remembered he fell, she spied his rolled-up prayer rug. During his fight against K'ail the prayer rug must have been ripped away from him. Biting her lower lip, she envisioned Fareed unrolling it, kneeling upon it, and praying quietly. The memory pained her, and as she had many times before, she prayed that he'd been reunited with his loved ones and could once again hear his daughter play her guitar.

Somewhat to Tasia's surprise, earlier that morning a messenger had delivered a sealed envelope to her from Zeus. Inside a message said that the Council had decided to follow her plan with Osaka Castle. Preparations were already underway. Zeus asked that she travel to Angkor, as she wanted. Guardians were to stay away from the castle in any case, so that their staffs couldn't be taken in the coming fight.

A demon shrieked somewhere high above them. Jerico knelt down to hold Rex still. The young dog growled and leaned away from Jerico's grasp but didn't bark. Again the demon shrieked. Tasia stared through one of the train's dirty windows, trying to locate the beast, tempted to step into the light and knock it from the sky.

"Just leave it be," Aki said quietly, reaching for her arm. "If Valeriya and I are going to scout out Osaka Castle, like that crusty old council wants, we don't have time to save you here."

Tasia glanced at her friend. "Are you sure you don't want to drop with us to Angkor? You'll be safer with me, with my staff."

"I've been to the castle before. And if we're going to fight the demons there, I should help with the planning."

"But you hate plans."

Aki shook her head. "I never said that. What I hate are other people's plans. My plans are brilliant. And of course, I adore them."

"Your plans involve about five words," Valeriya interjected. "How many times have I heard you say, 'Just kill the big bats?'"

"Well, what else is there to say? Fighting isn't the same as fishing, you know. You don't have to decide on whether to use a big spoon or a little one or some dirty old worm. You just find a bat and put a bullet in its eye."

Jerico scratched the top of Rex's head. "You defy the odds, Aki."

"How's that?"

"You make me look smart."

"Wow. That certainly is defying the odds. I must have talent. Maybe that cranky council should be bigger. They could use me, you know. And it wouldn't be hard to call it the Council of Thirty-Four."

Jerico smiled. "You'd offend everyone in that room in about ten minutes."

"That's because they need offending. If someone doesn't need it, I don't do it. The problem is, most people need it."

"Who doesn't?"

"Rex. He's safe. Though why he wastes his time with you, I'll never know. I mean, you don't read him poetry. You don't hold his paw and skip through fields of flowers. He might whimper a bit, but he seems too tough for you."

"Thanks, Aki."

"As always, my pleasure."

Tasia squeezed Aki's hand. It felt good to enjoy a little levity, and her friend's words had lifted her spirits. No longer did she reflect on Fareed's death, but on the looming encounter with her mother and brother. She was excited to be reunited with them, to let them know she was safe.

"We'll be back tonight," she said. "And then we'll find you at the castle. I don't know when the demons will fly into our trap, but when they do, you should be safe. Our snipers will surprise them."

"Just ask for Queen Aki. I'll be the one wearing a crown. Valeriya here will be my servant."

Valeriya rolled her eyes. She started to respond, but stopped, her smile fading as she turned to Tasia. "Will you really be able to control the Orb? And drop straight into Angkor?"

Nodding, Tasia tried to appear confident. K'ail had said she possessed the power to control the path of her drops, but he'd lied before. "It's going to work," she replied. "And after we see my family, we'll come back here. We'll look for your crown, Aki."

"And my servant with the pretty eyes."

"Her too."

Valeriya leaned down to scratch Rex's head. "Then you should go. But take care of this sweet boy, will you? He seems even more nervous than usual."

"He can tell something's about to happen," Jerico said. "He knows us."

"That's because he can smell your feelings."

Leaning forward, Tasia hugged Valeriya, then Aki. Tasia was surprised when Aki squeezed her hard and then kissed her on the cheek. She watched as Aki held Jerico tightly. She kissed him as well. Twice.

"Are you sure you don't want to come with us?" Jerico asked.

Aki stepped away. "Just go already. Be the hero of some new story. Some tale of knights and dragons. We'll see you soon."

The companions said their goodbyes. Aki took Valeriya's hand and led her back through the train, back from where they came. They spoke quietly, each holding a rifle with their free hand. They grew smaller and smaller. Finally, when they were about to step off the train, they paused, embraced, and then moved out of sight.

"I'm happy for them," Jerico said, leaning forward. He smiled, then kissed Tasia on the lips.

His touch immediately affected her, infusing her with a light and warmth that traveled from her lips to the rest of her body.

"I'm nervous about the drop," she whispered, still holding him. "What if I can't control it? What if we end up in Dubai or Paris or Risen?"

"I believe in you. We'll end up exactly where you want us to—in Angkor."

"And if we don't?"

"Then we'll fix things."

She nodded, stepping away from him. "You're good at fixing things."

"You can do this. I know you can."

Releasing his hand, she gripped her staff, took a deep breath, and started to walk to the end of the train. The Orb, so massive and brilliant, glowed on the nearby platform. The sky didn't appear to contain a single demon. Fareed's prayer rug rested where he had died.

"I need to pick up something," she said. "Just follow me, okay?"

"I'll watch your back."

She left the sanctuary of the train and hurried toward the prayer rug. It lay near a series of bloodstains, and she looked away from them, reaching for the rolled-up rug. Holding it with her free hand, she moved toward the Orb, shifting her thoughts to Angkor. She remembered what K'ail had said, that the only way to control a drop was to imagine your desired destination, to make it real before you even began your journey. And so she thought about her home. She envisioned its temples and jungles and statues. She remembered its sounds and smells. Her memories unfolded next, visions of her childhood. Climbing a banyan tree with her brother. Her mother drawing pictures in the sand. And her father telling her about the beauty around them, about flowers and beetles and monsoon-fed streams.

Holding Jerico's hand, Tasia called for Rex to follow them, and then stepped into the Orb. Immediately a white light enveloped her. She seemed to be torn apart and then thrown back together again. Crying out, she tried to keep visions of Angkor alive within her. She saw a temple, a tiger, an orchid. But the white light transformed into a sea of stars. A distant, alien ship appeared—malevolent and massive. Then the light came again, consuming her. She dropped and dropped and dropped, spinning and twisting, dying and being reborn, shouting in the throes of countless reincarnations.

Suddenly Tasia was on her knees. Her staff was forgotten, though she still held it in her trembling hand. She moaned, fell forward, and then vomited. Unable to remember her name or to comprehend her thoughts, she rolled to her side and stared up. At first, she didn't recognize the trees or sky above her. She didn't even know what they meant. But slowly, like the warmth brought by the early morning light angling down to strike her cheek, her mind cleared. She saw the trees and vines and leaves for exactly what they were.

Jerico said something to her, and though she wasn't able to fully comprehend his words, she knew that she loved him, and that she'd brought him to her home.

K'ail had given her another key to freedom.

CHAPTER 8

Aki was friends with the stable master of the Stronghold of Kyoto, and it hadn't been hard to convince him to give her two horses. Though the main army hadn't left yet for Osaka Castle, scouting parties had already departed, and Aki had told the old man that she'd been ordered to survey the citadel's top floor. She was to leave the Stronghold at once and needed his help in doing so.

In reality, Aki had been ordered to leave alongside the main force, but she'd never listened to her superiors and wasn't about to begin doing so now. Like Tasia, she was upset that the Council of Thirty-Three had decided to reclaim her staff, as well as Valeriya's. It seemed to her that, as the ones who'd helped to steal the staffs back from the demons, she and Valeriya ought to be able to wield them. After all, they were as strong or stronger than the Guardians who had originally lost the staffs.

In defiance of the Council, Aki and Valeriya had left the Stronghold early, just ahead of the main group. After parting from Tasia and Jerico, they'd taken the horses, ridden out of the hidden stable, and headed to the southwest, toward Osaka Castle. The journey would take them the better part of the day. Aki had explored the area enough to know the thickest parts of the forest that had sprung up after the cities of Kyoto and Osaka died. As long as she and Valeriya stayed beneath the forest's canopy, she didn't think any demon would spot them. An army of a thousand men and women, on the other hand, would be almost impossible to miss.

Now, as Aki followed a set of train tracks that had been overwhelmed by trees and bushes, she held her rifle in her right hand and the horse's reins in her left. The sky was barely visible through the leafy treetops and she wasn't overly nervous. Not only would it be difficult for a demon to see them, but the latticework of branches above provided a decent shield. Still, she reminded herself not to take their safety for granted. The demons were much smarter than she pretended.

Wishing that the clatter of their horses' hooves was quieter, Aki glanced at the sky, then at Valeriya, who rode beside her. "Do you find this war as tedious as I do? Because I'm ready for some new adventures. As soon as the fighting is over, let's get all dressed up and go to a museum or something like people used to. I mean, if you're going to take me fishing, the least you can do is let me wrap you up in something pretty—maybe a turquoise-colored dress to match your eyes. And you'll need to let me dye your hair and paint your nails. I'll even teach you how to walk in high-heeled shoes."

Valeriya smiled. "My grandfather told me about a theater in Moscow. He'd seen it once. People used to sing there, up on a big stage. There were lights and curtains, and the audience would dress up. The men wore ties and jackets. The women liked jewels and furs."

"So you'd let me?"

"Let you what?"

"Dress you up."

"As long as it's not in a fur. I'd never do that."

Aki nodded. "Fair enough. After all, you don't see the average fox prancing around in one of our skins."

Some sort of rodent darted across the train tracks and Aki's horse snorted. She tightened her grip on the reins, studied what she could see of the sky, and then lay her rifle across her lap. "Tasia let me paint her nails," she said, smiling. "And later, I saw her looking at them. I think they made her happy."

"Maybe just having you as a friend made her happy."

Aki nodded. "When we first met, I didn't think we'd be friends. She seemed too serious for me, like she was seventeen going on seventy. Luckily I was wrong."

"You? Wrong?"

"It does happen from time to time. Kind of like how Jerico's wit makes occasional appearances."

Valeriya pretended to push away Aki's words. "How were you wrong about Tasia?"

"Oh, I don't think she's as serious as she seems. I think she wants to have fun like the rest of us. But there is something different about her too. She's so much stronger than she looks. She's got a power I don't understand."

"How do you know that?"

"Because," Aki replied, sticking out her tongue, "I know everything."

At one point a torrent of water must have washed away part of the train tracks. Aki's horse left the tracks to follow a sandy, dried-up streambed. The stallion wanted to stay on the old waterway, but Aki forced him to head back to the tracks.

"Since you've always known everything, have you always known yourself?" Valeriya asked.

"What exactly is your question? You seem to be having a hard time with it."

"Have you always … liked girls?"

Aki ran her hand through her hair, which she'd recently dyed a dark green. "I started out with boys. Two or three of them if I remember right."

"And?"

"And for a while they were fun and exciting. They were new. But they were also more interested in what was under my skirt than what was inside my head. They were good at clawing and scratching and breaking the buttons of my blouse. And kissing them was like … trying to swallow a frog."

Valeriya laughed. "It was that bad, really?"

"Worse, actually. Though maybe I was just unlucky."

"You wanted a gentleman, I think. Someone like Jerico. Someone who'd smile at your pretty dress and your fancy necklace."

"He is a gentleman, isn't he? I call him Tasia's knight in shining army fatigues."

"He smiles when you say that."

"I know," Aki answered. "Maybe that's why I say it."

Valeriya swatted at a fly. "And what do you say about me, when I'm not listening?"

"You should ask what I think about you, not what I say about you."

"What do you think about me?"

Aki shrugged, pretending to be uncertain. "You're good with a hook and worm. You know the difference between north and south. And—"

"And I'm a gentleman?"

"And you're … interested in what's inside my head. And I enjoy being with you. And kissing you makes me feel like … a little piece of magic just exploded between us."

Valeriya smiled. "There's no frog involved?"

"The frogs left with the boys."

A pine cone fell from a nearby tree, and the two companions looked up, studying their surroundings. Valeriya exhaled when she saw a gray squirrel. "Did you know that frogs absorb water through their skin, so they don't ever have to drink?"

"I feel like a fool. How have I survived all these years, not knowing that crucial fact?"

"And frogs can jump twenty times their own body length in a single leap."

"Wow. That's amazing. Maybe we should recruit them to help us fight the demons. We could give them little spears. What else should I know about our future allies?"

Valeriya glanced at the sky, and then flipped the safety switch of her rifle off and back on. "Scientists identify how old frogs are by the rings in their bones. You know, like tree trunks and branches have rings? Frog bones are the same. They get them when they hibernate."

Grinning, Aki shook her head. "Another life-saving fact, for sure."

Distant rifle shots cracked, prompting Valeriya's horse to neigh. The two companions studied the sky, aware that somewhere, someone was fighting. More shots rang out. A faint scream lingered in the air before being carried away by an unseen wind. Birds took flight from a nearby tree, darting skyward. Though their horses snorted and stomped, Aki and Valeriya held their reins tight, keeping them in check. Soon the forest once again quieted.

"Back at Neverland, I wasn't sure if I could be happy again," Valeriya said, shifting her grip on her rifle. "But now I am. And that's because of you."

"I have that effect on people."

"I don't want to go back to who I was. To wandering around by myself."

Aki started to reply but realized that Valeriya's tone had

grown more serious. "You don't have to go back to who you were. You don't—"

"In the fight, at the castle, I'm going to be beside you. I'm going to look out for you. Because if you fall, I don't think I'll … want to keep standing."

"I won't fall. Not today. Not tomorrow."

"My grandfather promised me the same thing."

"But he knew how to fish. I know how to fight."

Valeriya took a deep breath, appearing to steady herself. "I want this to be the beginning of us … not the end of us."

Aki nodded, trying to stay strong, to block the fears that suddenly surfaced, fears she kept pressed down deep inside her. During her life as a Seeker, she'd seen so many couples split apart. The demons would kill one, and the other would try to endure—sometimes succeeding, but sometimes becoming a shadow of who they had once been.

Thinking about losing Valeriya made Aki's breath catch in her throat. She reached for her companion's hand, squeezing it tight. "We're not going to say goodbye. And neither of us is going to fall."

"You don't know that."

"This war won't be the end of us. We won't let that happen."

"Maybe not. But people don't always get to choose."

"We will."

Valeriya lifted Aki's hand, then kissed the underside of her wrist. "Tell me what I'm going to wear, when we dress up. Tell me how we'll look together."

A tear fell from Aki's long lashes, dropping to her cheek. Aware of its journey down her face, she forced herself to smile. "You're going to look so beautiful," she said quietly. "I know just the perfect dress for you. I saw it once when I dropped into Paris."

"So we'll go to Paris together?"

"That's right. We'll go to Paris. And we'll stand by the river, in our fancy dresses, talking about fish and frogs and hundreds of life-saving facts. The skies will be empty and quiet. And I'll take your hand, and everything will be new and fresh, just like it's supposed to be."

"The beginning?"

"The beginning. Because only then will we really know what it's like to live. And that will make everything new."

CHAPTER 9

The temple of Angkor Wat was just as Tasia remembered. Holding Jerico's hand, she led him forward, across a vast sandstone walkway that spanned a wide moat. Since no trees rose from the moat, the walkway was vulnerable to attack from above. Tasia rarely lowered her gaze from the sky, looking in all directions, sometimes dropping Jerico's hand so that she could spin around on her heels. As a child she'd swum across the moat many times before or after venturing into the nearby city of Siem Reap. She'd learned to swim without splashing, and knew where to hide beneath the walkway, in dark spaces where sandstone blocks had fallen into the murky water.

To Tasia's surprise, she didn't see any demons above the distant temple. The sky was empty of everything except for thin, nearly translucent clouds. She quickened her pace, finally crossed the moat, and headed toward the temple's outermost wall. Again holding Jerico's hand, she led him through a vaulted and ornate entrance. Rex followed at their heels. The belief that her brother and mother were nearby fueled her desire for speed. She wanted to run to them, to call out their names and rush forward until she embraced them.

Stifling the urge to abandon caution, Tasia stepped through the outer wall and stared at her home, which was still far away. Though large banyan and fig trees obscured most of her view, she still could see slices of the Stronghold of Angkor Wat. The legendary temple had been designed to house Hindu gods but looked as if it had been built by them. Rising from the top of the massive, terraced temple were five towers shaped like lotus buds, the central and tallest of which stretched upward for two hundred feet. The towers were situated on the highest of three rectangular terraces, each stacked on top of the other. Though Tasia couldn't see them from so far away, large swaths of the temple were covered in intricate carvings that depicted heroic images of the Hindu gods, the demons they fought, and the king who had ordered the temple built.

For centuries after its creation, Angkor Wat had stood apart from the jungle, but now the ornate sandstone mountain was covered in foliage. Birds had dropped seeds between the giant red blocks that comprised the temple, and massive trees stretched outward and skyward from these humble origins. The jungle canopy acted as a shield, making it difficult for demons to attack the Stronghold. Of course, sometimes they battered through the branches, but the ancient temple was protected by several Guardians and scores of Seekers. When branches snapped and cracked, these men and women rushed forward to confront their attackers.

Her feet no longer on stone, Tasia moved onward, following a trail that had been cut into the jungle. The foliage here was dense. She passed the ruins of an ancient sandstone library, then skirted a demon's moss-covered skull. Orchids grew from nooks in the curved and twisted trunks of sprawling banyan trees— purple and pink and white. Tasia remembered creeping along this same path with her brother in tow. Sayer had often wanted to join her, and when he'd turned ten, their parents let him.

As a child, Tasia hadn't always appreciated the beauty of her home, but now it added to her excitement and joy. She moved faster, releasing Jerico's hand so she could more easily climb over fallen branches. Her staff felt light in her grasp, and she thought about how her father would have been proud of her. She was returning home as a Guardian. She'd been able to control the drop from Kyoto, and her father had been right about her. She was different. But she was finally learning to embrace that difference, to understand that her uniqueness was a gift.

A wide sandstone stairway loomed before them. The smell of cooking fires and roasting meat hung thick in the air. Tasia glanced at the sky, then hurried up the stairs. Rex growled at a fleeing mouse. Soon they stepped inside the temple, which was dominated by walls that were several feet thick and a vaulted ceiling that protected ancient carvings and statues. A young boy appeared from a hiding place and waved to her. She smiled at him, reached the second level of the temple, and then started to climb higher. Soon she saw familiar faces—men, women, and children whom she'd known for many years. Embraces and greetings were exchanged. Most everyone seemed to be in awe of the staff she carried and wondered aloud how she had acquired it. But she merely smiled at their questions and asked the whereabouts of her mother and brother. Another set of stairs was ascended, another platform crossed. Unseen rifles fired in the distance as word of her victorious return spread and people celebrated her presence.

The highest level of Angkor Wat was reached by stairs so steep that they were almost vertical. Tasia told Jerico to be careful and then started to climb up, holding onto a thick rope with her left hand. She should have listened to her own words, however, because she'd only ascended a few of the narrow, steep steps when she slipped and banged her left knee. The blow hurt, but she held onto the rope and pulled herself up.

"And you're telling me to slow down?" Jerico asked behind her, holding onto Rex's collar with his free hand.

"I have to see them. I can't wait any longer."

"I know."

She hurried upward, climbing with speed and agility. Even when she neared the top, when she approached a height that people had fallen and died from, she didn't slow her pace. Upon reaching the stairs' summit, she leaned down, extended her hand, and helped Jerico. Two young girls greeted them, laughing. Tasia didn't recognize the girls but smiled and moved on, stepping into a corridor that led to the north. The passageway was lined with ornate, open-air windows, and Seekers stood at these gaps, aiming rifles toward the treetops above them. The Seekers turned to Tasia as she strode past, carrying her staff. Most recognized her but seemed uncertain as to why she was now a Guardian. Still, several celebrated the moment, nodding to her and shooting their rifles into the sky.

In the center of the upper level was a vaulted chamber that held ancient statues. Many people came here to pray, and Tasia wasn't surprised when she saw her brother. Calling out his name, she ran forward with her arms outstretched. Almost immediately, her mother appeared from around a corner, crying out, and limping forward as fast as her ruined leg would carry her. Tasia crashed into them, pulling them tight against her. In that instant, her many worries vanished. The affirmation that her loved ones still lived overwhelmed her. Holding them tight, she didn't try to restrain her tears or control her emotions. She simply clung to her mother and brother, shuddering with relief and joy, feeling free and unburdened.

Sayer finally broke away from her, asking about her staff, his eyes wide with disbelief. But Tasia shook her head, wanting to introduce Jerico. She wiped tears from her cheeks, took his hand in hers, and said that he had saved her, that she wouldn't be standing there if it wasn't for him.

"That's not really true," he answered, smiling. "I had help. And Tasia escaped all by herself. We just picked her up."

Tasia's mother started to speak, but Tasia asked Sayer if the medicine was working, if he felt better than before. He replied that he was fine, and that the now-dormant virus didn't bother him at all. His words immediately seemed to fill her with warmth, and she tousled his hair. "I missed you," she said. "I missed you a lot."

"I knew you'd come back," he answered.

Her mother reached for her hands, then kissed her brow and held her tight. The two of them rocked back and forth, clinging to each other as if waves threatened to knock them down. "How did you escape?" her mother asked. "I don't understand."

"It's a long story. And I'll tell it later. I'll tell you everything."

Tears fell to her mother's cheeks, streaming down her face. "You're right—tell us later. None of that really matters anyway. All that matters is that you're here. You're here to stay and there's light in the world again."

Tasia stroked her mother's brow, nodding. She would talk later about the truth, about the need for her to once again leave. And her mother would understand. She'd cry and shake, but she would know what must be done. After all, Tasia was now a Guardian. Her duties superseded everything else.

"I love you," Tasia said to her mother, her voice strained, cracking like old timber. She then turned to Sayer. "And you too."

Her mother smiled, hugging her again.

"Love kept me alive," Tasia whispered, then glanced at Jerico. "When things couldn't get any worse, I thought about the people I loved, and everything just got better."

CHAPTER 10

K'ail had been flying above Kyoto for most of the morning. He'd watched fellow gods appear from all directions, inspired to arrive at the human stronghold by the belief that soon the War for Earth would be over. K'ail had helped spread the word that the humans had captured all the staffs, that within days they would set them together, thereby summoning the gods' ship. When it arrived, the humans would attack it. And the gods were intent on being nearby when any such trap was sprung.

During his last conversation with Tasia, K'ail had sensed that she was hiding information from him. She was planning something, he was certain. And he would never underestimate her again. Yet she was naïve to assume that she was the only mortal in communication with the gods. And some of these mortals had been compromised. Their loved ones had been captured, and they would do anything to spare them from terrible deaths—including betraying their own species.

Soon enough, K'ail believed, he would learn about his foes' plans. And when their intentions were understood, they would be thwarted. Of course, the gods would allow the ship to be summoned, as each of them longed to escape the hell that was Earth. But once the ship appeared, the mortals would be annihilated. They would first fall in Kyoto beneath an onslaught of talons and fangs. But then the great ship in the sky would travel from continent to continent, laying waste to whatever pitiful bands of humans remained. The Dawn of Atonement would come and go. And K'ail would once again experience the thrill of life within the stars, of ruling a universe of his own making. The gods would conquer and enslave, as they had for millennia, searching for a new home—a planet as scorched and boiling and beautiful as the land that had created them.

The century spent on Earth had been a waste. Few precious metals had been found, metals necessary for travel through space. K'ail could only hope that the planets of nearby galaxies had been more fruitful. By now thousands more would have been studied. And gods would have landed on the most promising sites, ruling whatever species existed, raping the soil beneath them for the rarest of metals—substances able to withstand extreme heat and pressure. These metals once had been common on the gods' home planet. But they'd been mined until nothing remained of them but what had been forged to form the outside of the gods' ship. If more ships were to be created, if the gods were to travel even deeper into space, more of the precious metals needed to be discovered.

K'ail shifted his thoughts from the past to the present. He'd heard additional rumors of a human army marching to Osaka Castle. Why such a force would congregate there, he didn't understand. Wanting to see for himself, he flew to the southwest, away from Kyoto. Decaying buildings gave way to roofless houses and then to fields that were once used to grow rice but now sprouted trees and hidden worlds. K'ail dropped lower, soaring above the dense canopy.

The bullet struck him before he heard the crack of the gun, glancing off his forehead. Rage erupted within him, and he shrieked, lurching to his left, spotting a muzzle flash below. The second bullet didn't even hit him, and he twisted around, so that his back faced the ground. He let his wings go limp and he dropped from the sky, crashing through branches. More guns cracked, and bullets struck his back and shoulders. A woman screamed. Even upside down, K'ail was able to adjust the angle of his wings so that he drifted toward the sound of the woman's wails.

He crashed into the ground near her, leaping and turning and lunging toward a man who swung a rifle in his direction. K'ail's skewered the man's torso with his talons and pitched him toward a pair of other mortals. The three men collided, falling, and K'ail was upon them before they could rise to their knees. His fangs ripped through flesh and snapped bones. The men screamed as if set afire, dying swiftly, no longer able to harm him. K'ail killed the woman next. Then he leapt toward another man, covering his good eye with his hand the instant before the human shot at him. The bullet ricocheted off his wrist, and K'ail pounced on the mortal, driving him into the soil, tearing him apart with his fangs and talons.

K'ail turned. Only one woman remained. She didn't have a weapon and slowly backed away from him. Her face was lined with tears. She shook like a leaf in the wind. "Why ... why did you shoot?" she shouted at a dead man beside her. "You killed us all! You know that? You killed us all!"

Though the woman was pale and middle-aged, K'ail imagined that she was Tasia. He envisioned his enemy. He remembered her words and her mocking, victorious voice.

You defied me.

The woman started to run, sobbing. K'ail charged after her through the dense jungle, branches splintering around him.

You dared to challenge me—a god.

His prey fell, and though he could have devoured her, he let her get up and run again.

What will you think of, Tasia, as I feast upon you? Or will you think at all?

The woman shouted, pleading for help that would never arrive.

This love that you spoke of. Will it aid you now? Will it protect you from my hate?

A line of thick trees appeared, and the woman dashed ahead, trying to get between the trunks.

Love is nothing. A dead star. A footprint in ash. Love did not forge us into gods. Power did.

The woman leapt toward the tree line. K'ail pounced on her, bringing her down, breaking her legs with his vast weight. She screamed, thrashing against him, still trying to escape.

Love is a lie.

He used his talons to cut her—his movements deliberate, his joy growing.

Love is a lie and when I leave this cold rock never again will I think of you.

Screams echoed in the forest, causing birds to take flight from unseen places.

The boy will die too. But I shall kill his dog first. I shall break its back and watch him weep.

Gasping for air, the woman tried to crawl away. K'ail leaned forward, pressing down upon her, forcing her into the mud. She moaned—shuddering and shattered.

The end comes now. Can you feel it? Shed one more tear. Then it will be done.

The mortal wept, blood flowing like small, red streams from her many wounds.

Goodbye, Tasia.

Still struggling, the woman kicked at K'ail. With a twist of his taloned hands, he broke her neck. He reared back, shrieking, letting the world know that a god was within it. As more birds took flight from nearby trees, he lowered his head. The taste of his victim invigorated him, and for not the first time, he realized that he'd miss these moments.

Perhaps Earth, after all, had something to offer. The blood

of its top predator, its unrivaled creation, was as desirable, as perfect, as anything the universe had to offer.

Still pretending that it was Tasia he tasted, K'ail devoured the woman, shrieking again in triumph when she was no more.

CHAPTER 11

S till on horseback, Valeriya followed Aki toward Osaka
Castle, which loomed before them. The extraordinary
fortress rose from the middle of a series of massive
fortifications and moats—graceful and imposing, something
that appeared to have been created by a painter's brush. Aki
had told her that the castle was six centuries old. Each level of
the seven- or eight-story fortress featured an elegantly curved
roofline that sloped upward, making it seem as if a series of
smaller castles had been stacked upon each other. The structure
was as beautiful as it was imposing, reminding Valeriya of a
temple they'd passed earlier in the afternoon.

Many kinds of trees had sprouted from the castle's grounds.
These rose from cracks between the granite blocks of ancient
roads and walls. Fallen cherry blossoms covered courtyards,
muting the sound of their horses' hooves striking stone. As they
neared the castle, Valeriya glanced often to the sky. She could

see three demons high above, circling the citadel. Occasionally, someone from within the castle fired a rifle at them, but the demons were too high to strike, and Valeriya wondered why anyone would make the effort. All they accomplished by doing so was to give away their position.

The closer the companions got to Osaka Castle, the bigger everything became. Vast walls—made of giant granite blocks—provided a series of seemingly impenetrable fortifications that surrounded the fortress. Between the walls were moats, bridges, and gates. Holding her rifle ready, Valeriya wondered what ancient battles here were like. Swords were used, she knew that much. But thousands of defenders must have also stood atop the walls, firing arrows into masses of attackers.

Groups of Seekers began to appear. These men and women carried rifles and supplies. They led horses that pulled carts full of heavier equipment. A particularly large group of Seekers protected four machine guns that perched on tripods on one of the carts. Valeriya had never seen such a collection of weapons. Men and women also carried what looked to be silver staffs, but Valeriya could tell that the staffs were actually just painted bamboo poles. These Seekers were pretending to be Guardians. It seemed unlikely, however, that they'd fool the demons. They were too careless with the fake staffs, accidentally pointing them toward friends and piles of weapons.

Remembering Tasia's plan, Valeriya gazed toward the skyscrapers surrounding the castle. The buildings rose about a half mile away. Snipers would be positioned atop these structures, and when demons attacked the castle, they'd fly into a trap and find themselves encircled by expert marksmen. Seekers would strike them from all sides, killing as many demons as possible before retreating into basements and bunkers.

"We're the bait, aren't we?" Valeriya asked. "I mean … everyone in the castle is the bait."

"Do you have to bring everything back to fishing?" Aki replied. "Can't you think of another analogy?"

"But it's true."

"Have you been looking into these moats and wondering what's swimming around in them?"

Valeriya smiled. "You know, I'm not quite that simple."

"Really? I have my doubts."

Rolling her eyes, Valeriya tapped her heels against her horse's sides, urging the stallion forward. It responded and she quickly left Aki behind. Her stallion broke into a full gallop, but when Aki shouted, Valeriya pulled back on her mount's reins. Beneath the shade of an old maple tree, she searched the sky for demons, wondering why they flew so high above and hadn't yet attacked.

"You've ridden a horse before, haven't you?" Aki asked as she caught up. "Before we came to Japan."

"My grandfather showed me how to ride."

"Is there anything he didn't teach you? Can you turn yourself invisible too? Or shoot bolts of lightning from your eyes?"

"Just try to keep up next time. You won't break a nail, don't worry."

Aki glanced at her glossy emerald-colored nails. "Well, that would be a worry. A tragedy, actually."

Valeriya grinned, shaking her head. Although nervous about the looming battle, she enjoyed being outside in the sunshine. And Aki's company always seemed to lift her spirits. As the smell of roasting meat drifted over them, she explained to Aki how to ride faster, how to use her legs to hold herself tight against a horse. They trotted ahead, soon entering the shadow of Osaka Castle. Even more Seekers were present here. Each appeared to be busy bringing weapons and supplies into the fortress.

A woman shouted at Aki to help her unload a cart laden with boxes of ammunition. Aki looked to her right and then left, pretending that she didn't know where the request had come from. She urged her mount forward, arriving at a fallen tree to which people had tied their horses. After climbing down from her saddle, she reached into her pocket and then gave her stallion a carrot.

"That woman's still yelling at you," Valeriya said, pointing behind them.

"Well, she didn't say please."

"She wasn't trying to be polite, you know."

"Let's climb the castle. I want to show you the view."

Valeriya followed Aki into the citadel, which bustled with activity. Aki paid the people around her no attention, proceeding to a wide stairway. She hurried up the stairs, taking them two at a time. Holding her rifle in her right hand, Valeriya ran after her. They ascended several levels, each overflowing with Seekers. Valeriya wasn't sure how so many people had arrived before them. She'd thought that they would be among the first, but she was clearly mistaken.

By the time they reached the top of the stairs, Valeriya was glistening with sweat. Aki didn't wait for her but strode ahead, walking across a large room and passing through a doorway. She proceeded up a series of steel steps that cut through the castle's once elegant roof, then opened a wide, horizontal hatch. They stepped forward and were now outside, standing on some sort of open terrace or viewing platform that had been bolted to the roof. The companions paused to study the sky. Five demons were visible high above, circling them like giant birds. To their left, a man watched the demons through a large pair of binoculars. Two women, each holding rifles, stood beside him.

Valeriya saw that someone had fastened a series of large blue flags around the top of the castle. In the center of each flag was a depiction of a closed human fist. Every fist appeared to be a different color—shades of brown, black, white, and amber. The fists rippled in the wind, defiant and powerful. Below them on other terraces, men and women pointed rifles into the sky. A fake Guardian was also present, holding his painted bamboo staff.

"If we look too strong, the demons might not attack," Valeriya said.

Aki took her hand and started to lead her to the west. "Here, I want to show you something."

They walked across a catwalk to another terrace. Far below them stretched the castle's outer fortifications—walls and moats and towers. Beyond these sights, the modern city of Osaka rose far above the tree line. Skyscrapers seemed to huddle together as if cold and trying to generate warmth. Several of them were blackened from fires, but they hadn't collapsed. A few others must have fallen, as open spaces existed amid the gathering of buildings.

Valeriya had seen many dead cities and didn't think the view was unusual. She wondered what Aki wanted to show her but stayed silent. Instead she thought about traveling through Moscow after her grandparents had been killed. Much of the city had burned to the ground, and not even bandits seemed to dwell within it. It was then that Valeriya had hidden inside a zoo for several weeks, reading old signs about animals as a way of trying to escape the memory of her grandparents' deaths.

Aki pointed toward the skyscrapers. "Do you see that brown building? It's right between those two big ones."

"With the burnt top?"

"I was born in it. My parents were trying to get to the Stronghold of Kyoto for help. But I came early—surprise, surprise. I guess my mother screamed a lot, but they hid down in the basement, and no demons ever came. My father delivered me. He still tells the story about how I peed all over him."

"You did what?"

"I peed on him. When he was cutting the cord. Doesn't that sound like me?"

Valeriya smiled. "It sounds exactly like you."

"I think—"

The crack of a rifle interrupted Aki. Valeriya looked up and saw that a demon was dropping lower. Peering through her rifle's scope, she realized that the demon held a man in its talons. He was screaming. Suddenly the demon released him, and the man fell toward the castle. Valeriya didn't have a good shot at the demon, but fired nonetheless. So did Aki and a few other Seekers. The man screamed, flailing his arms and legs. Valeriya turned away from him right before he struck the far side of the terrace. His body landed with a sickening crunch.

After reloading her rifle, Valeriya reached for Aki's hand. She trembled and wasn't sure how to steady herself. Somewhere nearby, a woman was crying. "I liked … meeting your father," Valeriya said quietly. "Maybe he'll … tell that story to me."

Aki nodded. "They'll attack us tonight. I know they will."

"And we'll be ready."

"I don't want to die like that. If one of those big, ugly bats carries me away, just shoot me."

"That's not going to happen."

"Why not? It happened to him."

Valeriya started to speak, but then stopped herself. She didn't want to give voice to hollow, false words. And so she hugged Aki, holding her tight. "I won't let them do that to you," she promised. "I'll pull the trigger."

"I wish we had those staffs. The real staffs."

The crack of a nearby rifle startled Valeriya. She released

Aki, then glanced up. Demons were circling lower. There were more of them now. Maybe ten or twelve. Peering through her weapon's scope, Valeriya watched one loop around the castle. It kept its head up, so that she couldn't see its eyes. Still, she sighted her scope's crosshairs on its chest, her hands steady as she fired.

The demon flew on. Valeriya reloaded, aimed again, and pulled the trigger. Other Seekers did the same, and the air was filled with the sound of their loud, impotent shots.

Whatever the demons were planning, they didn't seem to be in a hurry. Aki and Valeriya would have to wait.

CHAPTER 12

J erico stood near the Orb in Angkor, watching Tasia say
goodbye to her mother and brother. As the sun set, they
hugged each other, talking quietly, swaying on their feet.
Tasia's staff rose above them, leaning from side to side as she
moved. She squeezed her brother's hand, kissed his forehead,
and then whispered something to her mother, who was in
tears. As birds squawked and crickets chirped, the three of
them continued to huddle together, seemingly oblivious to the
world around them.

Finally Tasia stepped away from her loved ones. Not
bothering to wipe off her tears, she nodded to them, promising
to return. After saying she loved them, she took Jerico's hand,
thanked him for coming with her, and moved closer to the Orb.
Rex followed them, whimpering without end, apparently afraid
of being left behind. Jerico kissed Tasia's brow, then hugged her
tightly.

"I need to know," she said quietly. "Because for my plan to work, I have to drop twice in one day."

"I believe in you."

"Maybe you shouldn't follow me. What if something goes wrong? You shouldn't have to suffer or die too."

"Nothing will go wrong. What you said makes sense. The demons drop twice in a day. And you're connected to them. So you can drop twice and lead me where we need to go. You'll protect me."

She took a long and deep breath, then looked up at him. "I love you."

"Tell me again when we get there. Tell me in a minute."

Tasia closed her eyes and bit her lower lip—a sure sign her thoughts had shifted to Kyoto. She was focused on envisioning it and leading them there. Jerico didn't want to distract her, so he leaned toward Rex and scratched the top of his head. Trying to suppress his own fears, he waved goodbye to Tasia's brother.

Without warning, Tasia stepped into the Orb. Jerico followed her, calling to Rex, seeming to tumble forward into the light. He'd always been able to maintain his thoughts during drops and this occasion was no different. Even as his body seemed to twist and turn, he was able to think about Tasia, to marvel at the strength she'd shown by once again leaving her family. Visions of her danced before him, and he felt his mind drifting away from his control. And so he focused his thoughts, blocking out the sea of stars that swirled around him. Then the light came again, and he lurched ahead, out of the receiving Orb.

Tasia was on her hands and knees, vomiting. Jerico stumbled toward her, placing his hand on her shoulder, realizing that she'd led them back to Kyoto. Though the city seemed to sway about him, it only took him a moment to remember why they had returned. As Rex appeared, Jerico whispered to Tasia, reminding her of her name, and that he was with her.

Continuing to heave, Tasia squeezed his leg, rocking back and forth. She moaned, her eyes wide, her forehead slick with sweat. Jerico had never seen a drop affect her so much, and edged closer to her, holding her tight. She felt hot, as if sick with a fever.

"I'm here, Tasia," he whispered, kissing the top of her head. "You did it. You brought us back."

A shot rang out in the distance, followed by another.

"Please, please say something," Jerico added, panic surging within him, consuming him. "Let me know you're okay."

She spit, wiped her lips, and looked up at him. "I love you."

His eyes immediately teared. "I love you too."

A man spoke, prompting Jerico to look up. Several Seekers were standing next to the torn corpses of a half dozen men and women. A demon must have been waiting for them near the Orb. When they'd arrived, it had ripped them apart.

"What can I do for you?" Jerico asked Tasia, rubbing her back.

"Just … let me lean on you. I want to get up."

He helped her to her feet. She nodded to him and he squeezed her hand. Only then did he realize that Trax stood among the Seekers. The thin scientist, Ishaam, was also present.

Trax stepped forward, smiling at the small piece of sandstone that Tasia held out for everyone to see. "What a lovely gift," he said, taking it from her. "We've been waiting for you both. Speaking for us all, Miss Tasia, I'm delighted to learn that you traveled to Angkor and back, that you controlled the path of your drops. I knew you would."

"Thank you."

"You're quite welcome. Now, if you'll follow me, Zeus would like the pleasure of your company. As would the rest of the Council."

Jerico shook his head. "Just let her rest for a minute. She's been—"

"No," Tasia interrupted. "It's alright. I can go."

"Wait. You need to wait."

"Thanks," she replied. "But really, I'm ready. I'm fine."

"And I thank you for your strength, my dear," Trax said. "So if you will, please walk with me."

Certain that Tasia hadn't yet fully recovered from the drop, Jerico took her arm as she stepped ahead, following Trax and Ishaam. The train platform, which had always seemed so empty to him before, bustled with activity. He glanced up and saw several demons circling high above. A pulse of light darted toward one, but the demon wheeled away from the Guardian's attack. Many Seekers were present, and they must have recently dropped into Kyoto from other Strongholds. Jerico didn't believe that they could control the path of their drops, as Tasia could, and so Seekers everywhere must have been simply stepping into Orbs and hoping that they'd arrive in Kyoto.

Somewhere distant, an explosion boomed. His pulse quickening, Jerico glanced in every direction. To the north a plume of heavy smoke drifted skyward. Gunfire sounded and a man screamed. Jerico had spent much of his life avoiding conflict with demons, and even Seekers usually opted to fight from behind fortified or hidden positions. It was strange to see men and women running around in the open, firing into the sky. Jerico wasn't sure what to think, but then it dawned on him that two armies were gathering—collections of demons in the sky and humans on the ground. The demons appeared to probe the human force, usually circling at safe heights, but occasionally diving to attack.

Trax led them into the underground Stronghold. By now Tasia seemed to be recovering her strength, but she remained unusually quiet. Jerico wondered if she were thinking about her family or the coming battle. If he'd been alone with her, he would have asked. But with Trax and Ishaam nearby, he didn't want to pry. And so he bent down and patted Rex's head. Rex licked the underside of his wrist, then jumped up, bumping against him.

Tasia kept staring straight ahead. She seemed oddly distracted. Jerico knew K'ail could communicate with her, and wondered what might have been said between them. Maybe K'ail had threatened her with something. Maybe he still held some sort of power over her.

Trax led them past the children's hospital. A young girl recognized Rex and called out to him. Rex bounded over to her, licking her face, prompting her to laugh. Other children appeared. One boy was bald and wore some sort of mask on his face that was connected to a portable machine. Reaching into his pack, Jerico searched for a set of toy train cars that he'd found a few days earlier. After handing his gift to the boy, Jerico said that he looked strong, that soon he'd be running around again. The boy nodded, cradling his new train cars.

Jerico smiled, but then saw that Tasia was still staring blankly ahead. Her continued silence troubled him. "Why don't you go on?" he asked Trax. "We'll be just a few minutes behind you."

Ishaam cleared his throat. "The Council is waiting for her. And—"

"And they can wait a little longer," Jerico interrupted. "Do you know what she just did? She dropped twice in a day. She brought me to Angkor and back. Give her a minute to rest before she has to answer their questions."

"A most agreeable proposition," Trax replied. "We'll see you there."

Jerico watched Trax and Ishaam depart. When they disappeared behind a corner, he turned to Tasia. "Are you okay?"

"I'm fine. Really."

"You seem … distracted."

"I'm sorry. I don't mean to be."

"But what's bothering you?"

She shifted her staff from her left hand to her right, glancing at the children, and then back at him. "There's something … I have to do. Some place I have to go. But I'm afraid of leaving."

"What are you talking about?"

"It's better if you don't know."

She didn't turn away from him and he searched her face for answers. "It's K'ail, isn't it?" he asked. "That demon wants something from you."

"He wants me."

"You said you could ignore him, right? That you could just … push his words away."

She nodded.

He took her free hand in his. "Then push them away. Don't let him get inside your head."

Glancing at Rex, she bit her lower lip. "He'll be inside my head until he's dead."

"Then let's kill him. Let's find a way."

"That's why I'm distracted. That's what I'm thinking about." She moved closer to him, squeezing his hand. "I want to think about you, about us. About my mother and brother. But if I don't focus on him, there won't be any us. He'll hurt me. And he'll hurt you."

Jerico saw that she was struggling to contain her emotions. He leaned forward, hugging her. "I wish I could hear him. I wish I had your powers."

"He spoke to me yesterday. But it was strange. I think he was killing someone when he called out to me. I think he killed a woman. And he thought about me ... while he tore her apart."

Swearing softly, Jerico kissed the top of her head, inhaling the scent of her. As he had many times before, he wondered if at some point she'd be overwhelmed by stress. She had been captured, tortured, and imprisoned. And even after escaping, her tormentor could still force his way into her mind. It didn't seem possible that she could go on, day after day, enduring such pressures. At some point, she would have to crack.

"It's going to be over soon," he whispered, kissing her brow. "One way or the other, it's going to be over."

"I'm ready."

"And in the meantime, I'm here for you."

"I know you are."

"I'm exactly where I need to be."

She nodded but squeezed his hand once more. "That love poem ... what did it say again?"

"The poem from Rumi?"

"Right. That was his name."

Jerico recalled the words that he'd read so many times. "'The minute I heard my first love story, I started looking for you, not knowing how blind that was. Lovers don't finally meet somewhere, they're in each other all along.'"

"It's perfect," Tasia whispered, then looked up, rising on her tiptoes to kiss him. "I could have never written it, but I know it's perfect."

He sensed so many things in the way she moved against him—love and longing and fear. "I won't let you face K'ail alone," he said quietly, holding her tight, wanting to make her feel better. "You don't have to do everything alone."

"Thanks."

"Rumi would agree with me."

A boy laughed. Tasia glanced in the direction of his voice. She then turned back to Jerico, kissing him once again. "I love you."

"And I love you … like the stars love the night."

She started to speak, but then smiled. "So you're a poet now? A warrior-poet?"

"No. But I can try to be one. I'll always try with you."

"And I'll always listen."

Jerico longed to feel all of her, and sensed her pressing harder against him, deeper into him, as if a river entering a sea.

But then, still holding his hand, she pulled away, leading him toward a place where all eyes would be upon them.

CHAPTER 13

T hough it was long past midnight, on top of Osaka Castle everything appeared to be illuminated. Six large, battery-powered spotlights probed the sky, hunting for demons. When one was located, if it flew low enough, dozens of Seekers fired their rifles, driving it away. Occasionally a lucky shot brought down a demon. The beasts shrieked as they died, plummeting through the darkness, crashing into trees or the castle.

Aki and Valeriya stood next to one of the spotlights, searching the sky. Behind them, a dead demon lay crumpled on the terrace. Aki had fired her weapon so many times that her ears rang and she felt slightly off-balance. Everyone around her feared that the demons would assault them all at once, diving down to overwhelm the defenders. And yet the demons continued to attack as individuals, avoiding the spotlights, appearing suddenly above startled groups of Seekers. These unfortunate men and women were often torn apart or thrown over the ancient parapets so that they fell to their deaths.

Though the screams of her comrades haunted her, Aki was surprised that the demons hadn't attacked with their full numbers. Something seemed to be holding them back. Were they waiting for the light of dawn? Or maybe more of them were arriving. Maybe their plan, whatever it was, required patience.

Not far away, five hundred snipers continued to remain quiet and hidden at the tops of skyscrapers. None would give away their positions until the demons attacked in force. Certainly these Seekers must have been tempted to bring down passing demons, but so far, they had kept to the plan.

Spotlights continued to swing back and forth, searching for the winged beasts. As there seemed to be a lull in the fighting, Aki lowered her weapon. Valeriya did the same, wiping sweat from her brow. Nearby, a tall woman with short, spiked blonde hair stepped toward them. She was a well-known Seeker called Slate. Dressed in a black leather jacket and matching pants, she carried a pistol in each hand. Slate had lived in Kyoto for several years, and she and Aki occasionally crossed paths. Their encounters weren't pleasant, and Aki wasn't sure why Slate seemed to despise her.

"Why aren't you firing?" Slate asked, pointing both her handguns at the ground.

"Because there's nothing to fire at," Aki answered. "The big bats are taking a break. Or do you want me to shoot at the moon?"

"You'll shoot at what I tell you to. I'm in charge of this section. I'm in charge of you."

Aki sighed, looking away. A headache throbbed at the back of her skull. Her ringing ears further soured her mood. Though she had argued with Slate in the past, she didn't feel like doing so now. She needed to focus on the sky and to keep Valeriya safe. Nothing else mattered.

Slate, unfortunately, wasn't ready for their conversation to end. "Did you hear me? What I say, you do."

Aki glanced at Valeriya and winked. "She likes to be heard."

"I was thinking the same thing," Valeriya answered, and then started to reload her rifle.

"You've always been weak, Aki," Slate replied, then looked up, searching for demons. "Do you know that?"

"I'm a bad listener, if that's what you mean. Actually, what was your question?"

"You should be a Hider," Slate added, "like all the other cowards in your family. You don't belong up here."

Valeriya twisted a dial on top of her rifle's scope, making a slight adjustment. "Aki helped bring back the stolen staffs. She belongs wherever she wants."

Slate started to reply, but Aki cut her off. "I fight so my family doesn't have to," she said, stepping toward Slate. "And choosing not to fight doesn't make them cowards. They help out in other ways."

"But they're so good at hiding."

"And you're so good at making friends."

The taller woman didn't move. "What happened to that toy sword you used to carry?"

Aki turned to Valeriya. "Is she really still asking questions? I already told her I'm not much of a listener. Maybe if my ears weren't ringing, I'd be doing better."

Slate shook her head. "Look at you, fighting in your jewelry, with your green hair. You're a child—a little girl who's always been lost in the world. You're like one of your own jokes."

"Really? I hope so because—"

"So when I tell you to keep firing, you'd better do it. I have authority here. My word is the law."

"The law?"

"That's right."

"You're in love with big, powerful clichés, aren't you?" Aki asked, looking at her nails. "Fine. Because your word is the law, I'll do what you say and keep firing. But since the demons seem to be taking a break, I guess I'll have to shoot at the moon after all. Do you think I can hit it? I'll bet you I can't. Maybe a wager of my hair dye against whatever kind of vegetable oil you comb yours with?"

Valeriya made a half-hearted effort to repress a laugh. "We're low on bullets, Aki. If we're going to shoot at the moon, we'd better get some more."

Slate glanced at the ammunition boxes strewn around them. Each had been opened and was empty. "Ammo is on the second level. Bring back as much as you can carry."

"So we're free?" Aki asked. "Do I have time to repaint my nails?"

"You have ten minutes. Take any longer than that and I'll have you locked up."

Valeriya extended her hand to Aki, then led her away. They started to descend the staircase. Seekers hurried up and down it, carrying weapons, ammunition, and bandages. Aki rubbed her ears, wishing that the ringing would quiet.

"Whatever did I do to her?" she asked, shrugging.

They reached the next floor and Valeriya turned around. "She's one of those people who hates the world. Because you don't hate it, she goes after you, trying to bully you around. But you won't let her. And that makes her—"

"Really mad."

"It makes her crazy."

Aki nodded, still descending the stairs. Far above them, a rifle cracked, and then another. "The big bats up there are just pretending. I finally understand their game. They're going to attack us in the morning with everything they have."

"Why then?"

"Because they like to fight in the light. They like to see us … when they hurt us."

A man carrying a large-caliber rifle bumped into Aki, apologizing. She patted him on the back and wished him well, continuing to make her way toward the second floor, believing that she was right, that the demons would launch their major assault after dawn. They'd come with the light, but what they didn't know was that the light would also help the hundreds of human snipers positioned in the nearby skyscrapers.

Aki finally reached the second level. She'd seen the supply depot before and knew where to go, heading toward a massive room that once served as a museum for tourists and was now filled with weapons and ammunition. People hurried about it, using crowbars to pry open wooden crates. In the far corner, several wounded Seekers were attended to by a trio of doctors.

On her way toward crates of rifle bullets, Aki stopped. A group of Seekers was gathered just outside of the room on a fortified outdoor balcony that might once have been some sort of guard post. Curious, she moved toward the group, asking why everyone was huddled together in such a small space.

A bearded man turned to her. "Just listen," he said quietly.

Aki nodded. Though her ears still rang, she could hear people behind her sorting through supplies. Far above, rifles popped. She didn't find any of these noises to be unusual and was about to ask the man what he was talking about when she heard a faint cry. Someone was weeping—a woman, maybe, but more likely a girl. She called for help, her voice distant and pained.

Moving through the men and women around her, Aki stepped closer to the edge of the balcony. She looked out into the forest that surrounded the castle. Again, the girl pleaded for help. She was sobbing.

An abrupt chill swept through Aki. Unconsciously she held her breath, straining to hear with more clarity. The girl pleaded, again and again. Suddenly Aki felt weak and reached toward a railing for support. Valeriya moved next to her.

"It's a trap," someone whispered behind them. "A demon is waiting out there—just hoping someone tries to help her."

Aki turned around. "You mean … no one's gone after her? No one's going to help her?"

"Not as far as—"

"What's wrong with you?" Aki asked, thinking about the little girl, Sasha, who'd been killed on the beach. Sasha had wanted to run free in the sunlight. Aki had promised her that someday she'd be able to. But that day had never arrived.

"Someone should help her," Valeriya said, her voice obscuring the distant pleas. "Ten of us should go out and get her."

A nearby Seeker shook his head. "We've been ordered to stay put. We can't leave the castle."

"And you're doing a lot to protect the castle?" Aki asked. "Standing here, listening to her?"

He shrugged. "We're just following orders. Besides, anyone who goes out there is going to get killed. And getting killed won't help the girl."

Aki swore, moving past the men and women around her until she was back in the supply depot. More than a dozen Seekers scurried around, seemingly oblivious to the girl's pleas.

Valeriya stepped to a crate and began grabbing magazines of bullets. She handed several to Aki. "I was alone once," she said quietly. "After my grandparents died."

"And?"

"And someone saved me. A boy, actually. A boy I didn't even like."

Again Aki's thoughts drifted back to Sasha. "Let's go get the girl. Before anything else happens to her."

Valeriya nodded. "Abandoning our post could give us problems with your friend up there."

"She's already got all the problems she needs."

"And it is a trap. You know that, right? We both know that."

Aki reached for Valeriya's hand, holding it tight, trying to suppress her growing fear. "Your grandfather taught you all about traps. Isn't that what you told me? That the two of you snuck around the woods and set traps for squirrels and rabbits?"

"Trapping kept us alive. Because it's quiet. It doesn't draw attention."

"Well, since you're such a master trapper, you know all about what's out there, what could be waiting for us. So just think like a hunter, think like the demon that wants to trick us."

Valeriya leaned toward Aki, hugging her tight. "Stay behind me. And for once, please, please keep quiet."

"Just put your hand over my mouth, like Jerico does to Rex."

"I will if I have to."

Aki took several deep breaths, trying to slow her pulse, to steady her thoughts. Though tempted to continue the joke, instead she kissed Valeriya on the lips. "I don't want to lose you."

"You're not—"

"I can't lose you."

"And you won't. Like you said, I'll be the hunter."

Far above, rifles began to crack once again, following each other like footsteps.

Aki swore, remembering how Sasha had scoured the beach for shells, skipping as she ran. Sasha had seemed so free, so unburdened. But now she was gone—forever destined to be little more than a fading memory.

"I can't live if I can't be proud of my life," Aki said quietly.

"If I didn't understand that about you, I wouldn't be with you."

Nodding, Aki kissed Valeriya again. "I'm glad you're with me. I wouldn't want to be with anyone else."

"Just stay behind me. Do what I do."

"I will. I promise. But don't stop to put a worm on a hook. That'd be asking too much of me."

Valeriya squeezed her hand, and then turned around and walked back toward the stairway. Aki followed in her footsteps, feeling blessed to have such a companion. She'd never expected to fall in love with Valeriya, but knew she had. Somehow this girl of the forest, this Russian hunter and trapper, had captured her heart. And though Aki always had been fiercely independent, she found solace in the feelings that Valeriya inspired within her—feelings of joy and grace, laughter and hope.

They entered the darkness together.

CHAPTER 14

The bed creaked only slightly when Tasia eased away from it. Jerico shifted in his sleep but didn't awaken. Dressing in silence, she glanced repeatedly in his direction, wishing it weren't necessary to leave him—and worse, to mislead him. But she had to face K'ail alone. He'd made her promise to fight him by herself, and while she placed no value on a promise to him, if she didn't face him, she believed that Jerico would die. Somehow K'ail would have him killed, probably within a matter of hours.

Tasia understood the risks she was taking by confronting her adversary. If she were to fall, she wouldn't be able to lead the attack on the demon ship. But she also believed that if K'ail killed her, he'd at least bring her staff back to her people. K'ail wanted his ship summoned. And perhaps someone else, maybe Zeus, could summon it and command the attack on it.

In any case, if Jerico was killed, Tasia knew she wouldn't

have the strength to lead the fight against the demons. She would try, of course. But she'd fail. Only with hope and love and belief flowing through her could she summon the demon ship, initiate the drop into it, and fight her way to victory. If K'ail had a way to kill Jerico, which she believed he did, and would, Tasia could never win.

She would defeat K'ail alone or die alone.

Silently, Tasia strapped on her pack, reached for her staff, and bent toward Rex. He lay at the foot of the bed, whimpering softly as she scratched his neck. Pulling a wrapped piece of dried fish from her pocket, she fed him the treat, whispering reassuringly. She then turned toward Jerico, her eyes glistening. On her pillow she'd left a note for him, and though she knew her words were inadequate, she had tried to explain her actions, to assure him that she'd soon return.

A tear ran down her face. Then another. Praying, she pleaded to see Jerico later that day, but also asked that if she fell, he'd stay safe, and would find happiness once again. Then she touched her fingers to her lips and blew him a kiss. Stepping away from him made it seem like she was cutting herself, but as her tears fell to the floor she turned around.

The hallway outside their room was dimly lit and quiet. Tasia took some deep breaths, trying to stay strong. She felt broken and unfaithful, as if she were betraying Jerico with someone else. She also worried about Aki and Valeriya, though they should be well protected within the castle. Once a sizable force of demons flew into the trap, five hundred snipers would knock them from the sky. And if anything went wrong, Aki would know where to hide. She'd been to the castle several times and could lead Valeriya to safety.

Attempting to focus on the task at hand, Tasia forced herself to walk down the corridor, nodding to several guards. They must have wondered what a Guardian was doing awake before dawn, but no one asked about her plans. The Stronghold was crowded with recent arrivals and people slept on makeshift beds. Unorganized piles of supplies were strewn about. A man coughed. The scent of steaming rice lingered.

Dawn was breaking when Tasia left the Stronghold, heading north on a wide street. She'd debated whether to take a horse but had decided that it would be wiser to travel in silence. Careful not to step on broken glass or anything else that would reveal her presence, she held her staff ready and often paused to study the sky. Scores of demons had flocked to the city and any of them could bring her down. K'ail wasn't her only concern. He never had been.

Tasia wanted to stay strong, so she didn't let herself think about Jerico, about how she might never see him again. Those fears would have distracted her. She didn't even muse over the coming battle or her friends or mother and brother. Instead she simply studied the sky and her surroundings, noting the many storefronts she passed.

Countless shops existed along the street, and though she couldn't read the many signs, she peered into stores and saw displays of clothing, shoes, umbrellas, televisions, dead bonsai trees, and musical instruments. The street was inundated with decaying cars, and also had a special, narrower lane that looked to have been used by people on two-wheeled platforms that featured an upright steering column. Locals must have stood on the platforms and darted around the city. Now their skeletons lay scattered on the cracked pavement. Though the clothes of every skeleton were nearly gone, many still wore faded, rotting backpacks. One small skeleton still gripped a leash tethered to a rusting robotic dog.

A few young trees had sprouted from the street's buckled pavement, and their leaves seemed to reflect the early morning light. Tasia spied a bird's nest and then thought about her father, wishing he could see her. He'd have been proud. She touched his ring as it rested against her chest, suspended from her neck by a new narrow cord of leather.

Ahead, a fire smoldered within a shattered building. Tasia glanced at the sky, then turned down another street, avoiding the flames. As she continued on, other sights rekindled memories of her loved ones and friends. She passed some sort of sword store and noticed the curved blades of ancient weapons. Maybe Aki had found her sword there—the blade that had taken K'ail's eye. Tasia also spotted a pet store, brimming with shelves of fish tanks. She wondered if Valeriya would enjoy a tank. It could be filled with colorful fish, and she could watch them explore their miniature world.

Tasia crossed a wide intersection and looked up. The sky had brightened. Two demons were high above and barely visible. Thankful for her staff's comforting presence, she moved to a nearby sidewalk, where a series of shattered storefronts provided her with some cover. To her surprise, she recognized a bookstore. Thinking of Jerico, she stepped inside. Nothing had been looted from its shelves, and the store looked like it must have a century earlier. There were rows of books and stacks of magazines. Tasia leafed through several of the books, but they were written in Japanese. She glanced around, saw a sign printed in English, and walked to a single shelf that held books with titles she could read. One novel was about a woman's journey to Mars, and believing that Jerico would enjoy it, Tasia stuck the book in her backpack.

Soon she returned to the street. She had imagined rushing toward K'ail, seeking to defeat him as quickly as possible. And yet now she was in no hurry to meet him. If this morning was going to be her last, she wanted to savor it. So she stepped into several other stores and collected gifts—a sapphire ring for Aki, a hunting knife for Valeriya. She also discovered a game with dice for her brother and a small jade pendant for her mother.

Though her backpack was heavier with these items, Tasia was glad to have found them. It felt good to consider what her companions liked, rather than how she might be taken from them. As she made her way through the ruined city, she continued to think about the people in her life, wondering what they'd do if the War for Earth ended. Her mother, she hoped, would remain in Angkor and help rebuild the ancient temple, as she'd often spoken of doing. Her brother would likely travel the world, perhaps bringing medicine to people in distant places. Aki and Valeriya seemed to be in love, and Tasia imagined them together, laughing as they taught an orphan how to fish.

A demon shrieked and Tasia paused, peering above. The beast encircled a position to her west. What did it see? A rifle cracked and the demon darted lower. She was tempted to fire her staff at it but didn't want to give away her position.

Tasia passed the ruins of a church that had fallen inward, as if its walls were so tired of resisting the elements that they had collapsed together, seeking a mutual resting place. She paused at the steps of the church, praying for her loved ones, and for strength.

K'ail's words interrupted her thoughts. *Why do you keep me waiting?*

"I'm not far," she whispered.

You failed to answer the question.

"I don't need to answer any more of your questions. I escaped, remember?"

Escaped from your prison, but not your fate.

"I'm writing my own fate," she replied quietly, starting to walk again.

Do you carry a staff?

"You'll see soon enough."

And the boy … is he with you?

"He's not a boy. And he's not with me."

You were wise to leave him behind.

Tasia shook her head, finally reaching the river that led to the golden temple. She paused, thinking about turning back, about running to Jerico and apologizing for leaving him alone. He would forgive her, she knew. But she would never forgive herself if K'ail acted on his promise to have him killed.

Banging her fist against her side, she continued onward, staying close to storefronts. "Could you really have Jerico killed?" she asked. "Just tell me that, so I know I'm doing the right thing."

Yes. All I would have to do is ask. He would be dead within an hour.

"Ask who?"

Gods ask. And the universe provides.

She circumvented some sort of utility truck that had crashed into a storefront. "You're not as strong as you think. None of you are."

Why would you say such a thing?

"Because if you were really gods, really so strong, you wouldn't need to keep trying to prove it."

We care what no one thinks but us.

"You kill and enslave. You rule through fear. Everything you do makes you weak."

We have nearly annihilated your species. We rule the universe. Weak is not a word often used to describe our kind.

Tasia started to speak but stopped when the breeze carried smoke to her. She wondered what was burning and why it was burning. Glancing behind her, she studied the sky, then stepped forward.

"The power to destroy doesn't make you strong," she finally replied. "It just means that you have power. If an ant was on the ground in front of me, I could step on it. I could destroy it. But why would I destroy something that isn't a threat to me?"

You are as naïve as a child running into a storm.

Tasia shook her head, wondering why she would rather talk with K'ail than walk forward in silence. Maybe because talking with him was how I survived being their prisoner? she thought. Maybe because that's how I learned so much about myself?

"People aren't born to hate," she finally said. "They're born to love but taught to hate. I was taught to hate demons, but when you're all dead, my hate will die with me."

K'ail didn't immediately respond, and Tasia studied the sky and then the nearby river. She saw several gray cranes wading through the shallow waters, searching for food. She thought about the worlds that the minnows in the water inhabited— forever-changing places of dark and light, turbulence and stillness.

I hate your kind because, as I said to you before, you destroyed the very land that gave birth to you. You murdered your father. Your mother. And you took for granted what we have spent lifetimes pursuing.

"I didn't murder—"

You raped your home for all that it could give to you.

"But I didn't do those things. Neither did my father or Calix or Fareed or Draven."

A breeze arose from the west, causing trees to twist and ripples to flash across waters.

I shall miss our conversations, Tasia.

"I won't."

You mislead yourself. Because you shall.

"You're so wrong. So arrogant and wrong."

But just because I shall miss them, do not expect mercy from me. When you deceived me on the island, you decided your own fate. And it will not be pleasant.

"Why the golden temple? Why don't we stop talking and fight right here? And now that I think of it, why do you pretend to be some kind of a poet? Or a philosopher? You waste so much time, pretending to be so many things."

The golden temple shall be a fitting place for your death. You should see something beautiful before your demise.

"Beauty is all around me. My father taught me that."

When I soon ruin you, I shall take all your senses except one. Which sense, Tasia, would you like to keep with you, as you lie dying?

Despite the staff in her hands, K'ail's words caused Tasia to pause, to scan the sky.

As you die, would you like to still hear or to see? Or maybe to smell a rose that I place against your lips?

"You don't scare me."

Tell me, Tasia. Which sense do you treasure most? I will let you keep that sense—my final gift to you.

Tasia held her staff in both hands, trying to draw power

from it. "Any child of mine ... won't hate. Do you understand that? Hate will disappear from Earth when we blow your ship from the sky."

You deny me still. A pity for you, because now I will take everything you possess. You have truly written your own fate.

The staff seemed to throb within Tasia's hands. She wanted to fire it. "I'll see you soon. With my eyes. The eyes you'll never take from me. The eyes that'll see you die."

He started to reply, but Tasia pushed his words away. She looked again at the distant cranes. They were majestic and pure and seemed as ancient as the low mountains beyond them. She would have liked to sit down and watch them. But instead she started to walk again—faster now, with a new sense of purpose.

K'ail's words reverberated within her, and regardless of how she had spoken to him, her fear of the coming fight grew— spreading and swelling into an ocean of unease that gripped her with such strength that she found it hard to breathe. K'ail would take everything from her that he could, and she might suffer as much as any man or woman ever had.

And yet she thought of her loved ones, of her world, and walked on, drawing strength from her feelings.

Behind her, the cranes took flight, their wingtips touching the water, their cries timeless and enduring.

CHAPTER 15

I t had taken Aki and Valeriya much longer than they expected to reach the crying girl. Part of the problem had been navigating the castle's many fortifications—moats and walls that were difficult to pass in the dim light of dawn. As they'd crept forward, the battle atop the castle quieted. Shots were rarely fired. Screams were seldom heard. And yet, high above, scores of demons flew in a circular pattern. Neither Aki nor Valeriya had ever seen such a gathering, and both believed that an attack was imminent.

The girl, when they finally reached her, no longer pleaded for help. Instead, she only whimpered. She sat in what looked to be a steel cage that might have once been used as a kennel for dogs. The cage had been placed within the middle of a clearing. Though dense trees surrounded all sides of the open space, for some reason it only contained grass and shrubs.

Hiding behind an overgrown evergreen bush, Aki peered

through her rifle's scope at the girl, who might have been five or six. She was about the same age as Sasha, the child who had died on the beach. Aki was more determined than ever to save her and would have rushed forward if not for Valeriya's demand for patience.

"There must be a demon out there somewhere," Valeriya whispered, using her rifle's scope to search for their foes. "Maybe in the treetops. Maybe somewhere else."

"Maybe it left," Aki said. "Anyway, she's still alive, right in front of us. We should save her now while we can."

"Wait. Just a little longer. Let me find it."

"We've already—"

"If we die, who's going to help her?" Valeriya asked. "Who's going to get her out of there?"

Aki swore, raising her rifle so that she could look through its scope toward a group of distant trees. "We didn't come here to wait."

"We didn't come here to get killed either."

"No, but—"

"Just be patient, Aki. Remember what you promised—that you'd follow me."

"Then tell me where to look. Where would you put a trap? Where would a big bat put one?"

"Where it's not seen, not expected."

"But the trees are obvious. Anyone would—"

Valeriya swung her rifle down, pointing it toward the distant path, peering through its scope. "The demon must be underground. In some sort of hole. We're taught to look up. But it must be down."

Aki's pulse quickened. She gazed through her scope toward distant shrubs. "I don't see anything unusual. There's no hole. Just a bunch of bushes."

"Look just to the west of the cage. Those bushes there, one of them is … upside down. I can see its roots. It's been moved."

"So a demon is under them? Just waiting?"

"I think so," Valeriya answered. "Maybe it's a small one. Maybe one trying to surprise a Guardian. But now that we know where it is, we can just—"

"Lower your weapons and turn around slowly," a voice said from behind them.

Aki twisted to her left, surprised to see Slate and two men. All three of the Seekers had their weapons pointed ahead, toward Valeriya and Aki. "What … what are you doing?" Aki asked.

"You deserted your post. You both did."

"No. We came here to save a girl. Don't you see her out there?"

"We're under attack and you deserted your post. That's a betrayal. A crime."

Aki was dumbstruck. She shook her head. "She's still alive! Look at her. Let me get her and then I'll go back to—"

"Hand over your rifles," Slate said, pointing both her pistols at Valeriya.

"That's not happening," Valeriya answered, standing her ground. "Because we've done nothing wrong."

Slate swung one pistol toward Aki. "I'd be within my rights to shoot you both. The Council would support me. We're at war and you deserted your posts."

"This is insane," Aki responded, leaning away from Slate. "You're insane."

"Take her gun," Slate commanded to the men beside her.

A bearded man shook his head. "I'm not authorized to—"

"Do it now!"

Valeriya held out her hand. "Wait. Just wait."

"You're both deserters!" Slate nearly shouted. "Three Seekers died up there while you were down here. If you'd been at your post, with the ammunition I asked for, you might have saved them. Now come with me or I'll have you both shot!"

Aki stepped backward, shaking her head. She could have killed the approaching men, but she didn't fire her weapon. One of the Seekers grasped her rifle's barrel and eased the gun away from her. Valeriya was also disarmed.

"We're going for a walk," Slate said. "So follow me."

Aki glanced at the little girl, then back at Slate. "Where are you taking us?"

"Shut up and walk."

"I'll shut up when I'm ready and that's not going to be anytime soon."

"You're such a little coward."

"And you're such a bow-legged bit—"

Still holding her pistol, Slate used the gun's butt to strike Aki on the side of the head. The force of the blow stunned Aki and she stumbled. Valeriya caught her, holding her up, yelling at Slate to stop. Aki tried to speak, but struggled to remain standing, as if gravity were suddenly a hundred times stronger. She heard Valeriya shouting. Tiny bits of light seemed to dance before her, and she closed her eyes, hoping the dancing lights would disappear. But they didn't, and a wave of nausea washed over her.

Someone pushed Aki forward. Valeriya stayed at her side, helping to hold her up. Aki's senses didn't feel connected to her body as Slate led them across fortifications and courtyards. What she saw and heard and smelled didn't seem to be a part of her reality. Her legs and lungs might as well have been made of bricks. Her mind was strangely weightless, lacking power and focus. She couldn't make sense of what she saw, of how once again Osaka Castle loomed before them, massive and magnificent. Leaning against Valeriya, Aki struggled to walk, to talk, to think. Blood trickled down from her wound, dripping onto her shoulder.

The group entered the citadel, and in a moment of clarity, Aki thought that they would climb to a higher level. Instead they reached the stairwell and started to descend. She stumbled, but Valeriya kept her upright, grunting with the effort. A corridor stretched ahead. They moved into it, their footsteps producing echoes. A door containing a barred window was passed. Then another. The next door was opened for them, and though Valeriya continued to help Aki, now she was shouting at Slate. Aki couldn't comprehend what was being said. Her head throbbed. She still saw bits of light. One of the men shoved Valeriya and Aki forward, and the door swung shut behind them.

Valeriya kicked the door with her right foot, shouting until it was clear no one would answer. Then she helped Aki toward what looked like a wooden bench. Aki sat down. She wanted to understand what was happening, but she felt so very tired.

Carefully, Valeriya helped her lie down, so that her head rested on Valeriya's lap. A tear rolled down Valeriya's cheek, reached her chin, and then fell. Aki watched as more tears came and went, leaving trails on Valeriya's face. She wasn't sure why her friend, her lover, was crying, but she was sad to see so many tears.

Then Aki's weariness overcame her, and everything became dim and then dark. Valeriya's tears disappeared, and the last thing Aki sensed was her lips being kissed. Then she felt nothing.

CHAPTER 16

Tasia approached Kinkaku-ji Temple with immense care and caution. The gold-covered three-story structure sat at the edge of a small lake. The temple's graceful rooflines arched upward, protecting balconies and chambers. Unlike most every building Tasia had ever seen, Kinkaku-ji appeared largely unaffected by the passage of time. Its golden face still shone brilliantly and was reflected in perfect symmetry within the lake's still waters.

Holding her staff with both hands, Tasia moved slowly toward the temple, staying beneath the cover of ancient pines. Her heartbeat raged within her with such strength that it seemed likely to burst from her chest and fly away, as if a bird that had broken free of its cage. She tried to keep her breathing calm and steady, but could only control the speed of her slow, hesitant steps.

Believing that K'ail was nearby, she paused next to a granite bench. While aiming her staff forward, she studied the sky, the tree line, the lake, and the temple. Yet nothing seemed amiss.

You came alone.

A shiver ascended Tasia's spine. She trembled, understanding that K'ail could see her. Though she sensed the presence of a powerful foe, the only demon she saw circled high above, and seemed unlikely to be K'ail.

And you shall die alone.

"Where are Fareed's bones?" she whispered, trying to stay strong, to draw strength from her staff.

In the center of the temple. As promised.

"And you?"

You shall see me soon enough.

"Gods shouldn't need to hide."

Soon that tongue of yours will be ripped from your mouth. The power of speech will leave you first.

Wiping sweat from her eyes, Tasia turned slowly around, peering into the nearby forest, searching for K'ail. He might have been trying to distract her, and she vowed to ignore his words. Instead she studied the land, remembering how her father had taught her to search for demons. The forest was unnaturally quiet. Birds didn't chirp and weren't even visible. K'ail was close, she knew. The back of her neck tingled. The corner of her left eye twitched. She tried to use her connection to K'ail to locate him, but some sort of barrier seemed to exist between them.

Again Tasia crept forward, her staff swinging in the

direction that she looked, always ready to fire. With each step her confidence diminished and her heart pounded harder. Her mouth was suddenly dry. K'ail had picked this location for a reason, which gave him an advantage over her. She thought about turning around and letting him come to her but felt compelled to gather up Fareed's bones. She longed to bury him and still carried his prayer rug in her pack. But even more powerful than this desire was her craving to kill K'ail. She needed him gone from her world, from the entirety of the universe.

The temple loomed before her, shimmering in the sunlight. Leaving the path that led to its main entrance, she stepped closer to the lake. K'ail might be inside the temple, she reasoned. He might await her just behind its main doors. Deciding to climb into a window, she continued on, focused on the structure, occasionally pausing to study the sky and the forest.

Suddenly the lake beside her seemed to erupt, casting spray in every direction. An immense demon sprang toward her and she only had time to squeeze her staff once. A brilliant bolt of light darted forward, piercing the demon's right wing. Then the vast weight of her foe smashed into her, driving her backward, into the ground. The air was hammered from her lungs and she struggled to breathe, to comprehend the fate that was befalling her. Shrieking, the demon ripped away her staff, throwing it toward the temple.

Tasia gasped, now in the demon's grip, still fighting to breathe, to resist. The beast's taloned hands tightened around her forearms, threatening to snap them in two. Her foe lowered its head, and even as terror overwhelmed her, Tasia realized that the demon had two eyes. It wasn't K'ail.

But K'ail's voice reached out to her. *Look above you, Tasia. Watch how I come to claim you.*

Gritting her teeth, she glanced up and saw the second demon, the one that had been circling far above. K'ail must have studied her advance from his position in the sky. He'd never even been in danger. And he'd been communicating with the demon in the water, describing her approach.

She thrashed in the demon's grasp—twisting and turning as if she were being held over flames. Yet she was unable to free herself. A sense of overwhelming horror, stronger than anything she'd ever felt, poured into her then. She began to weep, terrified of what K'ail would do to her, of being torn apart. The thought of losing her senses made it feel as if the imaginary flames below her were now inside her—cooking her flesh, boiling her blood. Driven by her profound dread, she kicked and clawed and bit at the demon above her. It leaned lower, opening its mouth, its fangs nearing her face.

K'ail landed next to the other demon and bent over her, his words materializing. *I shall leave your tongue intact for a moment. Instead I shall take an eye first. You may decide which one.*

Tasia tried to kick him, to find a weapon, but was powerless against the two of them.

Decide now or lose them both.

"No!"

K'ail leaned closer to her, a single talon from his right hand approaching her face. As she struggled and screamed, the talon dropped lower, finally resting against her forehead, pressing hard enough to draw blood. Tasia ceased her struggles, though her chest still heaved and the flames still raged within her. Tears welled at the corners of her eyes. She shuddered, trying to pray, begging to be reunited with her father. She must have whispered something out loud, because K'ail seemed to smile.

You pray to a god you cannot see. How foolish. How weak.

She gasped, struggling to breathe, to think.

Pray to me, a true god, and perhaps your pain will be brief.

"Please."

Pray to the only god you shall ever know.

"Gods are kind," she whispered, tears on her cheeks.

Pray to me or I shall blind you!

"They listen."

Close your eyes, Tasia. Because darkness comes for you. A final, eternal darkness.

The world seeming to collapse around her, she shut her eyes, weeping. She felt his talon drift down her forehead, cutting into her flesh, dropping over her eyebrow, to her right eye. The hard point pressed against her closed eyelid, and again she struggled against both demons, kicking and clawing and screaming.

Good. Let me feel your fear. Let me bathe in it.

"Please don't."

I shall enjoy the taste of you. Of your sweet, defiant blood.

She couldn't breathe. Couldn't think. "You win," she muttered, sobbing.

I know.

"You've always won."

The talon pressed harder against her eyelid. She felt her skin start to separate, to yield. Blackness seemed to pour into her, overwhelming everything that once had been lit, suffocating her hope and love and faith.

Do you feel the darkness nearing?

"Stop! Please, please stop!"

Her eye began to burn, to throb.

"No!"

You once called me a one-eyed bat.

"I was wrong! So wrong! And I'm sorry."

Such a frail creature. Look how easily you bleed.

"I'll pray to you. I'm ready."

Your blood awakens me. I long to see more of it.

"Please. Please don't!"

I shall strip the flesh from your bones, Tasia. But first, your eye. I wish to taste everything you have seen, everything I am taking from—

The crack of a rifle sounded, and the silent demon atop Tasia was thrown backward, falling away from her. She gasped, opening her eyes, scrambling out from under its bulk as the rifle cracked again. Screaming, she crawled and then stumbled toward her staff, diving for it. As she gripped the alien steel, power surged within her.

She spun around, aiming her weapon toward K'ail's ascending body. She fired once, but he wheeled away and her bolt of light barely missed his underside. Again and again she sent brilliant bursts of energy into the sky, but K'ail twisted and turned, avoiding her blasts. He soared upward with unimaginable strength and speed, and soon was too far above for her to strike.

"Tasia!"

Blinking repeatedly, hoping that what she saw was real, Tasia peered into the nearby forest. Jerico ran toward her and she stood up, holding one arm out to him. He reached her, hugging her with such ferocity that it hurt her bruised ribs. She wept against him, caressing his face with her free hand. Above, K'ail still circled their position, though he remained too high to attack. Then the demon drifted to the west, disappearing behind a nearby mountain. Whispering words she couldn't comprehend, Jerico eased his grip on her, yet they still clung to each other.

The flames within Tasia vanished. Once again, she could breathe. Though she trembled and ached, she could still see. Her eyelid hurt. It bled. But K'ail hadn't stolen her sight.

"You ... followed me?" she asked, fresh tears falling, nausea rising up within her.

Jerico nodded, wiping the blood from her forehead and face.

Biting her lower lip, she struggled to stay standing. The ground seemed to shake beneath her, as if an earthquake were about to swallow her up. Resisting the urge to vomit, she collapsed to her knees. Jerico supported her as she fell, dropping beside her, keeping her partially upright.

She wanted to thank him and hold him and kiss him, but all she could do was lean against him. Now that she was safe, whatever strength she'd once harbored had fled. Her mouth felt wooden. Her bones seemed to have gone limp. Time itself felt as if it had stopped, as if she were still perched between light and dark, life and death.

"Where's Rex?" she finally whispered, swaying as a wave of nausea seemed to wash over her.

"With the children, back in the Stronghold."

A bird chirped in the distance. A frog croaked. Now that one demon was dead and the other was gone, nature reawakened.

"How did you know … I was leaving?" she asked, still trembling.

Jerico kissed the spot on her forehead where K'ail had cut her. Then he kissed the top of her eye. "You were so distracted last night. You never went to sleep. And neither did I. But I pretended to, because I thought you might leave me."

"I had to. He made me."

"You're wrong. Leaving me like that was really wrong."

"I'm so sorry."

Jerico glanced up, then shook his head, clenching his jaw. "How could you do that? What if you never came back? I'd have spent the rest of my life wondering what happened to you. That note wasn't enough. You didn't say enough."

Tears dropped from his eyes, racing down his cheeks. The

sight of them caused her to shudder and she cried with him. "You're right," she whispered. "I betrayed you."

"Why?"

"K'ail promised to have you killed … if I didn't do what he wanted."

"He tricked you."

"I believed him. I was scared."

Jerico looked away.

A jolt of pain darted down Tasia's face, lodging itself somewhere deep in her chest. She blinked repeatedly, trying to remain calm, reminding herself that she could still see. "He's so powerful," she stammered. "He almost is like a god."

"Was he the one who flew away?"

"Yes."

"Why was he afraid?"

"Because of you."

"Because of the little piece of metal that I shot from my gun? If that's true he's not all-powerful. He's not some sort of god."

"Maybe not. But sometimes it feels like he is."

Jerico sighed, then wiped the tears and blood from her face. "Don't ever do anything like that again," he said quietly, shaking his head.

"I won't. And I'm sorry."

"If I'd missed, you'd be dead. I'd be dead."

"I know."

A gray crane stepped into her view, searching in the pond's shallows for minnows. Ripples spread out before the bird. It leaned downward, its long beak darting into the water.

"Tell me more about him," Jerico asked, looking skyward. "Why does he want you dead?"

"I thought he'd be alone. I thought I could beat him."

"You risked everything to face him."

She nodded. "He's the biggest threat to us all. To me. To you. And ... and he has Fareed's bones."

"Fareed's bones?"

She glanced at the golden temple. "I wanted to bury him. But K'ail ... beat me."

"He didn't beat us. And that's all that matters. You're safe and I—"

So the boy saved you.

Tasia groaned, trying to ignore K'ail's words. But she didn't have nearly the strength.

Maybe love is stronger than I thought.

"It is," she whispered.

I shall drop the bones. Watch them fall from the sky.

Tasia glanced up and saw that K'ail once again had flown into view. He looked to be five-hundred feet up and circled their position. Squinting, she watched him soar, wishing that Jerico had shot him instead of the other demon.

Small white shards fell from beneath the demon, drifting through the air and then disappearing into the forest.

Time will bury him. I have simply spared you the trouble.

"What's he saying?" Jerico asked, still holding her. "Tell me what he's saying."

"Fareed's bones … he dropped them into the forest."

Jerico started to speak but stopped, shaking his head. "Fareed wouldn't want you to die. Do you understand that? He prayed for you."

"I know."

"Then let's get out of here. Let's get back to the Stronghold, where we're safe."

Tasia squeezed Jerico's shoulder. While she understood that returning to the Stronghold was the logical and safe choice, she couldn't abandon her friend, even if he was dead. "I saw where his bones went," she replied quietly. "I just want to find one of them. I want to bury a part of him. Please."

"Why? Why is that so important with everything else that's going on?"

"Because I owe him. Because when he took K'ail's eye he saved me. He saved me and he didn't even know it and I want to give him some peace."

Jerico looked up at K'ail and then peered into the forest. "Don't leave me like that again. It wasn't right."

"I know. And I'm sorry."

"You would have been killed."

She nodded, once again squeezing his shoulder. "Sometimes he gets inside my head and it's hard for me to think straight. He says terrible things. And I just want him to be gone."

"Then let's kill him together. Once and for all."

A fish splashed in the pond, causing Tasia's heart to skip. She watched K'ail circle far above, promising herself that she'd be smarter—never again would she walk into one of his traps. If Jerico hadn't arrived, she'd be screaming right now, entombed beneath K'ail's vast weight, blind to the world around her. A shudder rippled through her, and she tried to force away an image of her own death.

"It's amazing," she said, fighting to change the direction of her thoughts, "how you shot that big, moving demon. Just once—right in the eye. From so far away. With so much at stake. I wouldn't have wanted anyone else in the world to pull that trigger."

Jerico shrugged, then kissed her forehead. "I had to wait. I couldn't rush things. And I'm sorry about that."

"Don't be."

"It was easy to follow you—though I didn't understand why you went into so many shops. What was that all about, anyway?"

"I found you a book. A new story."

His brow furrowed. "You went shopping on your way to fight K'ail?"

"Well, I wanted to find something for you," she replied, finally managing to smile. "Because I knew you'd be mad at me."

"And now you want to find Fareed's bones?"

"They're on the way back. I promise."

He leaned forward, kissing her lips. "You're right about Fareed. And I want to bury him too. So let's go find his bones. Let's give him peace."

She glanced up. K'ail still circled above them, so high that he almost looked like a bird. Grateful to still be alive, she thanked Jerico once again. Then she followed him as he stepped away from the golden temple. Its walls still seemed to shimmer and most everything around it was unchanged. The temple was as beautiful now as it had ever been, a testament to the goodness of people who once walked these same grounds.

"Love won," Tasia whispered to the demon above, and then ignored his angry response.

CHAPTER 17

The darkness was nearly complete, deep within the subway system. Using only a red-beamed flashlight, Ishaam moved slowly forward. Rats scurried ahead of the scientist, disappearing into fissures within the walls. The ceiling leaked and water dripped everywhere, falling into puddles, producing a sound nearly as rhythmic as the beats of Ishaam's heart.

Shaking, he stumbled, then regained his balance. He carried no weapon, even though he was far from the Stronghold of Kyoto. This part of the subway system was ignored and isolated. Ishaam already had passed through a series of defensive fortifications—narrow passageways, steel doors, and a minefield. Even though he'd studied a map of the minefield, crossing over it had demanded every bit of courage that he could muster.

A stone's toss ahead, part of the ceiling had collapsed, and a mound of concrete blocks, bricks, and dirt occupied most of the passageway. Holding the flashlight in his left hand, Ishaam struggled to climb over the unstable pile. Dust rose, filling his lungs, causing him to cough. Momentarily his fear was forgotten as his chest heaved. When he reached the top of the debris, he stumbled, falling sideways and sliding to the bottom.

The sight of the white demon, Li'kan, caused him to moan. With bricks still tumbling down, he leaned back toward the pile, as if the rubble behind him could somehow shield him from the menace before him.

You kept me waiting. And how that's made me hungry.

He saw her words in perfect clarity. Though no man or woman knew it, the long years Ishaam had spent at the Arctic Stronghold had given him the opportunity to learn how to communicate with a captured demon. "I'm … sorry," he replied, the red-beamed flashlight unsteady in his hand.

Never mind. Our game would be over if I dined on you. And that wouldn't be much fun, would it?

"Please. Just tell me—"

The castle. Why do so many of your little friends scurry into it?

"Wait. First tell me about my wife and sons. Tell me they're unharmed."

Well, physically they're fine. But I can't speak for how they feel. These past days haven't been particularly agreeable to them.

"You promised—"

Such a foolish, small-minded man you are. Back in your

Arctic Stronghold, you should have stayed quiet. Yet you became too close to your prisoner. You let him befriend you. You even told him about your family and how they enjoyed watching sunsets near the river. It's hard to imagine such stupidity.

"An unforgivable ... mistake."

When he informed me about your conversations, he gave me a wonderful gift. Of course, it came at your family's expense. What a pity for you.

Ishaam looked away from Li'kan, feeling so very broken. His intentions always had been good. But everything had turned out so badly. His prisoner had outwitted him, flipping everything upside down. "They're to be freed," he finally replied. "That's our agreement. If I tell you about the castle, you'll release them."

Of course I will. I'm not a demon, after all, regardless of what you all call us. Such a trite name. So uninspiring. Even the smallest of minds should know the difference between a god and a demon.

"This is the last time we'll meet. I won't give you anything else."

Soon there won't be a need. So tell me about the castle. Tell me or your wife and sons will endure ... so much ugliness.

"Please. Please let them go. After I tell you, let them go."

We've been good allies these past days—good friends, I might even say. So tell me and they'll go free.

Hating himself for the enormity of his betrayal, but willing to do anything to save his loved ones, Ishaam shook his head, then closed his eyes. "The castle … is a trap. A ruse. Yes, it's full of Seekers. But no Guardians are present. All the staffs are just … painted bamboo."

But why?

"The Council wants you to attack. But our best shooters are in the skyscrapers encircling the castle. And when you demons … you gods … attack, our snipers will strike. Five hundred rifles won't all miss."

Why fight this battle at all? Why the need?

"Because we'd rather fight you at the castle than on your ship."

Li'kan flapped her wings, causing dust to rise once again. Ishaam coughed, struggling with the foulness around and within him.

Your snipers won't expect us to attack them first. We'll come at them from behind and introduce ourselves. And then the castle will fall. How many of you little ones are within it?

"Another five hundred."

A thousand mortals slain in one day. Oh, it will be like a battle from the past. A fight of honor and glory. How exciting.

"My sons—"

In the days of old, after we were abandoned on your weary planet, we'd destroy entire cities. We'd knock your war machines from the sky, your ships from the waters. We fought like the gods we were, slaying you by the thousands. Those were the best of days, so far removed from today, from how we now hunt you—one at a time. What a tedious, unfulfilling task this war has become.

"Please release my—"

Almost all the gods are already nearby. I'll spread the word immediately. You've given me another gift. How fitting. What a treat. By the time you eat your next meal, a thousand fewer little creatures will scurry around this world.

Ishaam rubbed grit from his eyes. "My wife and sons—when will they come to me?"

Soon.

"Are they … really still alive?"

Voices carry so well in the sky. I could give one of your sons a ride and let you hear him scream.

"No," Ishaam replied, clenching his fists. "Please no. Just bring them back to me. Bring them here. If I don't see them by tomorrow … I'll poison myself. And then your spy will be gone."

We have other spies, little man. You deem yourself too important.

"I told you about the castle. I kept my part of our bargain. So please, bring them back. Let me hold them once again."

And what will you do with them, when our ship arrives? Will you go deep underground before we attack? That may save you. It may not. In any case your world will be in ashes. And you'll be alone.

"I'll be with them. That's what matters."

The white demon flapped her wings again. She was much larger than any male and occupied almost the entire subway corridor. *Soon we'll be free. The Dawn of Atonement will come and go. To soar in the stars again, well, it will be such a wonder to us all. You're so very generous. Thank you.*

Ishaam coughed, then nodded. "Gods … should keep their promises. So, please, bring them to me tomorrow."

If the fight goes well, they'll be released. You can dance together if you wish. Or just scamper away to somewhere deep underground. That would be wiser.

Ishaam nodded, feeling nauseous. "I think I'll leave now."

Look for me in the sky. I'll have blood on my fangs and joy in my heart.

Trembling, Ishaam turned away from Li'kan and climbed back up the pile of debris. He wept as he moved, wounded by his own betrayal. He'd dedicated his life to fighting the demons, studying them with such focus that he had eventually felt connected with them. Two weeks earlier, he could have said that he'd saved hundreds of human lives. But then, in a moment of profound stupidity, he had told the prisoner about his family. They'd disappeared five days later, and his nightmare had begun. He had gone from being a hero to a villain, to someone who was proud of himself to someone who hated himself.

The demons had tricked him. Not only were they the stronger species, but they were the smarter species.

And soon they would win the war.

CHAPTER 18

Aki awoke with a pounding head but a clear mind. She remembered Slate striking her with the gun, as well as stumbling back to the castle. Groaning, she lifted her head from Valeriya's lap and felt the bloody lump above her temple. "How long … was I asleep?" she asked, reaching for her companion's hand.

"A few hours. Slate came by a little while ago."

"And?"

"And she threatened to shave you bald unless you kept your mouth shut."

"I hope she tries."

Valeriya nodded and then stood up, leaning down to stretch her back. She pivoted to her left and right, moving her shoulders in a circular motion. "I asked her to save the girl. I even told her where the demon was hiding."

"What did she say?"

"That deserters don't get to beg for favors."

"That skinny, bow-legged, good-for-nothing wannabe."

Smiling, Valeriya continued to stretch. "You seem fine. I was worried about you."

"Well, my skull feels like there's a demon inside it, trying to burst out. But otherwise I'm great."

"We need to get out of here. Then we can save the girl and take her back to the Stronghold."

Aki agreed and then stood up, moving slowly. Though her head throbbed, she was no longer dizzy. Even her ears had stopped ringing. "I hate asking for help," she said, then walked to the cell's door and looked out through its barred window. "But we're going to need it with Slate. She'll turn people against us. She'll lie."

"We'll tell Tasia what happened," Valeriya replied, shrugging. "And with her vouching for us, no one will care what Slate has to say."

Tugging on the bars, Aki shouted into the hallway. She called for help, demanding to speak with whoever was in charge. Raising her voice caused her headache to intensify, but she persisted. Though she wanted to face Slate, she was more concerned with the imprisoned girl. They needed to save her. Otherwise the demon would grow impatient of waiting and simply take her life.

"You should rest," Valeriya said, rubbing Aki's shoulder.

"But we need to save her. Just like you said."

"And we will. But it won't do us any good if you pass out again."

Aki swore, enraged that Slate had struck her down. She felt betrayed, even though Slate hated her. "This isn't right!" she shouted through the window. "We were trying to save a little girl! Didn't you hear her cries, whoever you are, you steaming, stinking lump of cow dung?"

"And that's supposed to help us?"

Turning from the window, Aki looked at her friend. "We don't have any time. If we stay here—"

Valeriya raised her hand. "Wait."

"Wait for what?"

"Just be quiet for once and listen."

Aki closed her eyes, aware of the distant sound of rifles firing. The shots didn't come from the top of the castle, but from somewhere farther away. Scores of weapons fired. An explosion rang out. "I don't understand," she said, shaking her head. "If the fight's not here, where is it?"

"The snipers. They stumbled into our snipers."

More rifles cracked, one after another, the sounds blending together, echoing off unseen buildings and landscapes. They seemed to crescendo into a nearly nonstop pounding, as if countless hammers struck as many nails. But then, ever so gradually, as time passed and the battle evolved, the tempo of gunfire slowed. The voices of individual rifles rang out, defiant and powerful. Yet even these became fewer, and the pauses between their cries lengthened. Soon a near complete silence descended on the cell, interrupted only when a single gun fired, its distinctive crack repeating itself again and again.

"Our guns are too quiet," Aki said, shaking her head. "Something's wrong. Why is just one person shooting? That doesn't make any sense."

"It makes sense if almost every demon flew away. Or if we're losing. If our snipers are dead."

Aki turned toward the door's window. "We'll fight!" she shouted through the iron bars. "Let us out and we'll fight!"

"I have a bad feeling about this. One person shooting—that's just not right. I think the demons won. I think they're coming for us."

Swearing, Aki struck the door with her fist. "We're good at shooting the big bats! Let us help!"

Guns began to fire from the top of the castle, much louder than the shots of the snipers. Rifles cracked and machine guns rattled. A loud crash reverberated down from the fight. Then another. More guns erupted with a fury that Aki had never heard. Throughout her life, Seekers had fought in small groups, had avoided big battles. And yet now, hundreds of men and women were shooting above her. The sound of gunfire intensified, merging into a steady stream of clamor that echoed off ancient ramparts. Then, amid so much fury, another rumble seemed to shake the castle's foundation.

"What's that?" Valeriya asked, feeling the wall near her.

"The bats must be dropping things from high above. They've started doing it lately."

"This isn't good. We need to get out of here."

"We want to fight!" Aki shouted through the window, again

pounding on the door. "Just give us a chance to fight!"

Gunfire sounded from somewhere much closer and a man screamed. More shots rang out, ricocheting off stone. Crash after crash reverberated. A part of the castle must have collapsed because a distant rumble came and went.

Her headache forgotten, Aki called again and again for help, but no one answered. With each beat of her heart it seemed that a dozen guns fired. Deeper, more ominous crashes continued to shake the walls. Men and women screamed. The smell of smoke drifted downward.

The fighting seemed to be nearing them. A man yelled for help and then screamed in pain. Loud thuds caused dust to drift from the ceiling. A demon shrieked. A woman begged for mercy and was silenced. Gunfire continued to crackle but wasn't as constant as before. Another rumble, this one much louder, caused more dust to fill the air.

"We're going to be buried in here," Valeriya said, wiping dust from her forehead. "This place is going to fall down around us."

"So help me with these bars."

The companions tugged at the window's center bar, trying to dislodge it. Though the metal was ancient and rusted, it was also thick and immovable. They then yanked at the next bar, and then all the others.

"Let's kick down the door," Aki said, smashing her booted foot against it. The blow hurt her heel, but the door didn't move. Valeriya struck it as well, again and again.

A man shouted from nearby, and Aki peered through the

window, surprised to see a bloodied, white-robed medic run into the passageway. Her eyes further widened when Slate stumbled after the man, firing both of her handguns behind her.

"Help us!" Aki screamed.

Slate glanced at her but didn't pause, instead running forward, past their cell. A demon appeared next, so large that its wings struck either side of the corridor as it walked ahead. Aki reached for Valeriya's hand and pulled her away from the door, toward the room's nearby corner.

As they crouched down, Aki placed her finger to her lips, holding Valeriya close. Aki started to shake, fear spreading within her, consuming her. Though she'd faced many demons, there always had been a rifle in her grasp. Without a weapon she was powerless to protect herself, and that knowledge seemed to cut at her. The room, small to begin with, felt as if it were shrinking, pressing on her from all sides. Suddenly Aki found it hard to breathe. The air tasted like poison.

The demon shrieked. Aki reached for Valeriya's hand, squeezing it tight. Her companion was holding back tears, and Aki pulled her even closer. "We're not going to die here," she whispered, as much to herself as to Valeriya. "That door's really strong."

Valeriya nodded, then glanced around the room, as if looking for another means to escape. Something thudded against the door. The two companions crouched lower, drawing themselves tighter into the corner. The door was to their left.

Aki couldn't see its barred window and hoped that the demon hadn't noticed them. As rifles cracked in the distance, the door shuddered again, harder this time.

Aki fought against the urge to shout for help. Maybe the demon didn't know they were in there. Maybe it had heard their voices but wasn't sure which cell they occupied.

The door boomed and the demon shrieked. Aki turned to Valeriya, staring into her eyes, terrified of watching her die. As the door shuddered again, Aki leaned forward so that her forehead rested against Valeriya's. They embraced. They didn't speak or even whisper, simply expressing their affections through touch as tears fell to their cheeks.

Shrieking, the demon threw itself with renewed fury at the door. Aki heard wood splinter. The demon struck, again and again. Suddenly Aki was tired of hiding, of waiting for death. No longer could she endure the thought of Valeriya being torn apart. "Stay here," she whispered, then kissed Valeriya's lips. "When I'm fighting it, run."

"No. No way."

"Please."

"I'd never abandon you like that."

Aki shook her head, but stood up, stepping to the door. Valeriya moved to her side. The demon peered through the door's window, its large, red eyes blinking repeatedly. Blood covered its fangs and was smeared on its chest. The beast's wide mouth opened farther, and it shrieked so loud that Aki's ears hurt. Above them, the castle continued to rumble, as if falling on itself. A growing roar, like the crash of a stone wave, seemed to echo in all directions. Aki thought about people dying, about how the demons had come into her world and destroyed so many things.

"You should go home," she whispered to the demon. "You're not welcome here."

The demon lowered its shoulder and threw itself against the door. Wood splintered and a large crack appeared in one of the center planks.

"This is my friend," Aki said. "And you're not going to touch her. Do you hear me, you ugly, rabid, stinking bat? You're not going to touch her!"

Rearing back, the demon struck the door again and again. Valeriya shouted for help but stood her ground. Additional cracks appeared and one of the door's hinges was pulled from the wall, swinging inward, revealing three long nails. Valeriya reached for one and yanked it out of the hinge. Aki did the same, grimacing with effort, the door collapsing beside her. Valeriya pulled Aki back as wood burst apart, and the demon's taloned hands ripped at whatever remained. The beast leaned forward, sticking its head through the ruined entryway. As it shrieked, its fanged mouth opened and then snapped shut.

Aki felt Valeriya pull her from behind, until their backs were against the far wall. Despite her bravado and desire to live, she began to shake, finding it hard to breathe, as if all the dust in the castle were suddenly filling her lungs. The nail looked like a rusty stick in her hand, a laughable weapon against such a foe.

"I'll die first," Aki said, leaning toward the demon, toward her death. "Try to run past it. Please, please try."

"That's not going to happen!"

"You have to try."

"No!"

"Just run! If you don't—"

A loud boom from above interrupted her. The wall behind them shook, then buckled outward. A deafening roar filled their ears and the ceiling started to collapse. Stone bricks and blocks fell, slamming into the demon, driving it into the floor. Something struck Aki's shoulder and she cried out. Then the wall behind them toppled backward. Aki and Valeriya fell back with it, away from the shrieking demon, away from the cell and into an open courtyard. Above them, more granite blocks fell, dropping toward them. Valeriya tugged on Aki's hand, yanking her away from the danger. The world seemed to break then. The ground shook. The walls above them toppled. Men and women fell screaming.

The castle appeared to lean to one side. Then an entire level within it must have collapsed. The citadel seemed to suddenly fall to its knees, as if it were honoring its makers and its glorious past. The castle died then, falling forward, its vast walls and towers disintegrating into dirty, roiling clouds of dust and debris.

Aki and Valeriya stumbled away from the wretched scene.

Stones and Seekers fell from the sky. The land shook. Plumes of dirt shot into the air. A crack appeared in the ground, opening up, seeming to swallow the companions as they ran.

Aki only had time to scream as darkness and pain engulfed her.

CHAPTER 19

The forest was no longer the quiet place it had been when Tasia crept toward the golden temple. Birds darted among trees. Squirrels leapt from branch to branch. The air buzzed with insects. In the tantalizing warmth that accompanied late spring, flowers bloomed and ferns sprouted new fronds.

As Tasia followed Jerico, her near-death experience troubled her less and less. In fact, she felt more euphoric than shaken. She should be dead, and yet Jerico had saved her. The forest was so very alive around her, and she felt as if she were a part of it—soaking in the sunshine, growing and thriving. To have seen death reaching for her and to have escaped its grasp was intensely liberating. She was grateful and joyous, hopeful and renewed. Instead of walking past the beauty around her, she savored sights of moss-covered boulders, shallow streams, fallen pine cones, and slanting rays of light.

Although Tasia had nearly died on multiple occasions, she'd never felt such elation afterwards, and she wondered why this time was different. She could only conclude it was because she followed in Jerico's footsteps. He had rescued her. And while she'd never wanted to rely on someone else, or to be saved, it felt profoundly reassuring to know that he loved her. Once again, he'd fought for her, struggled for her, and won for her.

As they moved through the forest, Tasia tried to explain her emotions to him—how it had never felt better to be alive. Sunlight and warmth seemed to be everywhere, even in the dark forest. Her feet might as well have not struck the damp ground.

"I can't win by myself," she said, stepping over a fallen log. "This morning I thought I could. But I was so wrong."

"No one could."

"I think being imprisoned got me used to fighting alone. I didn't have a choice. But I don't want to fight like that again."

"There's no reason to."

Tasia glanced up, saw nothing, and dropped her gaze to the faint trail they followed. "It's so strange. I almost just died and I should be a wreck. But I feel really good. Really happy. And that must mean that my life is good. Because if I didn't care, I wouldn't feel like dancing."

Jerico turned to her, smiling. "I didn't know you could dance."

"I can't. I'd step all over your feet."

"But I'd be busy stepping on yours."

She grinned, shifting her staff from her right hand to her left. "Since my father died, I've been so sad and angry and confused. I've been lost. But you … you take away the loneliness. You make me like myself."

"You do the same for me."

"To feel happy … well, it's not something I expected. I always thought feeling happy would come later, after the war ended."

A large moss-covered tree had fallen across the trail, and they climbed over it—helping each other. Ahead, golden rays of sunlight slanted downward, having penetrated the forest's thick canopy. The air was damp and sweet with the smells of rebirth.

"You shouldn't have to wait to be happy," Jerico said. "None of us should."

"And I won't. But that's because of you. You've changed everything. Remember how I felt in the desert, after that demon almost killed me?"

"You were angry. We got into a fight."

"I got mad at you when I should have been thanking you. And I'm sorry for that. I blamed you for things that weren't your fault."

He paused on the trail. "You don't have to apologize for something you said after almost dying."

Smiling, she turned to him, reaching for his hand. She kissed him softly, wanting to savor him. His lips pressed against hers, somehow seeming to lift her up, off her feet. "I love you," she said. "And I love us. I love what we've become."

"Did you steal one of my poetry books? Because you're sounding a lot like Rumi."

She brushed an insect from his shoulder. "I'm sure he understood everything a thousand times better than I do. A million. But a few hours ago, I thought I was going to die. And now I'm alive, with you by my side. And all the bad things, the really terrible things that have happened to me, seem farther away. They're not pushing down on me as much. It's like … I can look up and see light."

"That's because you have hope," he replied, kissing the cut on her forehead. "You've always had hope. Actually, you're the one who taught me about it. Rex might have tried, but he's too much of a worrier. You're going to have to help him too."

"I like it when he wags his tail and leans into me."

"That's his way of giving you a hug."

"He's good at it."

They started to once again walk. Before long they neared the place where Tasia thought K'ail might have dropped Fareed's bones. She studied the damp, green ground, looking for anything that wasn't covered in moss.

"I want to find just one piece of him," she said quietly. "Then we can wrap him up in his prayer rug and bury him in a sunny place."

They continued to walk and search. Heat rose from the damp ground, causing them to sweat and slow their pace. Something crashed through the timber, and they spun, extending their weapons, relieved to see a pair of deer streaking away. The deer bounded over logs and rocks, moving with as much grace as speed.

Onward the companions went, following the ancient trail that monks had cut into the Earth a thousand years earlier. Since animals now used the trail, it was still visible, rising and falling, twisting and straightening. Before long they approached a moss-covered stone lantern that rose to Tasia's shoulders. She imagined a candle burning within it many centuries earlier. The candle's light, so small and fragile, must have illuminated a gathering place, a spot of hallowed ground.

Tasia touched the lantern, wanting to be a part of its history. Then she stepped forward, still searching, pausing when she noticed something long and white stuck in a hanging vine. She'd seen enough bones in her life to immediately recognize one. Believing that she'd found a part of Fareed, she hurried forward, then carefully pulled the bone away from the vine. Biting her lower lip, she asked Jerico to remove the prayer rug from her pack. Once he unrolled it, Tasia placed the bone on the worn fabric and rolled it back up.

"Thanks," she whispered.

"Let's keep looking."

They searched the surrounding area, finding three more bones. Finally, when the forest began to darken, they knew they had to leave. Now moving quickly, they walked back to the stone lantern and dug near its base. The work was difficult, as they lacked a shovel. Still, using a flat rock they managed to create a shallow trench in the dirt.

Kneeling, Tasia prayed that Fareed had found his family, that they'd all forever know peace and joy. She then placed the prayer rug within the disturbed soil. They buried Fareed with as much honor and dignity as possible, positioning his rug so that it pointed toward Mecca, as he would have wanted.

Tasia's prayers then shifted to everyone at Osaka Castle. She wasn't overly worried about Aki and Valeriya because she believed her trap would work. Once the demons flew into the area, five hundred snipers, positioned within a ring of skyscrapers would knock them from the sky. The castle was also heavily fortified, and any demons that approached it would be targeted by hundreds of other Seekers. Whatever beasts didn't fall would surely be driven off.

Even so, Tasia prayed for her friends and everyone else involved in the operation. She felt responsible for them, given that the plan was her idea. And so she asked whatever god or gods might be listening to look after Aki, Valeriya, and everyone else.

Now that Tasia had faced K'ail and buried Fareed, she was eager to return to her friends. Equally important, she wanted to help spring the trap, to watch demons fall from the sky like the ashes of a raging fire.

Taking a final glance at Fareed's resting place, Tasia stood up. Hand in hand, she and Jerico started down the trail again, heading back into the city. They spoke quietly along the way, reminiscing about the past and wondering about the future. They took turns describing what it would be like to live in a world free of demons and despair. Doing so wasn't difficult, they realized. Enough goodness remained that it was easy to imagine more of it.

Only when the sun had started to set did they leave the forest. The city sprawled out before them, dead and silent, nothing like the land behind them. Tasia searched the sky for demons, then made her way toward a road. In the distance a wolf or wild dog began to howl, its lonely cry seeming to echo off decaying buildings.

Tasia wondered what the cry meant to the animals that heard it. Were some afraid and others comforted? Was the howl a warning or an invitation? She wished she knew the answers, that she understood nature as well as Valeriya did.

K'ail reached out to Tasia then, and his words unfolded. Wincing, she remembered what he had planned to do her by the lake. She suddenly felt cold.

Turning to Jerico, she stepped closer to him. "He's … talking to me."

"Are you listening?"

"No. Not yet."

Jerico placed his hands on her shoulders. "You don't need to."

"He's being … persistent."

"So? Let him waste his time."

Tasia nodded and started to walk. But she felt K'ail reach out to her, again and again. As they passed by a burnt-out train, she still sensed his thoughts, his message. Though his voice continued to chill her, again she turned to Jerico. "If I hadn't listened to him, I wouldn't know how to control my drops, or how to summon his ship. I've learned a lot from him."

"And so you want to hear what he has to say? Right now? After he almost blinded you?"

"Not at all. But I think I should."

Jerico shook his head. Tasia said that she was sorry, but then opened her mind, allowing K'ail's words to unfold.

Your castle is gone. Your people are dead. As humanity weeps, the gods rejoice.

"What?" she whispered, the chill spreading from her limbs to her chest.

You have lived long enough, Tasia, to see your friends die. Congratulations.

She looked to the southwest, toward Osaka Castle. A distant light, a fire perhaps, seemed to twinkle. "We have to go," she said to Jerico, feeling as if she were falling, as if the ground had opened up beneath her. "We have to run."

"What? Why?"

"We should have won at the castle. Our trap should have worked. But K'ail says we lost."

"I don't understand."

Tasia thought about her friends. She remembered how K'ail's talon had felt on her eye and she shuddered at the thought of her companions being cut and killed. "Aki and Valeriya. They should have been safe, but I think they're in danger. Let's go, Jerico. Let's run!"

He turned around, studying their surroundings. "We need horses. The castle's too far. We should get to the Stronghold and find help."

A gust of wind swept into the city, and Tasia wondered if it carried the sounds of distant screams. She started to reply to Jerico, but stopped, her spirits so far from the height they'd reached a short time earlier. She had buried one friend that day and couldn't bury another. No matter how much she loved and hoped, she wasn't strong enough to look upon the ruined bodies of Aki and Valeriya. They had to be alive. She had to find them.

And so she ran toward the Stronghold, uncaring of what the sky held above her.

CHAPTER 20

Osaka Castle lay in ruins, strewn across the land. As the sun dropped behind the horizon, piles of immense granite blocks cast long shadows. Occasionally the retort of a rifle sounded, but far more often the victorious shrieks of demons dominated the air. The beasts circled the castle grounds, sometimes diving to attack one of the few human survivors.

When the fortress collapsed, it had brought down nearly every Seeker on it. Almost five hundred men and women had died in that moment, and demons now feasted on crushed and broken bodies, jubilant from their victory—which was so reminiscent of their early battles with human survivors.

Of course, the Seekers had fought until the stonework collapsed beneath their feet, and dozens of demons lay dead amid the rubble. Many more of the beasts had been killed near the skyscrapers in the fight against the snipers. Though they had won the battle, the demons had paid a steep price. Those that remained alive were consumed by bloodlust, and any human survivor unlucky enough to be found was maimed and killed. The screams of men and women reverberated as the sun set, seeming to echo off distant walls.

Valeriya and Aki lay under a grouping of massive stone blocks that had once comprised the castle's second level. The blocks had piled atop each other in a way that created a hidden chamber beneath a few of them. Immediately after the castle had collapsed, as dust still obscured the area, the two companions had climbed out of the fissure in the ground and then scrambled under the blocks, hiding from the demons above. Weaponless, they'd been forced to lie next to each other, whispering as the hours passed so that the screams were less prominent.

A granite block rested a hand's length above Valeriya's face. She closed her eyes, resisting the urge to panic, to flee from the confined space. They had agreed to try to escape during the darkest part of the night, so they would remain hidden until just before sunrise, when the moon dropped low in the sky. Valeriya had wept until her eyes stung and was now desperate with thirst. Her tongue was so dry that its surface felt like leather. Her lips were cracked and bloodied. And yet her grandfather had taught her about pain, taught her how to endure it. Pain, he said, can always get worse. To block some of it out, he believed, you had to keep your mind occupied, to plan your revenge or escape or where you'd next go fishing.

Dust drifted down from the stones above them and a demon shrieked nearby. Knowing that a cough would betray their presence, Valeriya held her shirt in front of her face, using the fabric to filter out the dirty air. She moved her tongue around the roof of her mouth, searching for moisture that didn't exist.

Despite their predicament, Valeriya knew they were lucky to be alive. If they hadn't been in the cell, they most likely would have been fighting atop the castle. When it fell, their deaths would have been swift and unavoidable.

Conflicting emotions surged within her. She was devastated by the great loss of life. And she felt guilty whenever she heard a distant scream. But she was also thrilled to still be alive and grateful Aki hadn't been harmed.

"Tell me a story," she whispered, her voice cracking. "It's too hard … to listen to them die."

Aki rolled to her left, so that their faces were only inches apart. "It hurts to talk."

"I know. But it hurts more to listen."

Shifting again, Aki put her right arm around Valeriya. "We're so lucky Tasia and Jerico weren't here."

"We'll see them again. We just have to wait."

Somewhere in the distance, a woman began to sob, pleading for mercy. Aki's eyelashes fluttered together, but no tears emerged. Her body seemed to have no more water to offer. "I'll tell you a story," Aki finally replied, whispering. "Though it's not funny."

Valeriya winced when the woman screamed. "Should we help her?"

"We'd die trying. Die like she is."

"Still, maybe we should try. Maybe we owe her that."

"We owe it to each other to stay alive."

"We do. But the world is bigger than the two of us."

"So we should run out there and die? We should fight those demons with our bare hands?"

Valeriya started to reply but stopped. A large cricket made its way across the stone above her. She wished it would chirp. But the insect kept moving in silence, so much at odds with the world around it.

"Only a few days after Tasia and Jerico met," Aki said quietly, "we all dropped into the Arctic. But almost as soon as we got into the Stronghold, she fainted. She fell like a bag of rocks, but we caught her and brought her to a doctor. When he was treating her, I saw Jerico trying to make her more comfortable. He pulled a blanket higher up on her. He straightened her pillow. And took her hand in his. I'd never seen a boy act like that. I didn't know if I should clap or cry or ask if he had siblings. Because it was obvious he'd already fallen for her. Any fool could see that."

Valeriya licked her cracked lips, aware that the woman had stopped sobbing. "If you'd met a boy like Jerico, would you be with him instead of me? Maybe you just never met the right person."

"I don't know. One time he crossed my mind like that.

Before I met you. But I think girls are more complicated. And I like complications."

"I'm complicated?"

Aki shifted again, grimacing. "Well, I'll list a few things for you. Let's start with the fact that you're beautiful and you like to pick up slimy fish. You grew up in the woods, but you're happy to let me dress you up. You don't really seem to like boys, but you ask me about them. You want to lie here and talk when we're both about ready to die of thirst. And you … you know how to touch me like no one else ever has. So, yes, I think you're a bit complicated."

"Maybe I'm too much for you," Valeriya said quietly.

"Ten of you would be too much for me. One of you is just about right … though two would be better. I could definitely handle two."

Valeriya closed her eyes, trying to ignore the sharp stones beneath her. She remembered how she and her grandfather had sat still for hours while hunting deer. At a young age, she'd learned how to overlook the ache of her back, the cold that seeped into her feet. Her emotions, unfortunately, had been much harder to master. Even now she continued to feel conflicted. "People out there are dying," she whispered, her throat aching. "And I'm safe in here asking you to tell me a story, so I don't have to listen to their cries. No matter how you look at it, that's disgusting. I'm disgusting."

"Well, listening to them doesn't help us. And it doesn't help them."

Nodding, Valeriya thought about the girl in the cage. "When it's dark, we have to go back to the little girl. She still might be there. And if she is, we have to get her out."

"And we will. We'll save her."

"Whoever we can save, we have to save."

Aki stifled a yawn, then shifted her position once again. "My hips hurt. And so do my elbows and ears and teeth. I think my teeth hurt the most, actually. They feel ten times too big."

A demon shrieked from nearby, and Valeriya flinched. Panic surged within her, and she felt as if the castle walls were once again falling. "Did you know that giant armadillos have the most teeth of any land animal?" she whispered, suddenly desperate to continue their conversation. "They have about a hundred."

"Then I'm glad I'm not a giant armadillo."

"Though some dolphins have even more. I think about two hundred and fifty."

Aki twisted again, rolling onto her opposite hip. "You should write a book about animals. I'm sure Jerico would read it."

A rifle fired once. Demons shrieked.

As Aki continued to shift her weight, Valeriya thought about those who had died. "We'll take the little girl back to the Stronghold," she said quietly. "And if the demons killed her parents, we'll have to teach her things. We'll let her know that she's not alone."

"And you'll teach her about animals? You'll tell her all sorts of life-saving facts?"

"Of course."

"Start by telling her about the trout we caught—those beautiful rainbows that drifted through the water and made you smile so many times."

In the distance, a man screamed. He wailed again and again before finally going silent.

Somehow bits of moisture formed and merged in the corners of Valeriya's eyes. Wiping away these half-tears, she thought about trout and sunlight and waters that flowed down from mountains—worlds within worlds, places she longed to see again but feared she never would.

Sometimes she seemed to live in a world of ghosts.

Would she become one too?

CHAPTER 21

T asia and Jerico, along with twelve other Seekers, rode horses through the dark forest. By now scouts had returned from the castle and reported that it had been completely destroyed, and that hundreds of men and women were dead. Tasia and Jerico had been told to remain at the Stronghold but dreaded what might have happened to Aki and Valeriya. They'd insisted on leaving, and a group of likeminded Seekers had joined them.

As her horse followed Jerico's, Tasia prayed for the well-being of her friends. She didn't allow herself to believe that they were dead. Instead, she told herself again and again that they'd somehow escaped and were returning unharmed. After all, Aki knew the castle better than almost anyone. Surely, she'd realized that it was about to fall, and had fled with Valeriya behind her.

Around Tasia, Seekers spoke quietly, asking each other how the demons could have known about the placement of the snipers. According to survivors, the snipers had been attacked from behind, killed before many of them could even fire their weapons. But the snipers were skilled at concealing themselves, and it seemed almost impossible that a large group of demons would have simply stumbled upon them, killed them, and then destroyed the castle.

The demons' attack, everyone seemed to believe, was well planned. Somehow, they must have learned about Tasia's trap. She could only surmise that someone had told them—someone on the Council of Thirty-Three, perhaps. But such a betrayal was nearly incomprehensible, and also meant that this person could communicate with the demons as easily as she could.

Reeling from the thought that a traitor could destroy them, Tasia wondered whom she could trust. She wouldn't share her most important plans in front of the Council again. Of its members, Zeus most likely was loyal. K'ail longed to kill him, and any foe of K'ail's was a friend of hers.

Almost everyone she had met here seemed honorable. Trax, she was certain, could also be trusted. And yet, she was increasingly convinced that someone had told the demons about her trap. And that someone was likely on the Council.

Tasia's mind continued to churn as the small force moved through the dark landscape. She prayed again for Aki and Valeriya, biting her lower lip as she thought about them, her stomach in knots. She longed to race toward the castle, to shout out their names, but resisted these impulses. Instead she whispered questions to Jerico, then wondered about how to best summon and destroy the alien ship. The end was near, she knew, and she needed to plan for every contingency. But her thoughts continued to dart back to Aki and Valeriya, and she whispered to the men and women around her, urging them to move faster.

The moon rose, drifted, and had nearly fallen by the time they neared what remained of Osaka Castle. Tasia had never been to the site, but she was astounded by the destruction around them. Huge mounds of debris seemed to stretch skyward. Mutilated human corpses lay everywhere and dead demons were strewn about as far as she could see.

Thinking of Valeriya and Aki and how they might have been maimed, Tasia rocked back and forth in her saddle, feeling nauseous. She glanced up, studying the sky. Although she had expected to find demons here, none appeared to be present. They must have returned to wherever they had gathered within the city, perhaps saving their strength for the next big battle.

Using her left hand to turn on a red-beamed flashlight, Tasia searched the nearby grounds, then looked up once again. Holding her staff in her other hand, she swung the light to and fro, wanting to entice any demon that remained. She continued to believe that one would attack her, but to her surprise, the night stayed silent.

"Aki," she called out, urging her horse ahead. "Can you hear me?"

Jerico and the other Seekers also began to ask for their missing friends. Red-beamed lights swung in every direction.

Again Tasia looked skyward, but she saw nothing but stars and the setting moon.

"Valeriya," she said, "are you out there?"

An owl hooted, but otherwise silence prevailed.

"We're going to find them," Jerico said from nearby. "Not everyone here died."

Tasia called out again to her friends—much louder this time, her voice filled with urgency and concern. Her horse snorted and stubbornly refused to go near a pair of dead demons. Tasia tugged the reins to the left, sending her mount in another direction. Everywhere she looked she saw piles of stone blocks, human remains, and fallen demons.

"Aki!" she half-shouted. "Valeriya! Where are you?"

No one answered. Panic threatening to consume her, she looked more carefully at the human bodies, terrified that she would see her friends. Though nearly all the corpses had been mutilated, she'd recognize Aki's dark green hair.

"Please, please don't let me see it," she whispered, trembling now, biting her lower lip so hard that she opened an old wound.

"See what?" Jerico asked.

"Her hair. I don't want to see her hair. I can't."

They continued to search, riding around piles of blocks and masonry. Tasia noticed several blue flags, each with a different-colored fist. One was blood-stained, and Jerico jumped down from his horse and picked it up. As tears rolled down Tasia's cheeks, he tied it to his saddle.

"They're not here," he said, shaking his head.

"Then where are they? Maybe they're buried under all this rubble. That's why we can't find them."

"No. That didn't happen. I'm telling you it didn't happen."

Tasia tried to slow her breathing, to hold her fear at bay. She reached for Jerico's hand, squeezing it tight. "I have to ask K'ail," she said quietly. "If he saw them die, he'll gloat."

Jerico nodded.

She looked up, projecting her thoughts into the sky. "Were you at the castle?" she whispered. At first, she only heard a woman's sobs. But then K'ail's words unfolded.

At the end. After I watched you beg.

"Did you see a girl with green hair? Did you kill her?"

Was she your friend?

"She is my friend. Not was but is. Did you see her?"

No. But I will look for her now, if she still lives. You just doomed her to an unfortunate death.

Wiping tears from her eyes, Tasia again squeezed Jerico's hand. She thought about K'ail, needing to ask him one more question. "How did you know about our trap?"

Gods breathe in knowledge as if it were air.

"One of us told you, didn't they? Someone betrayed us."

And you shall be betrayed again. So prepare to die, Tasia. Enjoy your last days.

"I'm ready to die," she replied, remembering how his talon felt on her eye—the pain, the fear. "But I'm not going to let us lose."

As if you could choose.

"I can choose to fight. To fight until we win."

And a castle may choose to stand. But is it still standing, Tasia? Is anything in your pitiful world still standing?

She looked at Jerico. "We are."

And so you shall fall together.

Taking a deep breath, Tasia ignored K'ail's next words. She focused once again on Jerico, rubbing her thumb against the back of his hand. "Let's keep looking," she said quietly. "He didn't see Aki die."

"Who betrayed us, Tasia? What were you talking about?"

"Later. We'll talk later."

Jerico started to reply, but then nodded and called out to Aki and Valeriya. As before there was no response, and when they moved ahead, Tasia prayed once more, begging whoever might listen for her friends to be safe. Her flashlight died then, and the night became darker.

Tasia's hope wavered at that moment but didn't vanish. She gripped her staff tightly as she called out, and her voice drifted across the castle's ruins.

The night was strangely quiet, as if ashamed of what it had witnessed.

CHAPTER 22

A ki and Valeriya crept through the darkness, ignoring the faint shouts of men and women. They both had found rifles and held them ready while making their way toward where they'd seen the caged girl. Aki's headache had finally disappeared, and she understood how lucky they were to be alive. To her surprise, the demons had left about an hour earlier, flying away with a flurry of shrieks.

She hated the fact that the battle had been a victory for the demons and was desperate to have a single ray of light pierce the darkness that seemed to entomb her. If the girl still lived, they would save her. And maybe she would grow up to be happy and complete. Maybe the war would end soon, and she'd never have to fight.

Against the wishes of her parents, Aki had become a Seeker. Though her mother and father always had been Hiders and she was raised to be one, Aki felt like someone from their family needed to fight for their future. They couldn't all disappear underground and pretend that the war didn't concern them. Aki reasoned that if she became a Seeker, if she fought and bled, her younger brothers and sisters wouldn't need to. They could grow up without ever fully understanding the fear that accompanied battle, or the pain that lingered when a fellow Seeker died.

And yet sometimes, despite the many emotional and physical hardships that came with being a Seeker, there were also special opportunities to find joy and salvation. Not long after her first battle, Aki had realized that Hiders would never understand the overwhelming relief that accompanied saving a friend during a fight, or the euphoria of a victory over the demons. They would never comprehend the depths of camaraderie that developed among Seekers as they faced death together, day after day.

The opportunity to save the little girl, to create one right from a night of wrong, was a gift that Aki needed to open. She understood the terror that the girl must have faced alone and wanted to take away some of her pain. Moreover, she felt guilty about adding nothing to the fight against the demons. While she and Valeriya had been imprisoned, Aki hadn't been able to aid her fellow Seekers. They had fought, killed, and died. Many had been tortured. All she had done was wake up from a nap and hide beneath some rubble.

The landscape was nearly pitch black now that the moon had set. Aki followed in Valeriya's footsteps, trusting her judgment. Back at the castle, people continued to shout, but Aki had no interest in responding. If she raised her voice, any nearby demon would be able to pinpoint her position. She already made much more noise than Valeriya as they moved between trees and bushes. No matter how much care she took, she often stepped on twigs, which cracked beneath her. Somehow Valeriya was silent, making as little noise as lengthening shadow.

They soon reached the edge of the clearing. Aki peered into the night, searching for the cage. She had a hard time discerning it but believed that she could see its outline. She started to move ahead, but Valeriya reached out to her, halting her progress.

"We need to listen," Valeriya whispered, her voice barely audible. "If a demon's here, the crickets will be quiet."

Aki nodded, straining to hear what the night had to offer. At first, she was aware of nothing other than the distant shouts and the sound of her own breathing. But then she heard insects chirping and buzzing around them. A breeze also caused nearby pine trees to sway, their needles rustling.

Valeriya started forward, her rifle pointed ahead. Switching off the safety of her own weapon, Aki followed closely behind. She thought of Sasha skipping along a beach, looking for shells. Aki hadn't been there to protect Sasha and dreaded the sight of an empty cage. If the little girl were gone or dead, Aki would have failed someone else.

The cage seemed to materialize before them. Valeriya abruptly stopped, then gestured toward a giant black hole in the ground. Aki almost fired into it before realizing that it was empty. Whatever demon had hidden there was gone. Switching her rifle's safety back on, Aki crept behind Valeriya as she walked around the hole, moving faster. The cage grew more distinct and visible, looming before them.

Aki hurried ahead, reaching out to the rusted steel. She saw the girl's limp body and shook the cage, terrified that the child was dead. But the girl turned toward her, screaming with fright.

Gasping, Aki dropped to her knees. "It's okay. You're safe now."

Valeriya stepped to the other side of the cage and struggled to open its door. Heavy wire had been twisted around a latch designed to hold a padlock. As the girl wept, Aki hurried to Valeriya's side and they fought to untwist the wire. Cursing at the old rusted steel, Aki grimaced, forcing it to bend. Finally they were able to yank the wire away from the latch and swing open the door. The cage was the size of a small room. Aki stepped inside it.

"Everything's fine," she said, reaching out to the girl, surprised and happy when the child practically leapt into her arms.

Valeriya joined them, stroking the girl's back with one hand while she still held her rifle. "What's your name?"

The child looked up, her dirty face lined with the paths of past tears. "Ziva," she answered, then wiped her eyes.

"How long—"

"They caught me yesterday when I snuck outside to find ants for my toad, Henry. Please don't tell Mommy. Please. I'll be in so much trouble. Mommy told me not to go out. She made me promise."

Aki smiled, stroking Ziva's brow. "How's Henry?"

"Good. But he's always hungry."

"Then my friend and I will bring him some ants. You don't need to. Okay?"

"The demon scared me. I didn't want to be eaten."

"And you weren't," Aki said. "And you won't ever be. So let's get you out of here. Let's get you back to your family and your toad."

"Can we go now?"

Aki nodded, settling Ziva into her arms and following Valeriya out of the cage. As they made their hurried exit, shadows emerged from the trees, morphing into immense creatures that crossed into the clearing, nearing them. Valeriya swung her rifle up, peering through its scope. But then a voice called out—a voice Aki recognized.

"Aki? Valeriya?"

Aki hurried toward Jerico, still holding Ziva. He leapt from his horse, reaching out to her. Tasia did likewise, and though she held fast to her staff, she still managed to embrace both Aki and Valeriya. The companions huddled together, oblivious to the world around them, expressing their joy at finding each other. Aki heard the concern within her friends' voices and was grateful to have them near. They had come for Valeriya and her, and even better, they were alive.

"What kept you?" Aki asked, smiling as her eyes welled

with tears. "Were you picnicking in the mountains?"

Jerico squeezed her arm. "How did you guess?"

"Did you feed her berries? And read her poems?

"Both, actually. You missed a lot."

Tasia hugged them so tightly that her staff pressed against Aki's head. "I was so afraid we wouldn't see you two again," she said, tears dropping to her cheeks. "I couldn't have been more afraid."

"Then you need to work on your bravery," Aki answered. "And speaking of bravery, this is Ziva. She got lost looking for ants and we're going to bring her home."

Tasia smiled. "Hi, Ziva."

"You're a Guardian?"

"She likes to think she is," Aki answered. "But I'm not sure she even knows which side of that staff is up."

Nodding, Tasia glanced from Ziva to her staff. "It is kind of hard to tell, isn't it?"

"It wouldn't be for me," Ziva answered. "It's the big end that shoots. So hold the big end up."

"I'll remember that."

The companions continued to embrace. As Ziva gave Tasia more advice about her staff, Aki felt light on her feet. Though the day's horrors wouldn't quickly fade, her friends still lived. There was still light in the world.

A stranger appeared from the trees, saying that they should all leave. Jerico offered his horse to Aki and Ziva. He helped them settle onto the saddle. Tasia did the same for Valeriya, who politely declined.

Looking down, Aki smiled at Valeriya. "Do you ever get tired of walking?"

"No. Not yet."

"When you do, let me know. I want to celebrate or something."

The group started forward. There were at least a dozen horses and all of them carried one or two riders. Five other survivors had been found. Like Aki and Valeriya, they had hidden under the rubble. They spoke at length about their ordeal, marveling at their good fortune.

Slowly the group passed beyond the castle's grounds, and the horses spread out. Aki spoke to Ziva, asking about her family and her toad, growing quiet only when exhaustion seemed to overwhelm the girl. As Ziva fell asleep in front of her, Aki held her tight.

She looked down to Valeriya, who still walked beside them. "Thanks," she said, nodding repeatedly. "Thanks for being with me today. And for helping me."

"You helped me too. When we were under those stones … you helped me a lot."

Aki reached down so that she could squeeze Valeriya's hand. "I'm sorry I got us into trouble with Slate. I forgot how nasty she could be."

"Do you think she's dead?"

"Oh, I'm sure she escaped. She ran right past us, remember?"

Valeriya nodded. "In a way she saved us. If she hadn't put us in that cell, we'd have been on top of the castle with everyone else."

"I'll blow her a kiss the next time I see her."

"But she also hurt you."

"Well, I—"

"And I'm not going to ignore what she did to you."

Aki heard the shift in Valeriya's tone. She had gone from being grateful to being angry. "Don't worry about her. Like I said, she's a bow-legged, skinny—"

"She's not going to touch you again. I'll make sure of that."

"You don't have to make sure of anything. I don't want you to fight my battles."

Valeriya looked up at her. "We're together, Aki. Your battles are my battles. That's the way it works."

"Is it? I didn't know."

"My grandfather told me once that when you care about someone, you start to look out for them. You stand in front of them, so they don't get hurt. And I know you don't need me to stand in front of you, but I'm going to at least stand by your side."

"Wow, I've got a bodyguard."

"You've got me."

Far above, a demon shrieked. Aki glanced up but wasn't frightened. Tasia and Jerico were ahead of her. And Valeriya was at her side. With such companions, it seemed, anything was possible.

"I'm going to take you to Paris," Aki finally replied. "And we're going to get all dressed up and dance in some forgotten café."

"Let's do it."

"And when we're dancing, we won't remember all the bad things that happened. We'll only remember the good—how we saved a girl and talked about your grandfather and knew that we'd travel to Paris together."

CHAPTER 23

As soon as Tasia returned to Kyoto, the Council of Thirty-Three held an emergency meeting. She had been summoned and so, holding hands with Jerico, she made her way toward the old underground movie theater. Rex trailed them closely, whimpering occasionally until Jerico turned to pet him.

Tasia's emotions were turbulent. She was euphoric that they'd found Aki and Valeriya alive, yet deeply saddened by the fall of Osaka Castle. Between the Seekers killed in the skyscrapers and in the fortress, nearly nine hundred men and women had died in the fighting. And while more than seventy demons had been slain, Tasia's trap had been a disaster. Many of humanity's best fighters had died, and at least in the near future, would be impossible to replace. The only consolation was that not a single Guardian had perished, nor had any staffs been lost.

Still, the weight of so many deaths was a burden that Tasia found difficult to carry. The plan had been her idea, and she'd believed that vast numbers of demons would be brought down. Instead most of the snipers had been surprised from behind, and when the castle fell, all hopes of victory that day were shattered.

Though Jerico had advised her to ignore the thought, she couldn't help but wonder if things might have unfolded differently if she'd been present. Maybe she would have sensed the demons' intentions and been able to warn her fellow fighters. Maybe K'ail had drawn her far away from the battle because he understood that she might alter its outcome.

The skin by the corner of her left eye twitched, and Tasia rubbed at it in frustration, telling herself repeatedly that she didn't have time to dwell on the past, that the present required her full attention. Jerico said something to her, but she barely heard his words. She saw him reach down to scratch Rex's head again, and she muttered a simple response, unable to focus on him. Instead she thought about how things had gone so terribly wrong with her plan, and how she could avoid a second such calamity.

When they reached the movie theater, Jerico held the door open for her. She thanked him, apologized for being distracted, and then entered the room. The Council of Thirty-Three was seated around the diamond-shaped table. Tasia started to head for the nearby seats in the theater, but Zeus cleared his throat and invited her up onto the stage. As Jerico squeezed her hand, she remembered her father's last words, reminding herself that he believed in her. And she needed to believe in herself, despite the previous day's setbacks.

As before, Tasia walked through a gap in the table and stepped into the middle of it. The stares of so many council members might as well have been hands pressing against her. Gripping her staff tightly, she managed to repress most of her fears and uncertainties, noting that Ishaam stood just outside of the table, not far from Zeus. Someone coughed.

"Hello, Tasia," Zeus said, rising from his chair. He was once again dressed in white. She was close enough to him to see that his eyes were red and inflamed. "As you know by now, yesterday's battle … did not go as we had hoped. It was—"

"A catastrophe," a white-haired woman interrupted, shaking her head. "It was as if we'd learned nothing in a century of fighting the demons. A big battle like that was what we did a hundred years ago. We lost almost every one of them, and yesterday was just as tragic. How could we have been so foolish and utterly reckless?"

Tasia didn't think the question was directed at her, so she merely stood still and waited for someone to reply.

"It was a risk," Zeus said. "We all knew that. Every damn one of us."

The woman shook her head. "This girl seduced us. She came in here with her youth and her staff and her strength, and she seduced us."

"She did nothing of the sort," Zeus replied. "She gave us an idea and we acted on it. We took her plan, refined it, and made it ours."

"She seduced us all!"

"She's a Guardian. She deserved the right to be heard."

A frail man stood up from his chair. "And where was this Guardian when the castle fell? Why wasn't she there?"

Zeus gestured for the council member to sit. "No Guardians were at the castle. That was always the plan, so that none of their staffs would be lost to the damn demons. She was just doing what she'd agreed to do."

Though Tasia didn't like how they were speaking about her, as if she wasn't present, she didn't interrupt. A part of her understood the council members' anger. Another part was glad that Zeus defended her. As the they continued to debate Tasia's merits, or lack thereof, she thought about K'ail's words from the previous day. Within his taunts, he'd told her how the demons had won.

Before she even realized that her lips had parted, Tasia said, "Someone betrayed us."

Zeus turned to her. "That's a serious accusation. Tell us more."

She eyed the men and women around her, studying the weathered faces of so many former Guardians and Seekers. "I'm not the only one of us who can communicate with the demons," she finally replied. "And someone, maybe someone in this room, told them about our plans."

Several members shouted angrily at her, and the Council

erupted in noise, movement, and rage. People pointed fingers at her, at each other, and turned to face one another as they debated the merits of her accusation. Struggling to remain calm, Tasia twisted toward Jerico and Rex, who stood before the front row of seats. Jerico nodded in her direction, again and again. The sight of his unwavering support took away some of her angst as Zeus called for silence. When the council members finally abided, he bowed his head appreciatively.

"We need answers," Zeus said, turning to Tasia.

She started to reply but then stopped, studying a man who continued to quietly insult her. Returning her gaze to Zeus, she shifted her staff from her left hand to her right. "The demon who was imprisoned with me, who tried to trick me back on the island, bragged to me last night about someone betraying us. And I believe him. That's why the demons were able to fly up behind our snipers and surprise them. They saw our trap before we ever had a chance to spring it."

"Maybe that demon, damn it to hellfire, was trying to mislead you," Zeus replied. "Maybe it wanted to spread doubt among us."

"No, that's not right. He wasn't misleading me. Like all of them, he thinks he's a god, and he likes to brag. It made him happy to say that one of us is a traitor."

Zeus shook his head. "But traitors need motives."

"Motives can be made," Tasia replied. "And hidden."

Several council members asked her questions, but she kept her attention on Zeus. She imagined him with a staff in his good hand, fighting K'ail so long ago. Believing that she could trust him, she vowed to seek him out in private, to share her thoughts about the coming fight.

Turning from him to again look at the council members, she nodded. "I don't blame you for being angry with me. I'm angry with myself. The castle was my plan, my idea. And even though I believe someone betrayed us, I have so much blood on my hands. And I can't wash that blood off. Not today. Not ever. I should have thought about the possibility of someone telling the demons. I should have known better."

No one immediately responded to her, though she could tell that her words resonated because most of the council members glanced around the table, as if looking for whoever had betrayed them.

Zeus nodded to Tasia. "The blame should be placed on our shoulders, not yours."

"What do you mean?"

"Because you've reminded us all of a terrible truth. A curse, really. The possibility that someone among us speaks to the demons. You see, twenty years ago, a Guardian admitted as much. The demons, let them burn forever, had captured his sister, and he shared our secrets to try to save her."

Several council members spoke at once, and once again the stage seemed to erupt with disagreements and accusations. Tasia shifted her staff from one hand to another but said nothing. She glanced at Jerico, who now knelt on one knee next to Rex. He nodded again to her, and as she had many times before, she wished she could converse with him as easily as she could with K'ail.

Tasia didn't see Zeus raise his good hand to silence the Council, but when he cleared his throat, she turned to him.

"Tell us more about what you think, Tasia," he said. "You know the winged devils better than anyone here. If someone among us does speak with them, how does that change what happens next?"

Having asked herself that same question, Tasia was ready to answer it, but didn't do so immediately. Instead, her gaze wandered from person to person. So many of the council members were easy to interpret. She saw animosity and encouragement, distrust and admiration. Prompted by so many varied stares, she wondered what she might think of herself, if their roles were reversed.

"I don't think I've ever seduced anyone," she finally replied, glancing at the woman who had accused her of doing so. "I'm not capable of that. And I'm not sure who I am, but whatever I say, I say it because I want to win. The demons killed my father. My friends. I hear their voices inside my head, and I know how much they hate us, how much they want to destroy us."

Zeus clasped his withered forearm with his good hand, nodding to her. "Please ... go on."

"Sometimes I feel alone, like all of us probably do." Glancing sideways, she looked at Jerico. "But I'm not alone. And there are so many people who I fight for. I'll die for them and they'll die for me. So if someone in this room betrayed us, if the demons have your child or your husband or your wife, please … forgive yourself. But the next time you speak to them, lie to them. Because the only way you'll ever see your loved one again is if we win. The demons think your love makes you weak, makes it so they can control you. But let it make you strong. That's what I've tried to do. What I'm trying to do."

Zeus glanced around the table before turning his attention back to Tasia. "We have to assume that if someone betrayed us yesterday, that same scoundrel already told the demons about our plan to summon their ship and to attack it from the inside. In that case, Tasia, what would you have us do, in the broadest terms possible?"

She shrugged, absently stroking her staff with her thumb. "Nothing should change. The only way to destroy the demon ship is to bring it here and to drop into it. The demons on Earth will know about our plan, but the demons in space won't. They're too far away to communicate to. And these are the ones we need to surprise. So we'll bring them here, and before they know what's happening, we'll drop into their ship and destroy them. And we'll need to defend the Orb so that the demons here can't follow us through it."

Several council members again replied at once, and Zeus held up his good hand. He then turned to Ishaam. "Will your team's bombs be powerful enough? To bring down a ship like that from the inside? We need it turned into the hottest of hellfires, Ishaam. A hellfire that none of those winged devils will survive."

The thin scientist wiped sweat from his brow. "A ship that travels from one galaxy to the next must inherently be immensely strong. But no matter how strong their ship is, the space within it will be confined. And potent explosives, set off in a confined space, will do vast damage—especially if placed near vital parts of their ship."

"Such as?" Zeus asked.

Ishaam pursed his lips. "To propel a city-sized ship through space must require almost limitless energy. But such energy tends to be unstable. If our bombs are placed near their ship's power source, it will come down, or more likely explode all at once."

"After we set those beautiful bombs, we'll try to drop back to Kyoto using the Orbs on their ship," Zeus said. "But in case it has some sort of hatches that we can open, I want parachutes made. How, Ishaam, is your team coming along with them?"

The scientist again wiped his brow, sweat glistening on his face. "We'll have a hundred by tomorrow, just as you asked. But if the ship is too high up, there won't be sufficient oxygen for any of our people to survive a jump. And mostly likely that will be the case."

As Zeus, Ishaam, and other council members continued to plan, Tasia turned to Jerico. He smiled at her and suddenly she wanted to be alone with him. While she knew she'd play a prominent role in the coming fight, she didn't want to plan for it. The council members, despite their flaws, were wise and good and wanted to win just as much as she did. They'd tried to protect all that was precious for many years, regardless of the hate and power that faced them.

Whispering her thanks to Zeus, Tasia stepped away from the center of the table and walked toward Jerico. He moved in her direction as well, and their hands clasped when they met at the edge of the stage.

"You're wrong about one thing," he said, smiling.

"What?"

"You seduced me. You didn't mean to, of course, but you still did."

"How?" she asked, squeezing his hand. "How could I do something like that?"

"Because you've always had hope. And I'm not sure if there is anything as powerful, or as seductive, as hope."

While the council members continued to debate, Tasia and Jerico walked away, holding hands. Rex kept pace between them, wagging his tail when Tasia leaned down to pet him.

"Take me somewhere," she said, turning her attention back to Jerico, raising his hand to her lips.

"Where?"

"Where doesn't matter. Just somewhere we can be alone together."

CHAPTER 24

After the sun passed its zenith in the sky, Aki and Valeriya crept out of the Stronghold of Kyoto. Valeriya carried a heavy canvas bag on her back, and despite Aki's questions about its contents, kept the secret to herself. Because many demons were around and distant rifle shots cracked every few minutes, they moved with care and patience.

Before lunch, they had returned the young girl, Ziva, to her parents. Ziva's father had been speechless, sweeping her up in his arms. Her mother had wept, kissing Ziva's face again and again. The reunion had lifted both Aki's and Valeriya's spirits. Aki had asked to meet Ziva's toad, Henry, and had held the damp, docile creature as Ziva fed it a scrawny worm. Later, as Valeriya told Ziva remarkable facts about toads, Aki whispered to Ziva's parents, explaining how they'd found her. Though the story prompted her mother to cry more and her father to grimace, they were grateful that Ziva had been saved. Aki then told them of the coming battle, recommending that they arm themselves and go deeper into the Stronghold.

Now, as she followed Aki down a buckled sidewalk, Valeriya thought about her grandparents, remembering how her grandfather had shown her how to start a fire by striking a piece of flint against her knife. The process was tedious, yet he'd taught her to be patient, to understand that the outcome was worth the struggle. He had smiled at her many failures, encouraging her with humor and his self-deprecating stories. In some ways, Aki reminded her of him. Though Aki was much more outspoken and far less patient, she also knew how to make Valeriya laugh. And she believed that her initial interest in Aki arose in part from how Aki reminded her of time spent, deep in the woods, with the man who loved the forest and her with equal passion.

Valeriya's grandfather not only had shown her how to hunt, trap, fish, and make shelters, but also spoke to her at length about the forest's many creatures. He constantly pointed out brown bears, lynx, tigers, deer, owls, and eagles. He honored these animals, sometimes whittling their faces into old pieces of wood. But even greater than her grandfather's love of animals and fish was his admiration for trees. He often explained the differences between a spruce and a fir, a birch and an aspen. He said that to him, trees were as beautiful as sunsets or mountains or rivers. Trees, he believed, had been on Earth since the beginning of time and would remain long after people were gone. They could be spoken to, prayed to, and slept under. They sang songs in strong winds. They danced.

The canvas bag on Valeriya's back contained a pair of small ginkgo trees. She had asked a gardener in one of the Stronghold's vast farms if she might take them from his nursery and plant them outside. To her surprise, he had nodded, telling her to find a sunny, open spot. The man had added that the ginkgoes, if they survived their first few seasons, would live to be hundreds of years old.

Valeriya wanted to plant the trees to honor her parents and grandparents. She would place them near each other, overlooking something beautiful. And in the many years to come, the trees would grow, their branches lengthening and approaching each other, providing shade and shelter to each other. Birds would nest within the trees, and eggs would hatch, bringing new life into the world. And whenever the wind blew, the trees would move as one, bending backward together, connected through their roots and their history.

Somewhere in the distance a demon shrieked, prompting Aki to pause and study the sky. She held her rifle in both hands, and her right thumb hovered near its safety switch. On either side of them, battered buildings continued to defy the elements. Though they were cracked and burnt, though many of their windows had shattered, they stubbornly refused to die.

"Can we cut across to the river?" Valeriya whispered.

"Can you tell me what's in the bag?"

"Once we reach the river."

Aki muttered something beneath her breath but nodded. She glanced at the sky again, then led them to a narrow alley that ran to the east. It was full of trash, skeletons, bicycles, and vending machines. The machines still contained cans of cola, beer, and juice. Valeriya had tasted sugar before but wondered what it must have been like to have a sweet drink tumble out of a machine and into your awaiting hands. The concept was as foreign to her as wings to a whale.

The Kamogawa River appeared in the distance—wide and shallow. They reached a path that ran parallel to it, crossed the path, and proceeded to what looked to once have been a park. A swing set had rusted and fallen. But a slide still stood. Though several bushes had grown from the pebble-covered ground, an empty patch of grass and weeds perched above the waterline.

Valeriya looked at the sun, noting how it illuminated the empty space. "This is perfect."

"For what? Did we come here to work on our tans?"

Smiling, Valeriya stepped to the grass, then set the canvas bag on the ground and carefully removed the small ginkgo trees. The gardener had wrapped up their roots in damp rags. "My grandfather loved trees," Valeriya said, removing a miniature shovel from the bag. "So I want to plant these here to remind me of him. And my grandmother and parents."

"I thought you had a fishing pole in there. And some of those world-famous spoons."

Valeriya studied the patch of grass, trying to decide where

to place the trees. "I'm planting them for us too," she added, turning to Aki.

"For us? What's that mean?"

"I don't know, exactly. But I think … we're beautiful together. So I want to plant something beautiful here for us. And if we don't die in a few days, if we somehow blow up that big ship, we can come back here and just sit in the sun. I can fish and you can paint your nails. And maybe we'll plant some flowers too. We'll make a new swing so children can come here and play. We'll make our own little Neverland. We could even build a zoo for injured animals. Once we'd healed them, we'd let them go."

Aki studied the area, nodding to herself. She wiped her right eye. "Where should we plant them?"

After picking up two stones, Valeriya placed them about thirty feet apart, in the center of the clearing. "Let's dig where the rocks are."

They took turns with the little shovel, creating and expanding two holes. While one dug, the other stood guard. The work was difficult, but they didn't hurry or complain. For Valeriya, digging into the Earth was strangely comforting. She was about to plant something wonderful, to give birth in a way. When they finally finished with the holes, they each picked up a sapling and placed it into the ground, then carefully covered its roots with loose soil. Valeriya removed a water bottle from the bag, and they took turns walking to the river and then watering the trees.

The sunlight illuminated the fan-shaped leaves of the

ginkgo trees, and a breeze made them flutter like butterflies' wings. "Thanks," Valeriya said, reaching for Aki's dirty hand.

"Your grandfather would be happy."

Valeriya nodded, not fighting against the tears that swelled in her eyes.

"Are you crying for him ... or for us?" Aki asked, moving closer to her.

"Maybe both."

A gust of wind caused Aki's dark green hair to sway. "If I die, don't be afraid to come here. I still want you to water the trees and build your swing and help your animals. Because if your hands are clean, then you're not living how you want to."

Tears fell to Valeriya's face. She felt fear growing within her, as if it were feasting on the same light and water that now sustained the trees. "You can't die," she whispered. "Please don't die."

"I won't if you don't," Aki replied. "I think we should promise each other that." She looked away and then tried to smile. "We'll make a vow, in front of your baby trees. We'll vow that we won't die, and that after we go dancing in Paris we'll come back here and work on your little Neverland. And then maybe we'll go to the real Neverland, just to steal some more ideas."

Valeriya hugged Aki, holding her tight. "I'm afraid to drop into their ship. We don't know what'll be inside."

"Probably just a bunch of hot air and some sleeping bats. Remember, all we have to do is drop in, set the bombs, and drop out. How hard can that be?"

"It'll be hard, Aki. Don't pretend it won't be."

"But I'm so good at pretending. It's one of my specialties."

"Probably your best."

Aki sighed, then leaned her head so it rested against Valeriya's shoulder. "We're not going to die, Val. Think of everything we've gone through, everything we've survived. We've come too far to die in some ugly alien ship. That's not going to be the end of us. I won't let it be the end, and I'm not even as good a shot as you."

The wind blew again, and the ginkgo trees swayed back and forth, as if restless to grow and sing and shelter. "Why is it that neither of us wants to run away?" Valeriya asked. "I know some people will. I've already seen a few sneaking off."

"We won't run away because we couldn't live with ourselves if we did," Aki replied, shaking her head. "That's not who we are. I might have green hair and you might need to cut your toenails, but we're not the kind of people who abandon their friends."

Nodding, Valeriya thought about Aki's words. "If I die, promise me that you'll water the trees."

"We're not going to talk about—"

"Please promise me. I want to leave something behind. Just one thing ... to show that I was here, that I saw this beautiful place."

A single tear fell from Aki's dark lashes, dropping to her face. "I'll water them," she finally replied, her voice much softer.

Valeriya kissed the tear on Aki's cheek, tasting her, wanting their connection to grow even stronger, like the roots that would one day intertwine beneath them. "I've fallen for you," she said. "I don't know how or why it happened, but I've fallen so hard."

"Well, I am irresistible."

"You are. At least to me."

Aki was about to respond, but Valeriya kissed her lips, savoring their fullness, their warmth. In the distance, the river ran, water tumbling over unseen rocks. And cherry trees, so large and healthy, swayed together in the wind like they always had—their white and pink blossoms carried skyward, drifting across the emptiness as if miniature planets in a universe of infinite wonders.

CHAPTER 25

The immense underground ammunition depot bustled with activity. Scores of Seekers came and went, often carrying armloads of rifles, protective vests, helmets, and other equipment. Long tables had been set up at the far side of the room, and volunteers worked to fill backpacks with specialized equipment for the mission. Each backpack contained five magazines of bullets, a flashlight, a handheld radio, rope, and medical supplies. Explosive devices, which were being assembled at the far end of the Stronghold, would be added later. A limited supply of parachutes would also be distributed.

Tasia and Jerico had volunteered to help with the backpacks and sat next to each other, with Rex resting at their feet. From time to time Tasia unwrapped small bites of dried fish and handed them to Rex, smiling when he gulped them down, seemingly without even chewing. Though Tasia worked hard, she also looked up occasionally, studying the people around her. They were a mix of old and young, Seekers and Hiders. Everyone moved with a strong sense of purpose and care. A powerful camaraderie had always existed within the Strongholds, but now it seemed even more potent. People helped and encouraged each other. And despite the stress created by the looming battle, very few arguments arose.

The next night the moon would be full, and Tasia's plan called for summoning the demon ship the following dawn. If she didn't, she knew the demons would set the Earth on fire, as K'ail had threatened. And so the staffs would be placed together, creating an Orb that would somehow call the alien vessel, though no one was certain how long it would take for the ship to arrive. Scientists debated this topic with great passion, some advocating that the vastness of space meant that an encounter could be days or weeks or even years away. But other great minds believed that the alien technologies were so advanced that space travel would be nearly instantaneous.

Tasia had never studied physics or astronomy, but had often thought about her conversations with K'ail, about how he'd hinted that his ship would appear soon after the staffs were placed together. After all, he had said that when the Orb was created the Dawn of Atonement would arrive—not after a week or a month, but that very day.

Someone coughed from the end of the table, and Tasia glanced toward a group of women who carefully folded parachutes. Though the parachutes hopefully wouldn't be necessary, Tasia wondered if she'd have the strength to lead people on a second drop within a short amount of time. Theoretically, once the bombs were set, any human survivors could step into an Orb and drop back to Earth. The problem was that for generations Seekers had been taught that only one drop per day was possible, that two drops would wreck even the strongest of minds. And while Tasia had dispelled this notion to a certain degree, she wasn't sure if she was strong enough to drop twice within an hour. Yet she also believed that people had never really understood the Orbs. K'ail had told her how they worked, how her mind could control her path. Maybe it was also possible to shield herself, and those who followed her, from the aftermath of back-to-back drops.

Thinking about Jerico and how the drops didn't disturb him nearly as much as they did her, she turned to him. "Do you think you could drop twice in an hour?"

He shook his head. "We did it twice in twelve hours and that was almost too much for you."

"The demons do it. I've seen them drop into one place and then leave right away."

Setting down a roll of bandages, he leaned back in his chair. "Dropping twice like that would be risky. Really risky."

Shrugging, she started to work again. "But I'm learning. I'm getting stronger. Maybe I could protect myself and everyone with me."

Jerico turned, pointing to a pile of parachutes. "You don't want to use those after we set the bombs?"

"No, not really. To use those, we'd have to find an exit from their ship. And how are we going to do that when the demons are after us? Even if we could, do you think the demons on Earth would let us just drift back to the ground? They'd kill us all in the blink of an eye. And all these parachutes are probably going to be worthless anyway. If the ship is too high up, there won't be any oxygen."

Sighing, he nodded, then leaned forward once again. "I've never been afraid to drop. And maybe that's why the drops don't bother me as much as they do you. Maybe the secret is to not be afraid. Maybe fear somehow … weakens the mind."

She thought about his words. "Maybe you're right. At least … maybe fear is a part of it all. I've always been afraid of the drops. I've always hated them. And the demons … probably enjoy them. The drops probably make them feel like gods."

"Exactly."

"Maybe if I believe in myself, if I lose my fear, the drops won't hurt me at all."

"The drops seem to magnify our thoughts. So if you're afraid, they're going to shake you to your core. If you're thrilled, like maybe the demons are, the drops are probably exciting."

About to respond, Tasia glanced up when someone suddenly loomed above her. To her surprise, Zeus stood next to her, his crippled arm bent awkwardly upward, his hand against his chest. "Would you please walk with me, Tasia?" he asked. "And you may certainly join us, Jerico."

Tasia nodded as Jerico whistled to Rex. She picked up

her staff and followed Zeus away from the workstation. Rex whimpered until Jerico promised him that everything would be fine, scratching his head. People paused in their efforts to look up as they moved past. Zeus walked faster than Tasia would have guessed, his white robes swinging from side to side. They soon entered the main corridor of the Stronghold, passing workstations, feeding halls, farms, and a school. Zeus led them into a large, empty room, shutting the door behind them. At one point the space had housed a convenience store, but now it held dusty tables and chairs.

Zeus didn't bother to sit down, nor did he ask them to. "I wanted to speak in private," he said, eyeing the door.

"About what?" Tasia asked.

"We most certainly do have a spy among us, so the days of discussing our most detailed plans in front of the Council are over. Some scoundrel in that group can't be trusted."

Jerico nodded. "Her idea about the castle was a good one. It wasn't her fault that—"

"I know, son. I know."

"What else do you want to talk about?" Tasia asked, reaching for Jerico's hand.

Zeus waited for a group of Seekers to pass by the glass door. "If you're right, the dawn after next, after we've placed all the staffs together, an Orb will form and that Orb will summon the demon ship."

"Go on."

"Well, the Council wants to defend that Orb, to keep the

demons in Kyoto from dropping into their ship and fighting you."

Tasia nodded. "That's what we talked about."

"But what if we only defended the Orb for a short time, say ten minutes? What if we then let the demons control it? They'd drop into their ship to fight you. And when your bombs went off, not only would the ship be destroyed, but so would every winged devil on it—meaning that very few would remain on Earth."

Tasia shifted her weight from one foot to the other as she debated his idea. "That would make our fight on the ship harder."

"Yes, yes, it would," Zeus admitted. "But the more demons that are on the ship when it blows up, the better. The opportunity to trap them all, to destroy them all, won't come again."

"I think we'd need more time," she replied, "before you let them come after us. Maybe twice that much time. Because we need to find the ship's power source and set the bombs there. But I understand what you're saying. If every demon drops into the ship, and we destroy it, we'll never have to face them again."

Jerico shook his head. "But that's a risk. The extra demons will make it harder for us to win up there. And if we don't blow up their ship, then we lose everything."

"You're right," Tasia responded, turning to Jerico. "But I think Zeus is right too. And I don't know about you, but I'm tired of the middle ground. I'd rather win everything or lose everything. At least then, one way or the other, things will be over. Because if we don't let every demon onto the ship, if we keep some here, we'll just have to fight them later, one by one. We'll spend the rest of our lives fighting them, worrying about the sky. We'll never be free."

"Let's be done with this damn war," Zeus said as he slapped his good hand against his thigh. "Let's bury it in the past. I say we put everything we have into your plan. We start by flooding that ship with our best fighters. The young and old will stay in the Stronghold, of course. But anyone who wants to fight will fight. And twenty minutes after you're gone, we'll let the demons capture the Orb and drop into the battle. We'll lure those devils into a trap of our making."

"A really dangerous trap," Jerico added. "A trap that could backfire on us."

Tasia shook her head. "Don't you want it to end? Isn't the chance to kill them all worth the risk?"

"Probably. But if we're beaten up there, if too many demons come at us and those bombs don't go off and we don't bring down the ship, none of us will survive. Not Aki. Not your brother. Not you."

Jerico's words affected Tasia, but not in the way he intended. Instead, they only served to steel her resolve. "If we kill them all, then Aki and my brother and I won't ever have to worry about them again. And I think that's worth the risk."

Rex whimpered, pawing at Jerico for attention. Jerico scratched his companion's head, told him to not be afraid, and then reached for Tasia's free hand. "I'm with you. Because I believe in you. And if you think it's best to get every demon up there, then that's what I want to do."

Zeus asked them to keep the decision private, adding that he'd only tell a handful of Seekers who he trusted. They would be placed around the Orb, and when the time was right, they'd pretend to flee in disarray.

"And one more thing," Zeus said, as Tasia reached for the door.

"What?" she asked.

"Tomorrow we'll prepare for our fight. But tonight we'll celebrate. We'll celebrate our unity, our resolve, our strength. I want to fill everyone's heart with happiness, even if only for a few hours. We need to remind people of everything we have to fight for."

Tasia squeezed Jerico's hand. "That's a wonderful idea."

"Will I see you both there?"

"For sure."

He smiled. "I admire you both. You're young. You care about each other. You have so much to lose in this damn fight, and yet you don't run away. I'm an old man. My back hurts. My knees ache. And my loved ones already have been taken from me. So I have less to lose. The fight means as much to me, but your fears certainly are stronger."

Tasia started to speak, and then stopped, wondering who Zeus had lost. "You fought when you were young, when you weren't alone."

He shrugged.

"I don't think you have less to lose," she said. "You still have hope. You still have love. And hope and love shouldn't be taken from you. Not by them. Not like that. So when their ship comes, when the battle comes, you should stand beside us and fight for the same things that we do."

A smile slowly dawned on Zeus's face. He nodded once, then opened the door, gesturing for her to go first.

Still holding Jerico's hand, Tasia stepped forward. She thought about the people she loved, knowing that she'd die for them, if needed. They were too beautiful and good to let disappear from the world.

Zeus would fight for them too. And she was glad that he'd be beside her.

CHAPTER 26

L ater that afternoon, Aki, Valeriya, and Tasia left the Stronghold and made their way to an abandoned aboveground department store. The three-story store was easy to find and Aki had been there many times. Though the two upper floors had been consumed by flames many years earlier, parts of the lower level were still intact. Aki had always believed that heavy rains must have started to fall, saving the precious merchandise below. She'd been grateful for whatever storm had put out the flames, as some of her best outfits had come from the dusty racks on the ground floor.

Earlier in the day, Aki and Valeriya had participated in guard duty, helping to protect the main entrance to the Stronghold. Only a few minutes into their assignment, a trio of demons had attacked their position. The beasts, fortunately, were driven away by a hailstorm of bullets, as well as the bolts of energy from two Guardians' staffs. The demons shrieked, disappeared, and then dropped three cars from a vast height. Though the vehicles slammed into the ground near Aki, no one was hurt.

Over the next few hours, small groups of demons had continued to attack their position, but with little of the aggression that they'd shown at the castle. The demons simply appeared and disappeared, their movements coordinated. It was as if they were trying to keep the defenders' attention, to ensure that a solid force of Seekers and Guardians remained at the Stronghold's main entrance.

At one point during the fighting, Aki had noticed Slate and had moved behind a wall. She wasn't surprised to see that her jailer had escaped the attack on the castle. Slate's sense of self-preservation always had been strong. Accompanied by a few men, Slate had inspected the nearby defenses and then disappeared into the city.

Now, as Aki glanced at the sky and entered the department store, she wondered if Slate knew she was alive. She debated telling Tasia about her situation but decided that her friend had more important worries. Besides, Aki could take care of herself. If Slate came at her again, she'd be ready.

The store was dimly lit, and Aki crept past endless, half-empty racks of clothes. She'd inspected almost every dress in the store and had a good idea for what she wanted to wear for the evening's celebration. To her delight, she'd also talked Valeriya and Tasia into wearing something nice. In rather dramatic fashion, she had asked them to grant her a final favor before the fight, saying that she'd love to see them as they were intended to be—dressed in silk and sparkles, not in cotton and camouflage.

Glass cracked beneath their feet, but the store was otherwise quiet. At one point, Aki kissed a naked mannequin, and the three companions burst into muted laughter. Aki hurried ahead, kissing each mannequin she passed, embracing several. It felt liberating to act childish, and the stress of the past days seemed to vanish as she complimented the plastic statues on their figures, smiles, or choice of attire.

The department store contained a salon, and Aki led Valeriya and Tasia into it. Before they could protest, she sat each down in a dusty leather chair. "I'm going to fix up both of you," she said. "And I don't want to hear any complaints."

While her companions voiced half-hearted protests, Aki took off her backpack and started to remove supplies. She placed a solar-powered generator on the floor. She'd charged it for the past two days and thought it would last long enough for her to do what she wanted. After turning on the generator, she plugged a portable light into it, then removed a flat, twelve-inch device that was her favorite hair straightener. Aki plugged it into her generator, opened it, and then tested both sides to see if it was heating up.

"I like your hair," Aki said to Tasia. "But let's try something different for tonight."

"I don't want it colored if that's what—"

"Does this look like a paint brush?" Aki replied, holding up the hair straightener.

"I don't know what that thing is."

"It's a flat iron. Some people call it a hair straightener."

"A flat iron?"

"Do you trust me?"

Tasia shook her head. "No, not really."

Sighing, Aki glanced at Valeriya, who was laughing. "You be quiet," she said. "Because you're next. And if you get on my bad side, I'll shave you bald."

"Which would hurt you a lot more than me."

"Oh, shut up," Aki replied, turning her attention back to Tasia. "Now I just want you to sit still. You'll be fine, I promise, even though your knight in shiny army fatigues isn't around."

Tasia leaned her staff against the chair. "I still don't know what that thing is. It looks like a magic wand."

"In my hands, it is. You'll see."

Again, Tasia half-heartedly protested, her voice light and unconcerned. Aki continued to banter back and forth with her two companions as she started to work on Tasia. She'd never straightened such thick hair before and wasn't sure what to expect. The first thing she did was to try to run a brush through Tasia's locks, which were almost unbearably tangled. But somehow her patience persisted, and the brush moved with increasing ease. Aki set it aside and then picked up her hair straightener.

"Now just hold still," she said, opening the flat iron.

"I am holding still."

"Your mouth is moving. So how still can you really be?"

Tasia shrugged. "Then I guess you're never still. Probably not even when you sleep."

Valeriya laughed as she and Tasia shared a smile. Scowling, Aki began to separate Tasia's hair, using small clips to gather sections of it together near her skull. She then lifted up the hair straightener, moved it close to Tasia's head, and pulled it down, along one section. The heated sides of the device came together as Aki moved it, clamping down on Tasia's hair. As Tasia squirmed in her seat, Aki lowered the flat iron, careful not to go too slow.

To Aki's surprise, Tasia's hair straightened beautifully. "This is going to be perfect," she said, mostly to herself.

While Tasia and Valeriya spoke about something unimportant, Aki worked, using both the brush and the flat iron. It didn't take her as much time to straighten Tasia's hair as she'd guessed, although her friend's coffee-colored locks were much longer than expected, falling well past her shoulders. After setting the flat iron aside, Aki brushed Tasia's hair with graceful strokes, marveling at how easy it was to do. Smiling, she reached down and gave Tasia a hand-mirror.

"Told you it was magic," Aki said, clapping.

Tasia picked up the mirror and studied her reflection. The hint of a smile crossed her face, lengthening as she continued to stare. "That's me?" she asked, shaking her head. "How is that me?"

Valeriya stood up from her chair, nodding appreciatively. "You do have a gift, Aki."

"Well, I'm more than just a pretty face," Aki replied. "You should know that by now. So stop thinking about trees and toads and wrap your brain around me."

Tasia touched her long, straight locks. "How long will it stay this way?"

"Until the next time you get it wet."

"It's strange ... seeing myself like this. I look like a different person. I almost feel like a different person."

Aki leaned down and opened her makeup kit. "We're not finished yet, ladies. Not even close."

"There's more?" Valeriya asked, sitting back down.

"Well, my fish finder, I'm going to braid your hair, color your nails, do your eyebrows, add some makeup, and then turn my attention back to our local Guardian. And of course I'm going to find you each a pretty dress. I'll come last, but certainly not least."

"Just tell us what to do."

Aki nodded, then stepped to Valeriya and began to brush her hair. She smiled as she worked, pleased to see a transformation occur within her companions. No longer did they look like Seekers. Before sunset they'd resemble girls from another time, from an era when people didn't have to worry about war and death and loss. And for that night, Tasia and Valeriya could be different people. Not better people, of course, but maybe less burdened by responsibilities and fear, maybe freer.

As Tasia asked Valeriya about her homeland, Aki continued to work. Occasionally she paused to kiss the top of Valeriya's head, and her fingers sometimes lingered on skin that seemed impossibly soft. As time passed in the salon, the outside world seemed far away. Aki fell into her own thoughts, quieter than usual, concentrating on the tasks at hand. She brushed and plucked and colored, treating Valeriya and Tasia in the same manner that a painter might approach a vacant canvas. The metamorphosis of her companions continued to please her, and she often paused to admire her work.

Finally Aki finished with them. As they thanked her, and shared smiles and laughs, she quickly worked on herself. Then she collected her belongings, put on her backpack, grabbed her rifle, and took their hands in hers.

"We have to find three dresses," she said, feeling light on her feet. "And something nice for Jerico to wear. We can't have him feeling left out."

Tasia turned to her, leaning forward to hug her. Aki thought that Tasia would quickly let go of her, but she didn't.

"A lot of bad things have happened to me," Tasia said quietly. "But all those things led me to you. And I'm really glad they did. Because you're something good … something amazing … that came out of all the bad."

Smiling, Aki tried to think of something clever to say. But as her eyes watered, her wit seemed to vanish. So she nodded, holding Tasia tight.

"So much good has come from so much bad," Valeriya added, joining the embrace, wrapping her arms around her companions.

Aki turned to Valeriya, kissing her lips, delighting in the feel of her. She then kissed Tasia's forehead, pulling her companions tighter against her, suddenly not wanting to let go.

CHAPTER 27

T hroughout that day, more than a hundred volunteers had helped to decorate the main corridor of the Stronghold of Kyoto. Children had used colored chalk to draw on the walls and floor—creating everything from sunsets to mountains to rainbows to family members. Teenagers had raided the Stronghold's farms and returned with armloads of flowers, which they arranged into bouquets of every size and configuration. These bouquets were attached to the walls near lighted candles. Dozens of elderly men and women, also wanting to participate, hung ancient Japanese kites from the ceiling. Most of the colorful kites were designed to resemble different kinds of fish, and they swayed silently. To entertain the many volunteers throughout the day, at the far end of the corridor two men and women beat giant stand-up drums, creating rhythms that rose and fell like summer storms.

Shortly after dusk, the Celebration of Life, as Zeus called it, began. More than three thousand people attended the festivity. Many were clad in old dresses and shirts they'd looted from nearby stores. Because most fabrics couldn't survive for a century, people tended to wear silk, which seemed immune to the ravages of time. Women dressed in old kimonos as well as outfits that had been popular in the days before the demons first attacked. Men wore dark pants and colorful silk shirts. Children ran around in outfits ranging from swimsuits to costumes to dresses with old price tags still attached.

Anyone who wasn't a child understood that the end, or the beginning, was near. The sun would rise tomorrow, and they'd make final preparations for the attack on the alien ship. And the following dawn they would either die or win. No middle ground existed, and no one really wanted such an outcome anyway. The prospect of victory was intoxicating. The possibility of defeat, while sobering, wasn't impossible to accept. People were tired of living underground, of losing loved ones to a never-ending war. The time had come to rise or fall.

Not long after the celebration officially began, Zeus stepped onto a makeshift stage and addressed the crowd, his voice booming and potent, so much at odds with his crippled arm and frail body. He spoke about his pride in everyone, about how unity was as beautiful as it was powerful. After cheers erupted, he told the audience not to be afraid. Yes, people would die in the coming fight. But dying so that loved ones could live free wasn't tragic or senseless, but rather noble and selfless.

Zeus promised to fight beside anyone who would join him,

saying that he'd be honored to bleed and struggle alongside friends and strangers. More cheers rang out and drums beat with increasing fervor. Zeus held up his good hand, asking people to believe that victory was possible, that five generations of struggle had led to this one moment. Their ancestors would be proud, he added, proud of both the past and present.

Amid more applause, Zeus announced that, as Tasia had suggested, he would write the names of his loved ones on patches that would be sewn onto his robes, and that he'd carry them into battle. Those he'd loved and lost would sustain him while he honored their sacrifices. As applause turned to cheers and chants, Zeus pointed at the ceiling, swinging his arm back and forth, encouraging people to get louder. He said that the demons should hear them, should understand that they weren't afraid. As his voice intensified, screams and drumbeats echoed off the walls, and the clamor crescendoed, seeming to shake the very ground. At the Stronghold's entrances, Seekers and Guardians fired their weapons into the night, driving demons away.

After Zeus stepped down from the stage, he was engulfed by throngs of supporters. Children ran and danced. Men and women embraced each other, tears in their eyes. Strangers vowed to fight for one another to the death. Friends swore to raise each other's children if necessary, promising to love them as if they were their own. The drums sounded with relentless vigor, then slowly quieted, soon replaced by the sound of stringed instruments. Century-old violins and cellos, which had been passed on from one generation to the next, filled the air with their passionate cries. People began to dance, holding each other tight, the music inspiring the very emotions that the long-dead composers had perhaps once hoped to create.

Near the edge of the revelry, Jerico swayed from side to side with Tasia in his arms. She wore a short black skirt and a tight red top. Her hair was straight and fell below her shoulders. Aki had highlighted her features with creams, powders, mascara, and lipstick. A rose-scented perfume emanated from her wrists and neck.

Although he'd fallen in love with Tasia when she wore nothing more than camouflaged pants and shirts, Jerico was transfixed by the transformation. Not because she looked more beautiful, but because it didn't appear that she was going off to fight. She seemed safe and happy. The future was ahead of her, and that future wasn't full of fear and misery, but hope and joy.

Leaning closer to her, he kissed her forehead. "Can I tell you something?"

"That I'm a bad dancer?"

He smiled. "It sounds a little silly."

"Then I won't share it with Aki."

Children raced past, trying to get an old kite to fly. Jerico watched them disappear into the mass of revelers, then smiled again. "I just thought of a line to add to my poem. A line about you."

"Really? What line?"

"You have to wait. It's not ready."

"But when do I get to read it?"

"On the very last page, remember? That's where the best poems always are."

She pulled him closer to her, resting her cheek against his shoulder. "You're a tease, you know that?"

"Sorry. But the words … just sort of fell into my head. And I'm excited about them."

In the distance, the music quieted. Tasia stayed tightly pressed against him, feeling his warmth. "I wonder how many people here are excited by words," she said. "How many people think like you?"

"Luckily for us all, probably not many."

"I'm the lucky one."

"Well, my poem might change your mind."

She kissed him, then again rested her cheek on his shoulder, swaying from side to side. "If you can't tell me your poem yet, then tell me a story. The story of you."

Rex barked nearby, surrounded by a group of older children. Jerico whistled at his companion, then returned his attention to Tasia. He kissed the top of her head, moving with her, his arms wrapped around her and his hands resting against the small of her back.

"The story of me?" he asked, then kissed her again.

"That's right. Tell it to me like I'm a little girl and it's the story of someone really special."

He smiled, slowing his movements but still holding her tight. "It's the story of a boy who was looking for something beautiful. He thought he found it in art, in the sky, in the words of people who'd lived long ago. And maybe ... maybe he did find it in those places. But he kept searching, looking for something more, something even bigger. And then he met someone who changed everything. She opened his world in a way that he didn't think was possible. She taught him about hope, about belief. And when he fell in love with her, it was like ... he'd been swimming underwater for his entire life and suddenly he was at the surface, looking over all the waves, seeing a beautiful world that he didn't even know existed."

Tasia bit her lower lip. "And what happened ... at the end of their story?"

"A storm caught them—beating against them, threatening to tear them apart. And if he'd been alone, he might have let it destroy him. But he wasn't alone. She stood beside him, and they fought against it, rising even after they'd been knocked down so many times. And though they suffered, the storm finally passed. Everything became quiet and clear. And in the days and years that followed, their love grew even stronger. It wasn't perfect but was real and ... enduring. It kept them warm for so long, and they created so many beautiful things together. And even at the very end of their lives, it still felt like the beginning, like everything was new and fresh and full of promise. They wouldn't end. They wouldn't be separated. Because colors can't be taken from the sky. Light can't be taken from the sun."

As they shifted back and forth, Jerico wiped a tear from

Tasia's cheek. She thanked him for the story, and he kissed her forehead once again, holding her tight. He was about to tell her that he loved her when Aki called to him. Glancing up, he saw that she and Valeriya were dancing nearby. They wore colorful dresses and high heels and had flowers in their hair. Jerico smiled, waving to them. Aki joked about his blue shirt, saying that she liked him more when he was Tasia's knight in shiny army fatigues. After all, knights didn't fight in blue.

Jerico laughed, then watched Aki rise to her tiptoes to kiss Valeriya, still moving to the music. The two of them leaned into each other, as if they couldn't get close enough, and Jerico promised himself to look after them in the coming fight.

The night aged. Yet the music and dancing continued. Children ran around, holding kites aloft, encouraging them to fly. People laughed and cried. Old men and women sat at tables, eating sweets and reminiscing about the best of their days. Though their lives had been difficult, everyone seemed to have experienced moments of joy, and it was these moments that they discussed and reflected upon.

Jerico turned his attention back to Tasia, caressing the top of her shoulder with his right hand. "When it's over," he said, "I'd like to hear your story. The story of you."

"But I'm not a poet. Not a storyteller."

"Neither am I."

She shook her head. "You're so much more than you think."

The music stopped. People began to applaud and separate. But Jerico continued to hold her, not wanting to let go. If he didn't let go of her, maybe the night would never end. Maybe he'd be able to keep her safe and warm forever.

But she stepped away from him and the spell was broken.

CHAPTER 28

The next morning, Tasia awoke in Jerico's arms. She expected him to still be asleep, as they'd gone to bed late, but his eyes were open and he smiled at her. Thinking about how he seemed to enjoy kissing her forehead, and how for him it appeared to be an expression of endearment, she moved toward him and kissed him on the brow.

"What did you dream about?" she asked quietly.

"I'm not sure. Something about Aki. I can't remember what, but probably something to do with her coloring my hair pink and painting my nails."

"A dream come true for her."

"Exactly. So let's keep it between us and not give her any ideas."

Tasia smiled and stroked the side of his bare shoulder. "I have to meet Zeus this morning. I have to plan. But after that … we'll time to do something."

"Like what?"

On the floor beside them, Rex whimpered, prompting Jerico to pat the side of their bed. Leaping up, Rex landed on Jerico's legs and then licked his outstretched hands. Jerico laughed, scratching Rex's head and jostling him from side to side. Rex gnawed at his hands, his tail wagging.

Tasia watched them play, enjoying their moment together. Each time Jerico pushed Rex away, the young dog pounced back, producing moans and smiles. Rex growled, digging at the sheet that covered them. Jerico pretended to throw something that Rex might fetch, but Rex wasn't fooled. He nipped and pawed, in constant motion. Jerico finally wrapped his arms around him and, laughing, pulled him down. Rex fought against him, then lay on his side and licked the back of Jerico's hand.

Thinking about Jerico's earlier question, Tasia asked, "What would Rex like to do?"

"Eat more of your treats."

"And what else?"

"Take a walk outside."

Aware that demons would dominate the day's sky, Tasia weighed the risks of such an excursion. "We'll have to be careful," she replied. "Because if something happens to us, we'll let everyone down."

"Then let's stay underground."

She shook her head, all too aware that it might be their last day together. "No, we can't hide like that. Not today. Not ever again."

"Are you sure?"

"Aki told me about a secret exit from the Stronghold. It leads right into the woods. There's a hidden trail that goes to the top of a mountain. She said the trees are so thick that you can't even see the sun."

"That sounds safe."

"I'll bring lunch. You can bring a book. And when we're up there, you can read something to me. And then … then we'll get ready to fight."

He kissed the back of her hand. "We're going to win."

Nodding, she bit her bottom lip. She was about to respond when she felt K'ail communicating with her. The intrusion was strong, cold, and unwelcome. "He's … he's speaking to me," she said, her voice much quieter. "He wants to tell me something."

"But do you want to listen?"

"No. But I probably should."

"You probably should be careful."

Tasia nodded, rolling to her side in bed, away from Jerico, and opening her mind to what K'ail had to say.

Tomorrow will be your last dawn. Enjoy it. Then summon my ship. Summon it or we shall set your world on fire.

"We'll bring it here," she answered, whispering. "And we'll bring it down."

When it arrives, I shall tell Ne'ith what you have done. How you killed her offspring. Her wrath will be as infinite as the universe. After she ruins your mind, I shall ruin your body.

"You had your chance. At the lake. But you gloated for too long."

That tongue of yours. How I long to claim it.

"I'm not going to—"

You will always be a mortal, Tasia. No matter how much courage is within you, you will not be able to do what must be done. After all, a flower, no matter how brave and steadfast, cannot resist the foot that steps upon it.

Tasia felt fear rising within her. But she didn't want to be afraid. If the day was to be her last, she needed it to be filled with joy. "We danced last night," she whispered. "And I didn't think about you once."

A dance? We heard your revelry. We laughed and tasted the blood of your guards.

"Even if I die tomorrow, even if you blind me, I'll still have lived more in my short life than you have in your long one. And maybe … maybe I am nothing more than a flower. I'll never fly like you do. I'll never explore the universe. But I wouldn't trade places with you either. You don't have anything I want."

As you are dying, your thoughts shall be different.

"You're wrong," she replied, trying to steady her breathing, her emotions. "When my father died, he was reminded of the good. He smiled at me and he wasn't afraid."

But was I upon him, Tasia? Was I there? Because if I had been present, he would not have smiled. And nothing would have reminded him of the good.

"He was—"

Are you with the boy now? Have you told him how I shall break his dog's back, then pull the bones from its spine?"

"I told him how I tricked you, a one-eyed bat who calls himself a god."

I shall find you on my ship. You will not understand it, Tasia. Nor will you know where to go. Do you think if I feared what you could do that I would ever let you set foot upon it?

"You underestimate us. You always have."

Ten thousand of us killed ten billion of you. And yet you think you can win.

Tasia's pulse quickened as she wondered if she could deceive K'ail once again, if he might provide her with the answer to a question she longed to ask. Sweat beaded on her brow. She closed her eyes, nodding, trying to convince herself. "Before I danced, I dropped into Angkor, and said goodbye to my mother. Then—"

You wasted the little time you had.

"Then I dropped back here. I dropped twice in an hour."

How?

"Because you taught me the secrets to the Orbs. You taught me how to control my path between them. And I taught myself how to drop without fear, but instead with strength ... and belief. You believe yourselves to be gods. And though you're not gods, your belief gives you strength. It lets you travel like gods, without pain, without fear. And that's how it was for me yesterday."

K'ail didn't immediately respond, and Tasia wondered if

she'd been wrong to tell him what she believed to be true, and what she hoped that he'd confirm through his reply. But then he spoke again, and his words comforted her.

You know too many secrets, Tasia. And that is why, when my ship appears, I will come for you. Ne'ith will come for you also.

"You won't hurt me again," she whispered. "You won't ever hurt me again."

Tell the boy to—

Tasia shut her mind to K'ail's threat, vanquishing his words. She tried to slow her breathing, sitting up in bed. Beads of sweat ran down her face, chasing each other, moving to her neck and shoulders. Jerico sat up as well, holding her hands within his.

"What did he say?" he asked, ignoring Rex's affections.

"What I needed to hear."

"Which was?"

Tasia turned to him. "He's going to come for us, Jerico, when we're on that ship. And he won't be alone."

"Neither will we."

"But how will we know where to go? To blow up that ship, we have to know where to go."

"Remember what Ishaam said? That he'd make a device to lead us to the ship's power source? As long as his device works, we'll know where to go."

"That's right," Tasia replied, having forgotten what the scientist had promised. "That'll help."

Jerico touched her forearm, tracing the scar from the wound

he'd stitched together. "Maybe we should stay here today. Maybe it's better if—"

"No, I don't want to stay. Just let me plan with Zeus. Then we'll leave together."

"If you're sure."

"I'm tired of being afraid," she replied, remembering how K'ail's talon had cut into her. "And I can only do what I need to if I'm not afraid. That's why we're going to hike up Aki's trail, that's why we're going to stand in the light."

"We'd better be careful."

"We can't run any more, Jerico. If we run, we'll die. If we hide, we'll die. But if we finally find our strength, if we're not afraid of what's above us, we'll win."

CHAPTER 29

S itting on a cracked plastic chair, Valeriya studied the scene around her. She and Aki were seated at a long wooden table located in one of the Stronghold's kitchens. The table was usually reserved for slicing vegetables and was scarred with the crisscrossed cuts of thousands of knives. Pots, pans, and stainless-steel ladles hung from hooks above them. On the other side of the room, immense wood-fired stoves stood idle.

The kitchen had been temporarily converted into a weapons depot, and scores of rifles lay at the far end of the table. A row of five Seekers worked to clean, oil, and load each weapon. The first part of the process involved disassembling a rifle. A wounded sniper then used fresh rags to wipe away grit from the weapon's inner parts. Oil was then applied where needed, wiped down with a different, finer cloth, and then the rifle was reassembled. The process was time-consuming and tedious, but Valeriya didn't mind. She knew any weapon that misfired or jammed would likely result in the death of whoever wielded it. So her focus was intense and her hands steady. Even Aki, who sat next to her, rarely spoke.

Valeriya's back ached from leaning over the table all morning, but she tried to ignore the pain. Occasionally she stood up and stretched, wondering which rifle would end up in her hands. Though another group of Seekers would test the accuracy of the weapons after they were cleaned, making minor adjustments to the scopes, Valeriya knew she and Aki would step outside the Stronghold and fire at distant targets. After all, if a rifle's scope were calibrated incorrectly, even to the smallest degree, bullets would sail wide of their targets.

"We'll finish in an hour," Valeriya said quietly to Aki. "And then we'll be free for the afternoon. What should we do?"

"I don't know. Sleep?"

Valeriya didn't want to spend what might be her last full day on Earth sleeping. "We can sleep tonight," she replied. "Or even later this afternoon. But before that … let's do something new."

Aki wiped her grease-covered hands on a dirty rag. "Something new you say. Well, we're dropping into an alien ship tomorrow. That'll be new. And if we're really lucky, we'll then try our hand at parachuting. That sounds fun and definitely new. So what should we add to our list?"

Smiling, Valeriya shrugged. "Something I've never done."

"I understand that. You said as much. And since alien ships and parachutes aren't enough for you, what do you suggest?"

"It sounds silly."

"Most things that come out of your mouth sound silly."

Valeriya reached over and wiped her greasy fingers on the back of Aki's hand. "Be nice or I'll dirty up your hair."

"Which would be the end of you. And every fish in the world would be happy."

"I'm not so—"

"Can you just tell me what you want to do? We've got a pile of rifles over there, and they aren't going to clean themselves."

Valeriya shifted on her seat, her thoughts drifting back to the previous night. She and Aki had danced until the music ended. She'd never danced before and hadn't expected to like it so much. That realization had prompted her to think about what else she'd never experienced and might not ever get to.

"I've seen children riding bicycles here," she said, absently creating a circular smudge on Aki's hand. "And I've never ridden one."

Aki's brow furrowed. "But what about in Neverland? Didn't they have bikes there?"

"They did. But I never rode one. I always thought I'd have plenty of time to learn."

At the far end of the table, someone cleared their throat. Aki didn't seem to notice. "Then we'll ride bikes," she replied. "We'll ride bikes all over the place."

Valeriya smiled, pleased by the prospect. "And what about you? Is there something you want to do for the first time? I mean ... we don't know what will happen tomorrow. So I think we should do as much as we can."

"After our ride, we could—"

A commotion at the doorway caused Valeriya to look up. To her surprise, Slate stepped into the room. As before, Slate wore black leather pants and a similar jacket. Her spiked blonde hair seemed even lighter than before. A pistol rested in a holster at each hip.

Slate stopped, scrutinizing them. "Well, what do we have here? A pair of deserters who were in jail, last I saw them."

Aki stood up from the table. "Stay away from us, Slate. Stay away or you'll be sorry."

"What a pitiful little girl you are," Slate replied. "You sit there with your hands on a weapon and your pretty friend beside you, but you were really born to be a Hider—like every other coward in your family. Why shouldn't we just feed them to the demons and spare ourselves the trouble of saving them?"

Without pause, Aki leapt at Slate, knocking a chair over. Though Aki was smaller, her quickness and rage took Slate by surprise. The two of them toppled to the ground, with Slate falling beneath Aki. Valeriya started to intervene, but Aki's fist rose and fell, smashing against Slate's face. Aki struck her again and again. Slate reached up, grabbed Aki's hair, and pulled her downward. But Aki's punches didn't cease, and her fists slammed into Slate's sides.

Two men from the other end of the table shouted for the fighting to stop and hurried toward Aki, but Valeriya purposely got in their way. She bumped against them, saw that Slate was pulling out one of her pistols, and then reached for a nearby rifle. Without thought she pointed it straight at Slate's belly.

"Enough!" she yelled.

When Aki relaxed, Slate yanked her pistol from its holster.

Valeriya lunged forward, jamming the rifle's barrel against Slate's chest. "It's over! Do you understand? Point that pistol away from her or I swear I'll put a hole in you!"

Blood oozed from Slate's nose. The pistol trembled in her grasp. Aki raised her hands, then carefully stood up. "No one in my family is a coward. Do you hear me, you bow-legged bitch?"

"Be quiet, Aki!" Valeriya shouted. "You've made your point."

Slate lurched to her feet, which prompted blood to flow more freely from her nose. She wiped it away. "You assaulted me. And there are witnesses."

Valeriya kept her finger on the rifle's trigger. "Just like you assaulted her at the castle. And I'm a witness to that."

"You're a deserter. Just like she is. Your words won't matter."

"And after tomorrow, maybe someone will listen to you," Valeriya replied. "But today people have more important things to worry about than you getting beat up."

Slate started to speak, then stopped. She wiped more blood from her nose, then put her pistol back into its holster. "I'll look for you on the ship," she said, glaring at Aki. "So you better have eyes in the back of your head."

"And you better find yourself a new nose," Aki replied. "Not that you had much of one to start with."

Slate lunged for Aki, but the two men got between them,

raising their voices. Still struggling, Slate was escorted to the door. One of the men began to berate Aki. Continuing to aim her rifle toward her adversary, Valeriya made sure Slate's hands didn't drop down to her pistols. Understanding the threat that Slate posed, she wondered how to deal with her.

Both men now argued with Aki, who didn't back down. Once again, Valeriya came to her defense, explaining how Slate had nearly knocked her out, how all they'd been trying to do was to save a little girl. At these words, the men relented. Aki turned for the door as Valeriya set down the rifle and followed.

Outside the kitchen, people came and went, carrying supplies. The Stronghold bustled with activity. Slate, fortunately, was nowhere to be seen.

"You handled that well," Valeriya said, shaking her head.

"And what would you have done if she'd called your grandparents cowards?"

"Probably nothing different."

"Then I handled it just like I should have."

Valeriya sighed. "And now we're going to have to worry about her tomorrow, as well as the demons. I wouldn't say that's a good thing."

"Well, it is what it is."

"Your knuckles are bleeding."

"I don't care about my knuckles. They'll survive. The good news is that I was tired before, but now I'm wide awake. Throwing that snake to the ground was like drinking ten cups of coffee. So let's finish cleaning these rifles, get something to eat, and then we'll find a couple of bikes."

Valeriya lifted up Aki's hands, inspecting her wounds. "I didn't know you had such a temper."

"Slate's a bully."

"She—"

"And what are the demons, Val? They're bullies too. They came to our world and just … swept us aside. They killed us, laughed at us, mocked us. My whole life I've fought them. And if Slate thinks she's going to intimidate me and push me around, that I'm not going to stand up to her like I've stood up to the demons, then she's dumber than she looks."

Valeriya tried and failed to suppress a smile. "I think you made your point with her."

"And tomorrow I'll make it with the demons."

"Perfect."

"Is that sarcasm I hear in your voice?"

Valeriya nodded, again and again.

Aki reached out to her, wincing as she gripped her hand. "Stop that. You look like a drunk puppet. Anyway, can we finish our job here? I'm hungry and need to eat. Then we'll find those bikes."

"You never answered my question."

"What question?"

"What do you want to try for the first time?"

"Well, I've always wanted to punch Slate. So I can finally cross that off my list. Our afternoon is suddenly free."

Valeriya grinned. She let Aki lead her forward, no longer

angry with her for the fight. What Aki had said about the demons was right, and her rage, buried so deep inside her, was understandable.

At dawn the following day, Aki would get her chance for revenge on the demons. All of them would. And if Slate snuck up behind her, Valeriya would just have to be ready.

CHAPTER 30

Ishaam's second journey through the abandoned subway tunnels was much different than his first. Though he was still fearful of the white demon, she'd promised him the safe return of his wife and sons if he told her about Osaka Castle. Because of her promise, he'd betrayed his people and the demons had won the day. Now he could only hope that Li'kan would honor her words. The thought of holding his loved ones again brought tears to his eyes, which tumbled onto his cheeks and his dusty shirt. He hurried ahead, often stumbling, nearly delirious with desire to be reunited with his family.

Of course, Ishaam understood that Li'kan might have deceived him, and was terrified that his wife and sons had been slain. Were the white demon to say as much, he would try to kill her. If he succeeded, he'd then take his own life. If he failed, Li'kan would take it for him. To prepare for the confrontation, he'd gone to an underground firing range and tested the pistol that was holstered and hidden at his lower back. From a distance, his shots were wildly off-target, but up close, he might be able to kill his foe.

Shaking with both anticipation and dread, Ishaam started to run, holding a red-beamed flashlight in his left hand. He saw the pile of rubble ahead and scrambled up it, falling several times, bloodying his hands and knees. But he reached the summit, slipped, and then slid down the other side.

"Father!" one of his sons shouted.

Ishaam called out to his boys, coughing on dust and grit. He wiped his eyes, saw his sons, and felt relief wash through him. His boys, fourteen-year-old twins, stood in front of Li'kan, their arms wrapped around each other. Ishaam lurched to his feet and ran to them, hugging them with all his strength. He wept, muttering their names, looking for wounds. His boys cried in return, clinging to him, asking to leave. He kissed their brows and continued to hold them tight. Only then did he realize that their mother wasn't with them.

"Where is—"

Your wife is still my guest. She's having too much fun to leave.

Ishaam coughed again, then pulled his sons behind him. He faced the white demon. "You promised me—"

I promised your sons wouldn't be harmed. And do you see any marks on them? Believe me, it wasn't easy to keep them safe. So many of the weaker gods wanted to gobble them up. But lucky for you, I can be persuasive. So here they are.

"Our arrangement ... was for all three of them to be

delivered to me," he replied, trembling. "Why isn't she here?"

Patience, little man. You must have more patience. Answer a few more questions. Then I'll bring her here tomorrow. After the fight.

"No. That's wasn't our—"

Li'kan flapped her immense wings, causing dust to rise. She stepped forward. *Do you want to watch your boys die? Is that your wish?*

Ishaam held out his right hand, as if he could push the massive demon away. "No, please no," he stammered, struggling to breathe, to collect his thoughts. "That's not what I'm saying. But my wife … she's not here. And you said that—"

Answer my question now or watch me poke holes in your sweet sons. And so I'll ask, just this once—when my ship arrives, how will they bring it down?

"I don't know. I'm not—"

If you utter one more lie, or even pause again before answering me, they'll both die. I think I'll start with the brown-haired one first. He's the more defiant of the two. I find him most tedious.

"Please. Just—"

How will all those little mortals destroy such a big ship?

Ishaam squeezed his sons' hands, feeling them, desperate to protect them. "Explosives," he finally muttered, nodding. "Explosives from the inside."

The white demon didn't immediately respond. Ishaam's sons tugged on his shirt, pulling him backward. But he maintained his footing, ignoring their pleas.

Where will they place these explosives?

"If I answer you, will you promise to—"

With incredible speed, Li'kan lunged forward, thrusting her hand toward Ishaam's brown-haired son. A single talon pierced the boy's right shoulder. He screamed, falling back, striking the rubble behind them. Ishaam cried out, dropping to his knees at his son's side, horrified by the injury. Blood flowed freely from the finger-sized hole. As his son shrieked, writhing in pain, Ishaam ripped off part of his own shirt and began to make a crude bandage, his hands trembling.

Should I taste him? I must confess that I'm quite tempted to.

"Don't!" Ishaam shouted. "Please stay away! I'll tell you whatever you want!"

The demon stepped back. *His wound will one day fade to a scar. He'll survive. But deny me again, my little friend, and I'll take his life.*

Ishaam nodded, his face wet with tears. "He's just a boy. He's innocent."

Tell me what I need to know, and he'll be free to go taint himself. Innocence, after all, never lasts.

"The bombs … will be placed near your ship's power supply," he said, cradling his son, who was going into shock.

And how will they find the power supply? As you must know, it's a big ship.

"We're making handheld power detectors. They'll—"

Disable them tonight, in secret. If you wish to see your wife again, deactivate them.

Ishaam didn't respond but nodded, cradling his boy and weeping.

And one more thing. As soon as our big, beautiful ship arrives, use the gun hidden behind your back to kill the young Guardian, Tasia. I want you to put holes in her chest. As many as possible. Then your wife will be returned to you. And the four of you can hide down here, in safety, when we kill everyone aboveground. After they're dead, we'll leave your dreary planet, and who knows, maybe your family can learn to be happy. At least you'll be alive. And you'll have each other. A perfect ending to a troubled story.

Ishaam whispered to his injured son, stroking his brow. The color seemed to have drained from his face. He was clearly in shock, and Ishaam held the bandage against his wound, while also trying to keep him warm. "Yes … I'll do what you say. I promise."

Tasia. I want her shot. Right in the heart. Again and again and again. Then you can come back here and retrieve your wife. She's quite intact, by the way, though I fear she may think her sons are dead.

"Please … please tell her they're alive."

Oh, you forget that she can't speak with me. We really haven't gotten fully acquainted. In any case, you can show her yourself tomorrow. Just disable those devices and then shoot that inconvenient Guardian. After she's dead, you can close your eyes and pretend everything was a bad dream. You won't ever see me again.

"I'll do it all," Ishaam promised, then kissed his son's cool forehead. "Please let us go. He needs help."

Yes, I see that. I expected him to be more of a fighter, to tell you the truth. He was such a defiant little creature. But he should be fine. I didn't sever any major arteries, and your doctors seem quite capable. If you get him to them soon, he'll live to bother someone else. Probably you, of course.

Ishaam nodded. "I'll do what you say."

I know you will. Afterwards come back here tomorrow and claim your wife. She'll be most happy to see you.

Grunting, Ishaam lifted up his injured son, careful to keep pressure on his wound. He cradled his boy in his arms, like he had countless times many years earlier. Some color seemed to be returning to his son's cheeks, which filled Ishaam with hope. Without another word to the demon, he turned, then struggled to carry his son up the pile of rubble. His other boy tried to help, pushing him from behind.

Somehow, they made it to the top of the debris. Ishaam half stumbled, half slid downward. His injured son mumbled something, and he kissed his forehead again, remembering how once he'd held him all night when a fever had struck.

"You come first," Ishaam whispered. "You both have to come first."

Li'kan's words twisted their way into his mind.

Remember, in case your little gang of heroes manages to drop into our ship, I want them to be lost. Those power detectors had better not work. Let your friends stumble around, and maybe they'll enjoy some new sights. And don't forget to shoot Tasia before she steps into the Orb. That way she won't even be able to lead them to us. To be honest with you, since we're such good friends, I'll admit that she's troubled us enough already. How K'ail let her escape, I'll never understand. So fill her with holes and let's be done with her.

"I will. I promise."

Then I'll let you go, my little spy. Enjoy your time with your sons. What amazing stories they'll surely tell.

Ishaam nodded. Shuddering, he struggled forward. Though grateful that his boys had been returned to him and that they would survive, the thought of his wife still suffering tormented him. And nearly as bad was the understanding that he'd have to once again betray his people.

If Ishaam had believed that the Guardians' attack tomorrow would be a triumph, he might have tried to somehow double-cross the white demon. After all, maybe there was a way to save his wife without disabling the devices and killing Tasia. But he'd thought for many hours about the looming assault and didn't see how it could possibly succeed. The alien ship would be too vast and well defended. The small band of Guardians and Seekers who dropped inside it would be quickly overwhelmed.

Since the attack was doomed to failure, Ishaam didn't see how he could support it at the cost of his wife. The better choice, he believed, was to betray his people in order to save her. Then at least the four of them would survive. They could stay underground until the ship had departed. And once it was gone, maybe they could lead some kind of decent lives. Maybe they'd finally be free.

His son opened his eyes. He whispered something, and Ishaam wept in relief and joy, knowing that his boy wouldn't ever have to face a demon again. His betrayal would allow his sons to survive, to create their own destinies. The War for Earth would soon be over, soon be lost. Humanity would be pushed to the edge of extinction, but Ishaam's family would stay strong.

"You'll grow to be men," he whispered, as tears obscured his vision. "And I know you'll both make me so proud. You'll be everything I tried to be."

His uninjured son tugged on his arm. "Why were you talking to that demon? It wasn't saying anything."

Ishaam ignored his son's question, still thinking about the past and the future. "I thought science … would save us. But I was so wrong. And I'll never be able to forgive myself. But at least I'll be able to look at you both and know that there's still goodness in the universe, that I love you and you'll always be free."

CHAPTER 31

A s Aki had explained, the secret exit from the Stronghold led directly into a newly formed forest. What had once been an open-air market was now inundated with trees of every shape and size. Vines covered rows of stalls, some of which had collapsed into misshapen, decomposing piles. A barely discernable trail ran through the center of the market—now home to a variety of creatures. Birds chattered in the trees above them. Foxes hid in dens under mounds of decaying plywood and merchandise. And monkeys chased each other atop the rubble, screeching loudly. Whatever human remains once covered the grounds had been devoured long ago.

Careful to stay quiet, Jerico followed Tasia. Rex was leashed to a harness, and Jerico kept him close. Though Rex sniffed at droppings and sometimes strained against his harness, he refrained from barking, as he'd been taught. Somehow, he seemed to sense that his companions were trying to stay silent.

Tasia gripped her staff and followed the trail as it led away from the market. The trees were so thick around them that almost no sunlight struck the ground. Ferns appeared to thrive in the damp dimness and reached higher than Jerico's knees. As the trail started to rise, he tried not to think about the coming dawn, about all that could go wrong in their assault on the alien ship. Instead he focused on the scenery around him.

Aki had said that monks originally carved the trail into the mountain almost two thousand years earlier. At the mountain's summit rose a simple stone temple. Aki believed the temple would make a perfect place for a picnic and had teased them by saying that they could exchange vows and read poetry together.

The trail continued to climb. Small rocky streams crossed it in places, and soon their feet were wet. Two mountain bikes lay near a big boulder, and Jerico wondered if a pair of friends had been riding up the trail when the demons first attacked. The rusting bikes still looked strong and defiant, as if they'd rather have been resting at the mountain's summit.

From time to time Jerico studied the forest's canopy but he could barely see the sky. Only where large trees had died did openings exist in the green shield above. And beneath these openings, younger saplings rose straight and true, appearing to race toward the sunlight.

The distant cracks of rifles erupted and Tasia turned around toward the city. Jerico noticed how her grip on her staff tightened. To his surprise, she shook her head but said nothing.

He was certain that the coming fight occupied her thoughts, as it did his. The two of them had spent the morning with Zeus, discussing everything that K'ail had told Tasia, and how she believed his boasts might affect the battle.

The crackle of gunfire lingered for almost a minute, so at odds with the rhythmic and natural sounds of the forest. Jerico's rifle was slung over his right shoulder, and he glanced at its various components, ensuring that a stray twig wasn't stuck somewhere. As Rex paused to sniff at the base of a tree, Jerico leaned down to scratch his companion's head.

Tasia asked him then to tell her about his parents, prompting his mind to wander back into the past. They started to walk again, and he spoke about growing up in various Strongholds, about never having a true home. He'd dropped through every Orb by the age of thirteen. When his parents had gone off to fight, he'd often occupied himself by spending time in libraries and museums. His siblings had been more interested in making friends. And while Jerico had enjoyed laughing with various companions, he'd also relished the silence of solitude. Deep within abandoned buildings he read about the past and daydreamed about the future. He imagined so many things— what it must have been like to sail across seas, or to ride in a hot-air balloon, or to try to hit a white ball with a wooden bat. The stories that his ancestors once read fascinated him, and he often asked himself what they might have wondered upon coming across the same words that he did.

Tasia probed deeper, inquiring about his best memories

and moments. After answering her, he realized that one of his favorite things about her was her interest in others. She asked about someone's past and beliefs not because she was bored, but because she seemed convinced that everyone had something to offer. And she was genuinely attentive to what people had to say.

As the companions spoke, they climbed higher, crossing more streams. Sweat beaded on their bodies as the temperature rose. At one point they came across the remains of a crashed plane. They also saw deer, a leopard, and an immense salamander. Rex delighted in these discoveries, tugging against his leash, eager to smell whatever scents had been left by the fleeing creatures.

Finally the trail flattened, and before long they came to what must have been an ancient cemetery. Rectangular, moss-covered slabs of granite stretched skyward. Also present were old statues of bald, big-bellied men, as well as stone lanterns. A tall granite gateway appeared in the distance. Beyond it, a simple temple sat near the edge of a cliff. The temple featured a graceful roofline that curved upward at the corners. Though some tiles had fallen from the roof and most of the temple was inundated with moss, it was largely intact.

Tasia walked toward a stone bench that stood behind the temple, near the cliff. Because of the cliff, they were able to see above the trees in front of them, yet still were sheltered by the canopy above. Far below, the distant city of Kyoto stretched away from them. Buildings that once might have been white were blackened by the passage of time. They flowed toward a series of mountains to the north, merging into each other. Jerico tried to locate the Stronghold, but he realized that it was hidden behind a rise of faraway treetops. He carefully laid his rifle on the ground, sat down on the bench, and extended his hand to Tasia.

"You wore me out," he said, smiling as she took his hand and sat beside him.

"I think Rex wore us both out. And himself."

Jerico looked at his companion, who lay on his side, his tongue dangling. "I'd say he was thirsty if he hadn't slurped up so much of those streams. But I think you're right—he needs a break from chasing salamanders."

"That big one scared him."

Grinning, Jerico took off his backpack, then pulled out a water bottle. He offered it to Tasia. She thanked him, drank deeply, and then handed it back. After taking several gulps, he licked his lips, then set the bottle aside. "I've got some food in here too," he said. "Some dried fish, it goes without saying, but also some chocolate."

"Really?"

He smiled. "I have my sources."

"I haven't had chocolate in months. Maybe years."

"Then it's been too long."

She started to respond but stopped. "That's what everyone's doing, isn't it?"

"What do you mean?"

"Eating chocolate. Living like … the end is just around the corner."

Thinking about how he'd seen countless couples holding hands and embracing each other, Jerico nodded. "I think everyone wants to live as much as possible. In case we round that corner tomorrow."

A woodpecker began to hammer away at a tree in the distance. Tasia turned toward the source of the noise and then looked back at him. "Can I ask you something?"

"As long as Aki didn't put you up to it."

"Oh, she's tried. But I've resisted."

"Really? I'm impressed. She doesn't like resistance."

Rex raised his head to snap at a troublesome fly, then lay back down and sighed.

Tasia smiled, though her grin didn't last long. "Do you have regrets?" she asked. "I mean—if you could go back in time, would you do anything different?"

Jerico wiped sweat from his eyes, thinking about his past. "Only about a million things. Maybe more."

"Tell me one."

"I'd eat more chocolate."

"What else?"

A bright-green leaf fell from above, fluttering, spinning, and then landing on Jerico's lap. He picked up the leaf, turning it over in his hands. "I'd spend more time with my brother and sister. They wanted to do things with me, but I wasn't always there. Usually I was in my own little world."

"I'm sure you were good to them."

Shrugging, he stroked the leaf with his thumb. "What about you? What would you change?"

She started to speak but then stopped, glancing at the sky. "I'd listen to my father more. Sometimes he'd try to talk to me, but I'd think about other things. My mother wasn't much of a talker, so I don't think she ever minded. But he was different. He wanted to tell me things. He tried to tell me things. But I didn't always listen."

"You told me how he taught you about beauty, about how he thought you were different. You must have been listening."

"Sometimes."

"But that was enough."

"I don't like regrets. I don't want to die with them."

"You're not going to die with regrets."

The unseen woodpecker once again pounded away on a distant tree. The rhythmic thumping sounded artificial, yet was also timeless and comforting. Jerico was glad that the demons weren't going to set the Earth on fire. Regardless of how Tasia's plan unfolded tomorrow, woodpeckers, whales, and every other creature would survive.

He started to ask Tasia what she was thinking about when he noticed that she looked uncomfortable. She shifted beside him, drawing purposeful and deep breaths, as if trying to steady herself. "What?" he asked. "What's wrong? Is K'ail talking to you again?"

"He's trying. But I'm ignoring him."

"Good."

"But that reminds me, I need to tell you something."

"So tell me."

She bit her lower lip. "If I have to die tomorrow, so that we can win, then I'll die."

The woodpecker stopped its assault on the tree and suddenly the forest was silent. Jerico had known for many days that Tasia was ready to sacrifice herself in order for humanity to survive. In the coming fight, if faced with the choice to save herself or those she loved, she would die on the alien ship. She'd bring it down and fall with it.

"If we have to die to win, then we'll die," he said quietly. "Not you. But us."

"But why us? Why not just me?"

"Because I can help you. Because then maybe you won't need to die."

Nodding, she brought his hand to her lips and kissed it. "You've already given me so much. Not presents but … promises."

"Promises?"

"You promised me things and they came true. You told me not to be afraid of falling for you, and I trusted you, and you were right. You told me that you'd save me, and you did."

He thought about her words, sensing her fear. He couldn't imagine losing her or watching her be hurt. "You saved me too," he finally replied, suddenly at a loss for what to say.

The woodpecker pounded away at the tree again, prompting

Rex to growl. Tasia leaned down and scratched his head, telling him that everything was fine. Her hair, which Aki had so carefully straightened, clung to her damp forehead.

"If you don't mind ... can you tell me another story?" she asked. "Maybe something sweet? Or a poem? K'ail's still trying to talk to me, and it's easier for me to ignore him if I'm listening to you."

Glancing above, Jerico wondered what she might like to hear. She seemed unusually vulnerable, and he realized that the weight of the looming attack was threatening to overwhelm her. Though she had always been so strong, everything soon would be at stake. She'd led so many people to this moment, to this cross in the roads of fate.

"I once read a story, a true story, about an emperor who was madly in love," he finally replied, wanting to please her. "He lived a long, long time ago, and though he had many wives, he loved one more than all the rest. In a time when men ruled the world, she was his equal. And he always wanted her beside him. But then one night, after giving birth to their child, she began to die. No matter how much he loved her, no matter how great his power, he couldn't help her."

"And what happened?"

"Well, when he realized that she was dying, he wanted to give her one last gift, one last part of himself. So he asked what he could do for her, and she answered by wondering if he might build her something beautiful. And then, every year afterwards, on their anniversary, he could light a candle in this beautiful place and think about her."

Tasia bit her lower lip. "And then?"

"She died in his arms, and in the years that followed, he spent all his energy and fortune building her a memorial the likes of which the world had never seen. He called it the Taj Mahal, and when finished, it was the most beautiful sight anywhere. She was buried within it, and before long, he was put to rest beside her. And for centuries afterwards, people from all over the world came to visit their tombs. Poets said the Taj Mahal looked like a teardrop from heaven. And as far as I know, it's still there."

"Where is it?"

"Next to a river. In India."

Nodding, Tasia squeezed his hand. "Of all the stories you could have told me, why did you pick that one?"

He glanced at the sky, unsure how to answer. The world around him seemed to possess a strange weight, as if the air were an invisible blanket that pressed down on him. Though afraid of dying, of watching Tasia die, he understood her vulnerability and didn't want to add to it. She had enough to worry about.

"Well," he finally answered, "if I die tomorrow, I just want you to know that I'll die at peace. I'll die like she did. And you don't ever have to build anything for me, but ... but maybe you could light a candle and think about us."

Tasia looked up, prompting tears to fall from her lashes. "Promise that you'll take me there. To the Taj Mahal."

"Why?"

"Because your promises always come true."

He glanced away, then looked back at her. "I don't—"

"We have to believe that we're going to win tomorrow. I know it's hard right now. But we've come so far, and tomorrow's not going to be the end of us. You said that to me, back when we were climbing the Freedom Tower, before I was carried away. You said that it couldn't be the end of us, and somehow … somehow I knew you were right. Even when I was in that awful prison, I knew you were right."

He leaned toward her, kissing her lips, pulling her against him. "I hope I didn't make you feel worse," he said quietly. "With my story."

She kissed him back, her fingertips stroking his cheek. "You gave me another thing to fight for. Because I want to visit the Taj Mahal with you beside me. How can we die without seeing the most beautiful building on Earth?"

Somehow, amid the tears that fell to her face, she smiled at him. And he sensed such strength and hope and belief in that smile. "I'll follow you anywhere," he said, his voice unsteady as emotions threatened to overwhelm him.

"Everywhere. Let's follow each other everywhere."

"There's so much more to do. To be. I want to explore something magical. Want to see it for the first time. See it as if it were an ocean or a star. Or you."

She kissed him again, holding him tight. "I love you," she replied. "But I won't ever have to light a candle to remember you because you're always going to be beside me."

CHAPTER 32

D eep in the Stronghold, Aki and Valeriya sat at the edge of a large children's playground. Although it was nearly time for dinner, the indoor park was unusually busy. Many families, especially those with a parent who would be involved in the attack, had come to the playground. Children chased each other, dogs barked, balls sailed and bounced, and swings rose and fell. Someone had dressed as a clown and was painting fish, flowers, butterflies, and tigers on children's cheeks. Music hummed in the background.

Standing in an impromptu line, Aki and Valeriya waited for their turns on bicycles. Aki had just finished a game of hide-and-seek with her younger brothers and sisters. Yet she still watched them as they played tag—running around obstacles, leaping over toys. She smiled at their laughter and the way they happily dodged each other. At the far side of the playground, her parents walked, arm in arm. She'd spent several hours with them earlier in the day, reminiscing about her most cherished memories and eating her favorite foods. They'd tried to talk her out of joining the assault but had finally given up, knowing her well enough to understand that once she committed to something, there was no going back.

As Aki stood, holding Valeriya's hand, she thought about what her parents had said—how they were proud of her. She'd never sought such praise, but still, it had been heartwarming to hear. Wondering why their words meant so much, she remembered turning thirteen and deciding to learn how to fight so that her brothers and sisters wouldn't need to. She was given a rifle two years later, and shortly thereafter had snuck away from her family to participate in her first battle. Her parents, who always had been Hiders, were furious with her, but after countless arguments they finally came to realize that she'd follow a path of her own making. And that path, while it led to violence and conflict, also relieved their family from pressure, as at least one of them had joined in the War for Earth.

Still deep in thought, Aki was surprised when she found herself and Valeriya suddenly at the front of the line. For a second time, she explained to Valeriya how to balance her weight on a bike, and how pedaling made everything easier.

"But if I pedal ... doesn't that mean that my weight is changing from side to side?" Valeriya asked.

Aki pointed to a little girl—who might have been five years old—as she maneuvered a pink bike between groups of standing parents. "Watch how she does it. See how she always keeps her feet moving? Because her bike keeps going forward, it stays stable."

"That doesn't make any sense. It seems that—"

"Does it make any sense that someone as sophisticated as me would fall for someone as simple as you? Or that Tasia is one of the most powerful Guardians around? Not everything can be explained, Val. You just need to trust me and do what I say."

Valeriya put her fingers to her lips. "Wait a minute. Why are you more sophisticated than me?"

"The highlight of your day is putting a worm on a hook. Need I say more?"

"I'm sure you will."

Aki sighed, cringing when two children ran into each other and nearly toppled. "Just keep pedaling. Do that and you won't—well, you might not—make a fool of yourself in front of all these little boys and girls."

"Thanks for the encouragement."

Squeezing Valeriya's hand, Aki kissed her on the cheek. "I'm just a realist. You should know that about me by now."

"You're a child yourself. You fit right in here."

A woman dismounted from a bike and began to walk with it toward them. Aki nodded. "This one looks good. It's about the right size for you. I'll help you get on it and you'll just fly away."

As Valeriya muttered something in response, Aki thanked the stranger. Aki then took the bike, lifted it up, and turned the pedals so that the one next to Valeriya was near the ground. She moved to the back of the bike, holding the seat post.

Valeriya glanced at the bike, then at Aki, hesitating. Suddenly Aki didn't want her companion to fail. She knew Valeriya longed to ride and laugh like the children around her, and that Valeriya had never played with toys or thrown balls.

"You can do this," Aki said, nodding. "You've already done so much in your life, and you're good at so many things. You know how to fight and fish, how to hunt and kiss. Riding a bike will be easy compared to all that stuff."

Valeriya took a deep breath, then gripped the bike's handlebars and swung her right leg over the seat. She sat down, placing both her feet on the pedals. Aki grunted, struggling to keep the bike up straight. She told Valeriya to start pedaling, and as Valeriya leaned forward, the bike rolled ahead. Aki switched her grip so that she held Valeriya's arm and was able to better support her. But the bike leaned too far to the right, and Aki had to pull Valeriya in the opposite direction. She started to jog, aware that people were scattering in front of them.

"Don't overcorrect," Aki said, trying to keep Valeriya steady.

"Easy for you to say!"

"Everything's easy for me to say."

"Should I go right or left? Oh, I think I'll go right."

Aki laughed, nearly running now. Though Valeriya still moved the top half of her body too much from side to side, the bike was going fast enough that it wasn't in immediate danger of falling.

"I can't hold you any longer," Aki said. "I'm going to let go."

"Wait! I'll slow down!"

"You can do this. I'm letting go right … now."

"No!"

Aki giggled, releasing Valeriya's arm. She wobbled on top of the bike, yet kept it upright, pedaling fast. Clapping, Aki called out encouragement as Valeriya turned to her left, avoiding a large group of children. Braking, she almost lost her balance, but she continued to pedal, her feet in constant motion. She shouted something, but Aki couldn't make out her words.

Glancing around, Aki looked for a free bike, spied one, and ran toward it. Though it was too small for her, she hopped onto it and headed toward Valeriya. She called out again, laughing, complimenting her companion. A ball bounced in front of Valeriya, and rather than changing directions, she ran straight into it, sending it careening away.

"Don't be afraid to turn!" Aki shouted, getting closer to her. "If you don't turn, you're going to crash."

"What?"

Aki laughed again, standing up on her pedals as she pulled alongside her companion. "You look like you've been riding a bike since the day you were born."

"You're such a liar."

"Watch out for those boys ahead. They don't see you coming."

"I can't—"

"Turn to your left."

"But—"

"Turn!"

Valeriya veered away from the boys, nearly losing her balance. But she steadied herself and finally stopped pedaling. As her bike coasted, she slightly changed course, drifting back to the right, and then to the left. The tension vanished from her face and she grinned.

"You're doing it," Aki said. "You're really doing it."

"Kind of."

"No, you're officially riding. You're almost as good as that five year old."

Laughing, Valeriya began to weave around groups of people. She nearly hit an old man, apologized, and then pedaled harder. Aki kept up with her, staying alongside her, smiling at her obvious joy.

"I'm going to kiss you," Aki said. "Just lean over a little."

"No."

"We can do it."

Valeriya shook her head, but Aki moved toward her. Though she tried to do the same, Valeriya leaned too far in her direction, and their shoulders bumped together. Aki's handlebar got hung up on one of Valeriya's brake cables. The two bikes, now connected, veered to the left. Aki grimaced, tried to slow down, and could only clench her teeth as they headed straight toward a large trashcan. Both bikes struck the container, lurched to the right, and sent Aki and Valeriya tumbling to the ground. Bottles rolled away from them as children laughed, mimicking their fall.

Once Aki saw that Valeriya wasn't hurt, she smiled. "Sorry about that."

"About nearly killing us?"

"Yeah. That's right."

Valeriya shook her head, then half-heartedly pushed her away. "I've noticed that people don't kiss on bicycles, Aki. Maybe there's a reason for that."

"I'll admit—beds are a bit softer."

Wincing, Valeriya stood up, then pointed to the all the trash on the ground. "It looks like you've got some serious cleaning up to do."

"And where are you going?"

"To do some more riding. I need to learn how to turn a bike before I try to kiss on one."

Aki shrugged, brushed off her knees, and rose to her feet. "What can I say, Val? You looked so cute and happy. I just couldn't resist."

Shaking her head again, Valeriya tried and failed to repress a smile. "Those boys are still laughing at us. At you."

"You did look great ... riding that bike. You're really good."

Valeriya started to respond but stopped. She untangled her bike from Aki's and then picked it up. "I can't stay mad at you," she said. "Do you know that?"

"Is the sky blue? Still, tell me why."

"Because there's no one like you."

Aki shrugged, smiling. "That's because the world couldn't handle two of me."

"Thanks for teaching me how to ride. And to crash."

"You taught yourself how to crash. I can't take credit for that."

Valeriya climbed onto her bike, shook her head, and pedaled away. Aki stood motionless, watching her. Before long, Valeriya turned on her seat, waving as her bike wobbled. Rising to her tiptoes, Aki waved back. She clapped and shouted encouragement.

Then a man walked past, pulling a wagon filled with boxes of ammunition. Aki's thoughts shifted to the coming fight. And as she glanced back at Valeriya, she realized that her companion might be riding a bike for the first and the last time.

Rubbing her brow, Aki tried to repress her fears. But they came at her fast and unexpectedly, as if demons intent on ripping her apart. She struggled from their onslaught, unable to fire a rifle at them or to take shelter behind something. And so she simply suffered—not letting herself cry, but finally bending down to pick up the trash at her feet.

From time to time Aki glanced up, watching as Valeriya drifted in and out of groups of playing children, her feet in constant motion.

"I won't let you crash tomorrow," she whispered, shaking her head. "No matter what I have to do, I won't let you crash again."

CHAPTER 33

Several hours before dawn, Tasia quietly slipped out of bed. In the dim light of a candle, she saw that Jerico slept on his side beneath a sheet and a thin blanket, his right arm tucked under a pillow. Rex, who rested at the end of the bed, noticed Tasia rise and wagged his tail, whimpering quietly. She put on a robe, leaned down, and kissed the top of his head. When he whimpered again, she thought about what he might be thinking, sensing his unease.

"Everything's okay," she whispered into his ear. "Try not to worry so much."

He licked her wrist, rolling over, inviting her to scratch his belly. She rubbed his chest and his tail continued to wag. She then picked up a boneless fillet of dried fish from a nearby table and broke it into several pieces, feeding them to him one at a time.

If Jerico fell that day but humanity survived, Rex was to

be looked after by a woman who ran the children's hospital. If the demons won and humanity was destroyed, Rex would have to fend for himself. He hadn't been trained to hunt, and Tasia worried that he wouldn't survive on his own. Yet if every human were gone, Rex at least would have a chance to scavenge and learn new skills. And Kyoto, with its river and mountains and wildlife, seemed like a place where he might survive.

Breathing deeply, Tasia moved to the far side of the room. The previous night they'd arranged all of their equipment on a long table. Jerico's rifle lay next to her staff. Two full backpacks leaned against each other. Ishaam had dropped off a handheld device that he said would allow them to locate the alien ship's main source of power. It was propped up next one of the backpacks. The table also carried two brand-new uniforms— camouflage with gray and black patterns. Of course, for all anyone knew, the inside of the demons' ship might be white, but after lengthy debates, the darker colors had been chosen.

All the uniforms worn by the attackers were similar and each had a patch sewn onto both shoulders. One patch was a replica of the blue flags that had flown at Osaka Castle—highlighted in the center by a stitched image of a human's clenched fist. The patches featured different-colored fists, ranging from white to black, amber to red.

The other patch on each uniform had been created by dozens of volunteer seamstresses. Everyone planning to drop onto the alien ship had submitted the names of their family members and friends who'd been killed by the demons, and these names were sewn in white lettering onto a blue patch.

Tasia picked up her uniform and studied the names on her patch. Her father's was at the top, followed by Calix, Fareed, Tempest, and Draven. Jerico's patch listed his family members, as well as several names that Tasia had never heard him mention. The patches had been her idea, and Tasia was pleased that so many people would be honored in the coming fight. There was a story behind every name on every patch. These people had loved, fought, and died in the shadow of the War for Earth. They should never be forgotten.

Tasia traced the names on her patch with her forefinger, then carefully set down her uniform. Although she tried to keep her breathing in check, thoughts about the approaching fight consumed her. She knew at that very moment, a specialized group of engineers was setting up a defensive perimeter around the spot where all of the thirty-three staffs would be placed. Once the Orb was created, an elite force would have to protect it long enough for more than five hundred Seekers and Guardians to step into it. Machine-gun and laser-rifle emplacements would encircle the Orb, as well as a hundred of the best snipers still alive. It was imperative that the entire assaulting force had time to drop into the ship. If only a fraction of the force arrived within it, they'd be cut off and quickly annihilated.

Again and again, Tasia thought about the plan for their attack. She'd be the first person to step into the Orb, and she would be followed by Jerico, then every other Guardian. Once they dropped into the ship, they'd form a perimeter around the receiving Orb, protecting it as hundreds of Seekers arrived to join the fight. Only when everyone was present would they turn on their hand-held, power-seeking devices. These would lead them to the ship's engine room, where they'd activate and hide their explosives. With luck, they'd be able to hold off attacking demons long enough to return to the Orb and drop back into Kyoto. A hundred Seekers would also carry a parachute in case some sort of open-air exit was present and the ship wasn't too high up.

The plan was straightforward, yet so many things could go awry. For instance, the atmosphere within the ship might be toxic to humans. There wasn't time to make breathing systems, and planners could only hope that since demons appeared to breathe without trouble on Earth, that humans could survive on the demons' native air. However, even if the atmosphere within the ship didn't pose an issue, many other problems were also foreseeable. The assaulting force might emerge into a position far from the ship's power generators, resulting in a lengthy search and fight. K'ail had once told Tasia that thousands of demons lived on the ship, and the human force could never repel so many enemies. The element of surprise would aid the Guardians and Seekers initially, but if their bombs weren't set off soon, all would be lost.

Tasia took a deep breath, trying to control her fear. The skin at the corner of her left eye began to twitch. Her stomach ached and she reminded herself to eat a large breakfast. She couldn't believe that within a few hours she'd summon the alien ship, and wished the fight was days away. There were still so many things she wanted to do. She longed for the warmth of Jerico's body, the smell of the forest, the sound of her friends' laughter. Though she'd said goodbye to her mother and brother, she ached to see them again, to say that she loved them. She wasn't ready to leave the beauty of them, and of everything else around her—to never again see sunsets and eagles and oceans.

Biting her bottom lip, she lowered herself to her knees and bent forward until her palms touched the floor. She prayed as Fareed had, beseeching whatever god or gods listened to help her achieve victory. Then she prayed for her loved ones and friends, pleading that they be protected. She didn't ask for forgiveness or for distant dreams to come true. All she wanted was for the alien ship to be destroyed. Nothing else mattered.

Tasia continued to pray, silently explaining to whoever listened that the demons thought themselves to be gods, but love and kindness didn't exist within them. They might be the most powerful species in the universe, but they were evil. They killed and conquered, enslaved and annihilated. For a century, humans had struggled against them. And while humans were far from perfect, Tasia promised that people, if they won, would be better in the days ahead. No longer would they wreck their own planet and the species that inhabited it. Instead they'd try to make their world a more beautiful place.

Finally Tasia prayed for her loved ones, asking that if they must die, that they do so quickly and without pain. She didn't pray for herself, but for those who'd stand beside her during the fight, and for everyone who would stay behind.

The bed creaked and Tasia turned, realizing that Jerico was staring at her. "Are you okay?" he asked quietly.

She thanked whichever god or gods might have been listening, and then stood up. "I think so."

"You should come back to bed. At least … try to sleep."

"I can't sleep."

"But you can rest."

"If we win, I'll rest. If I die, I'll rest. There's no reason to do it now."

"Tasia—"

"But," she said more softly, "I'll lie with you."

"That sounds perfect," he replied, then lifted up the sheet and blanket.

She lay down beside him and tried to relax with her head on his chest, feeling it rise and fall. "Our minds are so strong," she whispered. "But our bodies are so weak."

"You're plenty strong with that staff. Stronger than them, even."

"K'ail warned me about a white demon. He said she'd come for me. He'll be there too. And he knows what you look like, so you really shouldn't be right next to me."

"Of course I'll be next to you."

She kissed his chest. "K'ail wants me to watch you die."

"Then he'll be disappointed."

Rex whimpered, stretched, and moved closer to them. Tasia exhaled slowly, tracing the contours of Jerico's body with her fingertips. He did the same to her, and it occurred to her then that his touch was the most wonderful thing she'd ever felt.

"If Guardians fall," she said, "grab a staff. It'll make you so much stronger."

"I will."

"And once we hide those bombs, let's run. The timers will be set for only a minute or two—depending how far we're from an Orb."

"We'll run like the wind."

His words didn't register with her. Instead she thought about K'ail's warnings. "The white demon … she'll get inside my head. She'll try to destroy me."

"Just like K'ail tried. Like they all tried. But you're still here."

Raising her head from his chest, she kissed his lips. "There's still so much I want to see with you."

"Remember what your father said—that you should believe in yourself."

"I will. I do." And she realized, saying it out loud, that it was true. Maybe it hadn't been once. But here, now, it was.

"You told me once that love is stronger than hate," Jerico said, holding her gently. "You said that's what you really learned from K'ail—that the demons grew strong because of their hate, but that you grew strong because of your love. So when I'm standing beside you, when everything seems like it's about to end, just remember that you're not alone. Your father will be with you. I'll be with you. And we'll fight with a weapon that the demons don't have, that they've never understood. And that's why we'll win—because the universe created them and it created us, but the best, most magical parts of it are in us."

CHAPTER 34

Several hours later, before dawn was about to unfold, Tasia, Jerico, and the other thirty-two Guardians crept out of the Stronghold, followed by a sizable force of Seekers. The group entered the dormant bullet train, heading toward the nearby platform that held the Orb.

Tasia moved slowly, cautiously. Their plan called for all the staffs to be placed together, not more than twenty feet away from the existing Orb. If K'ail had spoken the truth, the thirty-three staffs would rest together and create a single Orb, which would somehow summon the alien ship. Soon afterwards, the Guardians should be able to step next to the new Orb, reach forward, and remove their staffs. Tasia would then lead everyone toward the other Orb, drop through it, and enter the ship.

Upon arriving at the end of the train, Tasia studied the darkened platform where Fareed had died and was glad that she and Jerico had buried his remains. Nearby, a single white stone had been left on the platform—marking the position where the staffs should be placed. Men and women were already situated around the stone, in fortified positions with their fingers on the triggers of machine guns and laser rifles.

Tasia breathed slowly, searching the sky and distant buildings for demons. They were close, she knew. She could sense their conversations, their presence. The demons were expecting the staffs to be reunited, and she was certain they would attack just as soon as the Orb was created.

Her pulse quickened as she stepped from the train. Holding her staff with her right hand and a rifle with her left, Tasia approached the white stone. Nodding to those who followed her, she placed her staff on the ground, its thick end pointing up. Jerico stepped next to her. Then the remaining Guardians approached, leaning their staffs against hers. She sensed the chatter among the demons intensifying, and knew she was being watched. Yet the Guardians weren't attacked. For maybe the first time in the hundred-year war, demons and humans wanted the same thing—for the staffs to be reunited.

The last Guardian approached the collection of staffs. Tasia nodded to her, praying that K'ail had told the truth, that his ship would come. The Guardian held her staff out, then hesitated. Tasia whispered words of encouragement, yet the woman seemed frozen with fear. A demon shrieked in the distance. Glancing up, Tasia looked for danger, her heart now racing, her lungs expanding and contracting as if she'd just run up a long stairway. The woman's apprehension seemed to somehow infect the group. Guardians fidgeted, muttering quietly, holding their staffs together.

"It's time," Jerico said, reaching forward to grasp the woman's staff. He leaned it against its brethren, then looked away.

Tasia expected a sudden flash of light, but nothing of the sort happened. And yet, once the staffs were united, she felt a wave of power wash over her—a force of unrivaled creation. She closed her eyes as the power seemed to drive her back, away from the staffs. Though her feet stayed still, her thoughts fragmented, traveling in what felt like a thousand different directions. She saw stars, galaxies, and creatures both great and small. For the briefest of moments, the universe seemed to reveal itself to her—its mysteries and secrets open to her interpretation. She sensed divinity, magic, and constant creation. Then her thoughts cleared.

Blinking as so many wonders faded away, Tasia glanced from the staffs to Jerico. "Did … did you feel that?"

"Feel what?"

She turned to the Guardian next to her. "What about you? Did you see … those stars?"

"I didn't see anything."

Tasia took a deep breath, trying to steady herself. She was about to ask another question when she saw the staffs seem to glimmer. Though their outsides were still silver, something deep within them appeared to glow. "It's happening," she whispered, stepping back, fear and anticipation coursing through her, seeming to turn her blood cold.

The group of Guardians moved away from the staffs, which glowed brighter. In the distance, demons shrieked. More Seekers were arriving. Tasia saw that Zeus was nearby, and that he held a pistol. Ishaam, who was also armed, stood at his side. Not far behind them, Aki and Valeriya gripped their rifles and studied the sky. Trax had positioned himself behind them.

The staffs appeared to pulsate with energy. To Tasia, the power was as tangible as the ground beneath her feet. Yet she didn't know if anyone else felt it. She thought she heard a strange hum, but when she asked Jerico about it, he replied that all he could hear were the distant demons.

Continuing to brighten, the staffs became more difficult to distinguish from each other. They seemed to merge, as if individual flames that had been brought together by the hunger of a larger fire. Again Tasia felt a wave of energy wash over her. The enormity of its presence overwhelmed her. Compared to it, she was nothing more than a single leaf in an endless forest. She doubled over, gasping, somehow aware that across the universe, demons were mindful of the same new power. A signal had been sent, a signal that was able to instantly travel across distance and time, bridging an unimaginable gap between worlds.

"They're coming," she whispered. "And we shouldn't have called them. We've awoken something ... something we should have left sleeping."

Rifles began to crack, and demons shrieked. Knowing that the alien ship had already been summoned, that there was no turning it back, Tasia set down her rifle and reached into the Orb, wincing as energy surged through her. She saw stars, bit her lip so hard that it bled, and pulled a staff away from the brilliant, pulsating mass.

Immediately the Orb darkened. Other Guardians followed her lead, then swung their staffs toward the sky, firing at hundreds of demons that dove from every direction. Machine guns erupted. Laser rifles sent bursts of light darting upward. And the sun crept over a row of distant mountains.

Demons smashed into concealed bunkers, ripping men and women apart. Yet many of these beasts were brought down by Seekers and Guardians who fired their rifles and staffs with unrelenting skill and speed.

In the faint light of dawn, demons continued to dive down, killing and maiming, seeming to revel in the size and scope the battle. Pairs of Guardians stood with their backs to each other, sending bursts of energy darting skyward, driving their attackers away.

A demon landed near Aki and Valeriya. Tasia saw it lunge for them, and she ran toward it with her staff extended, leaving the protective cover of her comrades. She fired her weapon again and again, bringing down the beast. Yet as the demon died, it thrust its wing against her, and she was knocked backward, the air hammered from her lungs.

While she knelt on the ground, struggling to regain her breath, Jerico hurried to her side. He stood above her, firing his rifle repeatedly, his legs still but his arms in constant motion.

His lips parted and he must have said something to her, but she didn't hear him.

Instead, K'ail's words forced their way into her mind. She didn't have the strength to push them away.

Today everything shall end for you, Tasia. Everything.

"No," she muttered, struggling to her feet, swinging up her staff. She fired at one demon after another, missing most, though some of her attacks struck home. Undaunted, the demons dove at them, full of rage and power and belief. Men and women were torn apart, some dying in each other's arms, some all alone. Blood pooled around clusters of those still fighting—slick and dark, spreading out from lifeless Guardians and Seekers.

But even worse than the sights around Tasia was the oppressive, debilitating knowledge that from somewhere unseen, from somewhere deep in space, the alien ship sped toward them, unimpeded by distance and time, immune to the rules that otherwise governed the universe.

CHAPTER 35

From a height of a thousand feet, K'ail watched the battle ebb and flow. It was somewhat surprising to him that so many of the gods wished to confront the mortals now, when their ship drew closer with every passing heartbeat. But bloodlust was intoxicating, and scores of reckless gods dove at their adversaries, killing many but also suffering from attacks below.

K'ail had no interest in dying before the Dawn of Atonement had come and gone. Greater than his need for the taste of human blood was his desire to soar once again through the universe, among the stars, as he was destined. Soon Earth would be little more than a troublesome memory. Although time had been wasted on the planet, K'ail would live much longer. He was convinced that his best days still lay ahead, waiting to be savored.

From a safe height, K'ail continued to watch the battle. The humans appeared to be succeeding in their defense of the Orb. Gods fell from the sky, slamming into buildings, trees, and the train platform. Yet many mortals already had been killed. K'ail could see lifeless clumps of their tangled bodies scattered around some of their fiercest weapons. Even better, several Guardians already had been slain, and their staffs were in the grasp of the gods.

K'ail could sense Tasia's presence and knew she still lived. But she wouldn't last for long. Two humans had been forced into agreeing to kill her. They were to shoot her as soon as the ship arrived. Tasia's demise would batter—but not break—the spirits of the mortals. Yet K'ail doubted that any other Guardian had the skill or strength to step into the Orb and drop into his ship. And even if a small force of humans succeeded in doing so, their disabled power detectors would render them harmless. The gods could annihilate them at their leisure.

The rising sun warmed K'ail's broad back. He glanced above, looking for his ship. Soon it would arrive, having traveled at many times the speed of light, after bending space and time. When their ship appeared, every remaining god would attack anyone defending the Orb, overwhelming the humans. K'ail would be among the last to arrive, flying straight into the Orb when no one was left to protect it.

A bullet glanced off his shoulder and K'ail soared higher. To his surprise, Tasia's words unfolded in his mind.

"We're winning."

Soon all of you shall be dead.

"Soon I'll be on your ship."

K'ail peered below, wishing that he could spot her amid the chaos. *You cannot win, Tasia. The rules of this game already have been written.*

"I'm standing on a dead god. And I'm watching one fall from the sky."

Then enjoy the spectacle while you still draw breath.

"We're going—"

You fail to understand what you fight against. If you did, you would not have summoned my ship.

"I'm ready for it."

As a beetle is ready for a fire.

"I'm no beetle."

K'ail spied a group of humans that was far away from the Guardians and their accursed staffs. He dropped toward them, circling lower. *I pity you, Tasia. You will never know what it is like to soar among the stars, never understand the glory, the ecstasy. Your mind is strong, but your body is so very weak. You were betrayed by your maker.*

"The universe made me. Just like it made you."

When you fall, I will sweep down, gather up your body, and bring you to my ship. In the years ahead I will touch your skull and smile. You shall be with me always—forever reminding me of our fight, of my victory over you.

Tasia didn't immediately respond. Finally, she said, "You're alone, K'ail. You'll always be alone."

And everyone you love shall soon be dead. So enjoy these last moments. Tell the boy goodbye.

"You can't kill love. And that's why—"

K'ail pushed Tasia's words aside. Though he would never admit it to a fellow god or to a mortal, the girl's comments about love had always bothered him—not because he feared that the emotion would lead the humans to triumph, but rather because love was something he'd never known. And K'ail wanted to savor every experience that the universe had to offer. He was jealous of Tasia. He saw how love empowered her and knew she drew strength from it. Without love, she would have fallen a long time ago.

Angered by Tasia's convictions, K'ail circled lower, eyeing a group of fleeing humans. They were running from the fight, and though several carried rifles, there wasn't a Guardian among them. Inspired by his rage and suddenly feeling invincible, K'ail dove toward them, shrieking.

The mortals looked up, screamed, and fired their weapons. Bullets ricocheted off his chest and legs. One even struck K'ail's hand, which he held before his eye. But he wasn't as much as scratched, and he landed among them, his wrath exploding. Dropping their rifles, the mortals stabbed at him with spears, trying to keep him at bay. He charged forward, battering their weapons aside. His talons rose and fell while his fangs opened and snapped shut. He ripped the humans apart—wounding some, killing others. As always, their screams and the taste of their blood invigorated him. He felt the joy of youth, of unrivaled power.

Before long, K'ail stood above the torn bodies of five men

and three women. Glancing up, he saw that his ship still hadn't arrived. Yet it soon would. And in that moment, everything would change.

K'ail leapt up, flapping his immense wings. Fueled by the taste of blood and the anger within him, he flew toward the nearby battle, no longer able to stay clear of its call.

CHAPTER 36

A ki crouched next to Valeriya beside the body of a dead demon. She'd already gone through more than a hundred rounds of ammunition, and her hands were blistered and raw. Her ears rang from the sound of so much gunfire. Yet she and Valeriya were both unharmed. Their proximity to the remaining Guardians had helped keep them safe. More than twenty staffs still fired upward, driving demons away.

Tasia and Jerico stood right next to the Orb. During a lull in the fighting, Aki had seen Tasia whispering to herself. But now she was fighting again. Jerico protected her backside, firing at demons that sought to sneak up behind her. As he attacked their foes, she also faced the onslaught from above, sending bolt after bolt of energy toward the winged beasts, driving most away and downing others.

The battle was an odd mix of lulls and eruptions. At some

moments, the demons merely circled high above them. But at other times, a demon would dive toward them and, if it avoided their attacks, land within a group of defenders and tear them to pieces. Chaos reigned during these confrontations as people fought and fled. Sometimes, after killing a dozen humans, a demon would take flight once again. But often the strongest Guardians surged toward the threat, killing the demon before it could inflict any more damage.

Still, Aki didn't think that the fight was going well. No one knew how long it would take for the alien ship to arrive, and it didn't seem possible to defend the Orb all day. Certainly when night fell, whatever demons remained would have the advantage. People couldn't fight if they couldn't see. And while spotlights could be brought to the battle, Aki suspected that they'd be destroyed.

A commotion away from the Orb caused Aki to turn. An unarmed woman was running toward the Guardians, screaming. At first Aki couldn't hear her words, but then they became clear, tearing at her soul.

"Demons are in the Stronghold!" the woman shouted. "Help us! They're killing everyone!"

Aki nearly dropped her rifle. "My family," she muttered, turning toward Valeriya. "They'll find my family."

Valeriya glanced at the Orb, then back toward the Stronghold. "Let's go!"

Not thirty feet away, a demon landed atop a machine-gun emplacement, ripping the weapon from its tripod and then killing the women who operated it. People shouted, fled, and regrouped.

Aki ran toward Tasia, who still fought back to back with Jerico. "Demons are in the Stronghold!" she shouted. "And my family is—"

"Go!" Tasia replied, gripping her arm. "Save them!"

Aki reached for Tasia and Jerico, and their hands came together. Valeriya also stepped forward, but then a demon dove straight down at them, only to be driven away by Tasia.

"Stay alive!" Jerico shouted as the friends split apart.

Aki nodded and was about to reply when a nearby explosion sent her reeling. She stumbled away from the Orb. A man fell, screaming, from the sky. Aki didn't watch him land but ran forward, not even bothering to enter the train, instead hurrying alongside it. Valeriya dashed next to her, reloading her rifle. Several dozen Seekers joined them in charging back toward the Stronghold. A demon crashed into a group of them, and a desperate, crazed fight ensued.

Her side aching, Aki reached a dormant escalator and leapt onto a handrail, sliding down. She reached the lower level with too much speed, falling forward to her knees. Valeriya dropped with more grace, then helped her up. Distant gunfire and screams echoed off the walls around them.

"No!" Aki shouted, overcome with fear. Her loved ones had never fought against a demon and didn't even possess weapons. She thought about her younger brothers and sisters as she charged forward, knocking slower Seekers aside. The corridor widened around them. They came across the carcass of a demon beside scores of dead people, causing them to pause. Most of the victims were older men and women, and they looked to have confronted the demon holding little more than knives and spears.

Far ahead, a dog started to bark.

"That's Rex!" Valeriya said, her chest heaving. "Jerico left him at—"

"The children's hospital," Aki interrupted, then started to run again. Her feet barely seemed to strike the ground as she raced forward. An injured man pleaded for her help, but she ignored him, holding her rifle with both hands. Veering off the main corridor, she ran through one of the Stronghold's largest farms. A muddy path had been cleaved straight through rows of vegetables, and two dead women lay near a fallen apple tree. Aki reached the far side of the farm, slipped on some mud, and turned toward the children's hospital.

The sight of the large black demon stole her breath. It stood outside of the hospital, held at bay by rifle fire from within the structure. Unseen children screamed, and Rex ran around the beast from behind, biting at its leg. The big demon pivoted, striking Rex with its taloned hand. Rex yelped from the force of the blow and was sent flying backward. He landed on the floor, slid ten feet, and lay still.

"Leave him alone!" Aki yelled, firing her rifle at the side of the demon's head. It twisted in her direction, and to her horror she realized that it wore a helmet. The beast stepped closer to her.

Valeriya reached for her arm, pulling her back. "This way," she said, her voice sounding strange in Aki's ringing ears.

Knowing that they had to get the demon as far from the children as possible, Aki nodded, reloading her gun. To her surprise, Valeriya dropped her rifle, then blindly reached into her backpack. As they moved backward, Valeriya pulled out a grenade.

"That won't hurt it," Aki said, as the demon looked back and forth between them and the children.

"Maybe not."

The demon leaned toward the children.

Aki fired at it once more. "Get over here, you ugly, stinking bat! That's right! Come get us!"

Rearing back, the demon shrieked, then charged at them. Valeriya shouted at Aki to run, and she didn't need to be told twice. Spinning around, she hurried after her companion. Aki's anger turned to fear—the big demon was surprisingly fast, scrambling forward, flapping its wings to give it extra speed. Valeriya reached an escalator, slid down its railing, and landed hard on the lower level. Aki followed her without pause. The demon wasn't more than thirty feet behind her and continued to shriek, beating its wings. Valeriya turned down a little-used corridor. Unseen Seekers fired at the demon, but their bullets had no effect, and only seemed to further enrage it.

"Hurry!" Aki screamed, dropping her rifle, running as she never had.

The demon quickly closed the distance between them,

reaching for Aki, its talons nearing her head. But then Valeriya veered into another passageway, burst through a pair of doors, and stumbled into an abandoned part of the subway system. Aki lunged past the open doors, screamed when the demon smashed its way through them, and caught up to Valeriya.

"Don't stop!" Valeriya shouted, pulling Aki ahead.

The demon fell onto the rusting, forgotten train tracks. They didn't watch it rise but ran forward together, urging each other on. Century-old concrete columns supported the ceiling, and Valeriya began to weave through them. Aki surged ahead, calling out when she realized that Valeriya had stopped.

"Wait!" Aki screamed as Valeriya pulled the pin from the grenade, then tossed it at the column nearest to the demon. A thunderous explosion ripped through the confined space, knocking her backward. Chunks of concrete flew in every direction—deadly missiles that slammed into distant walls and an abandoned train. The ceiling buckled and then fell, cascading onto the tracks, sending up plumes of dust and debris.

Aki curled up into a ball, shielding her head from whatever might come next. A distant rumble reverberated throughout the tunnel as debris continued to fall on her, pelting her back. Grunting as something struck her shoulder, she coughed and opened her eyes, but she could barely see. An impenetrable wall of dust filled the air.

"Valeriya!" she shouted. "Where are you?"

The demon shrieked. It must have moved, because stones and debris clattered to the ground.

Aki struggled to stand. She then limped ahead, toward where she'd last seen Valeriya. "Tell me where you are!" she pleaded. "Please!"

But only the demon answered her—shrieking once again.

Aki coughed, shuffling forward, still blinded by the dust. Though she didn't know it, the demon grimaced from the pain of its shattered wing, then moved in her direction.

CHAPTER 37

Crouching in the ruins of a laser-rifle emplacement, Ishaam studied the dead bodies around him. Several men and women were torn apart, their faces still depicting fear and agony. Shuddering, Ishaam wept, clutching the sides of the old bulletproof vest he wore. The screams of so many of his people assaulted his mind and conscience. To his horror he'd just watched a young boy run into the battle, shouting for his father. Though the two had been reunited, they hadn't lasted long. A demon had dropped from the sky, ending their lives before devouring three others who came to save them.

Ishaam understood all too well that if Osaka Castle hadn't fallen, if so many skilled snipers hadn't been killed during that battle, the demons around him might have been driven away from the Orb. They might have been defeated. But there weren't enough capable Seekers left, and with every passing moment, more defenders fell. Even worse, by his count nearly half the Guardians had been slain and their staffs taken away.

His betrayal had doomed his people.

Beating his hand against his hip in despair, Ishaam struggled to stay standing. The burden of the sacrifice he'd made to save his sons was too much for him to carry. He loved his family more than life itself, but the sight of so much suffering around him, reminding him of what he'd done, was unbearable. And the white demon hadn't even brought back his wife, as promised. Only if Ishaam disabled the power detectors and killed Tasia would she be returned.

Although the previous day Ishaam had deactivated all the devices, as he watched Tasia fight and struggle, he found the notion of killing her increasingly difficult to consider. If he shot her, and the demons won, his family might live, but he'd be dead inside. And what would his sons learn from a dead father?

Gripping his pistol, he continued to watch Tasia, who wasn't more than thirty feet away from him. She stood next to Jerico, and during a sudden lull in the fighting they embraced. They were in love, he thought despondently. And while they could have run away together, instead they'd stayed to fight, facing almost certain death.

The sun had nearly reached its zenith, and Ishaam realized that the battle had already lasted for more than five hours. Though the ground was littered with the carcasses of scores of demons, humans had died in the hundreds. He counted eighteen Guardians, including Zeus, who held a staff and fought alongside Tasia. Most of the machine-gun and laser-rifle emplacements had gone silent. Barely more than two hundred Guardians and Seekers kept half that number of demons at bay. Soon the fight would end, even more quickly if Ishaam shot Tasia. Seeing her die, the remaining Guardians and Seekers might lose hope, opting to try to save their families, who huddled together back in the Stronghold.

Ishaam ducked as a demon swept over him, smashing against one of the few laser rifles that still fired. As screams pierced the air, he turned away, looking up, blinking repeatedly.

The sky seemed to be on fire. A second sun appeared to move across the emptiness, descending, glowing with such brightness that it was hard to look at. An abrupt roar, like the sound of distant, unrelenting thunder, dominated everything—even the chaos of battle.

The demon ship had arrived.

Clouds beneath it vaporized in the sudden presence of its extreme heat. Ishaam found it hard to breathe as the air around him warmed further. Sweat ran down his brow and into his eyes.

Original, firsthand accounts from the demons' attack a century ago still existed, and Ishaam shook his head in wonder at the accuracy of those descriptions. Impossibly large, the still glowing, city-sized ship was sleek, yet managed to resemble a demon's hand and talons. Four long, immense shafts protruded from a rectangular base. The shafts were smooth and, in some ways, elegantly shaped, ending in upturned points, like the bows of ancient sailing boats.

Ishaam realized that nearby demons were no longer attacking but were simply shrieking and circling. Human fighters had also stopped firing their weapons. Everyone seemed transfixed by the size and magnitude of the ship. Ishaam could still feel its heat, even though it was positioned miles above. The scientist within him wondered how it could possibly have traveled across the universe in only a matter of hours. Everything he had learned about physics was laughably incomplete. The knowledge that he'd been proud of, that he'd gained from a lifetime of research, amounted to little more than nothing. He felt as if he were an ant trying to understand geometry. The calculations and theories necessary for such space travel were far beyond anything he could comprehend.

He shook his head, trying to clear his thoughts. A stone's toss away, Tasia shouted as she attempted to organize the stunned men and women around her.

Kill the girl now or your wife dies!

"I'm going to—"

Now! Kill her now or I'll drop a pretty head from the sky!

Ishaam reeled from the white demon's words. Shuddering, he stood up, holding his pistol. He stumbled toward Tasia, struggling to breathe, to bring smoke-filled air into his lungs.

Run!

He wept, tripping on a body, squeezing the pistol, tears on his cheeks.

Shoot her!

An explosion nearly knocked him down, but he stayed on his feet, nearing Tasia.

Now! Now! Now!

Somehow, he saw his boys then, remembered them being born, remembered holding them tight. And he suddenly realized that they'd never be safe if the demons won the day.

"I'm so sorry," he muttered, thinking about his wife. "I love you."

The Guardian dies now! Shoot her!

Running, he neared Tasia, still holding his gun. She was only a few feet away from the Orb and looked up to him in surprise. But before Tasia could speak, a tall woman dressed in black, with spiked blonde hair, pulled two pistols from twin holsters and pointed them at her.

"No!" Ishaam screamed, leaping in front of Tasia.

The pistols discharged and two bullets slammed into Ishaam. One penetrated his old bulletproof vest, and the other hit his exposed hip, spinning him sideways. He cried out in pain, falling at Tasia's feet, aware that Zeus was struggling with the blonde-haired woman. People were shouting.

Ishaam looked up, his gaze drifting to the alien ship. Though it still glowed slightly, whatever covered its outside seemed to be turning from red to black. Despite the searing pain within his chest and hip, for the briefest of moments, the scientist within him couldn't help but admire the countless technological marvels that comprised the ship. Then he remembered his wife, realizing that she was probably dying right now, screaming beneath the white demon. Weeping, he thought of her, and then his sons, imagining their faces, and how they'd each felt in his arms.

Tasia knelt beside him, as did Jerico. She pressed her hands against his wounds, but he knew too much blood was flowing from him. He would die without ever seeing his sons again.

"My boys … are safe," he whispered, trembling. "And my wife … will forgive me."

Tasia shook her head. "I don't understand. What happened?"

"Hostages. All hostages. But now … all free."

"Your sons were—"

"Wait," he said, feeling a strange coldness flood into him, as if he were a sinking boat that filled with icy water. He struggled to reach for the power detector that hung from a strap around Tasia's neck. "This … won't work. Find … another way."

Her eyes widened. She glanced at the device, at the demon ship, then at him. "What way?"

"Look for … light. Reach … for power."

"Reach?"

He tried to respond but found that he could no longer speak. The echoes of his wife's voice reverberated deep within him. He saw her smile. He touched her outstretched hand.

Then his boys called to him, telling him that they were safe, that they loved him. And he saw them, running ahead, with an open sky above them. They were happy and free. A wonderful new world awaited them.

The faces of his loved ones stayed with him, even as his thoughts finally stilled, and he no longer worried about what tomorrow would bring.

CHAPTER 38

A s the battle raged around her, Tasia gently lowered
Ishaam to the ground. He had died swiftly, and while
she pitied him, she didn't have time to process all he'd
said or wonder why he had betrayed them. Instead, she stood
up, squeezed Jerico's hand, and stepped toward the Orb. Raising
her voice above the din of gunfire and death, she shouted for
the remaining Guardians, as well as a heavily equipped group
of Seekers, to follow her.

Tasia thought about the nearby ship. She repressed her fears,
reminding herself that she could travel through the Orbs with
as much ease as the demons. As her father had alluded and K'ail
had confirmed, she was connected to her enemies in so many
ways. The Orbs of their creation weren't something to be afraid
of, but to embrace. She was going to use them to destroy the
demons and save everyone she loved.

Glancing above, Tasia studied the alien ship, trying to forge a bridge between herself and it. Someone shouted something to her, and a demon crashed into a nearby group of Seekers. But she paid no attention to the chaos around her. Instead she thought about her love for Jerico, how she could end the war, and how easy it was going to be to drop inside the ship above her. She whispered that she wasn't afraid, that she wasn't alone. And for the briefest of moments, when she needed to most, she believed herself.

Holding her staff, Tasia stepped forward. As always the brilliance of the Orb enveloped her completely, and she felt herself dropping through an impossibly bright light. A distant roar emerged from the light, which then transformed into a swirling sea of stars. The light exploded, seeming to blind her. She tried to envision the ship, keeping it within her mind's eye. And though the light pierced her consciousness, her thoughts didn't shatter, as they had during other drops. She controlled her emotions, aware of the past but also the present. The smiling faces of her loved ones flashed before her. She saw her home. A battle was occurring beneath her, around the Orb. K'ail maimed and killed. Seekers fought and died. A rushing noise, like a torrent of water, dominated all else.

Tasia stumbled from the receiving Orb, and though she fell to her knees, she remembered who she was and why she had dropped. Jerico appeared beside her, then Zeus, and the other Guardians. Rising, Tasia stepped away from the Orb, turning around, trying to comprehend the scene that surrounded them. She'd expected the interior of the demon ship to resemble the inside of her prison, and while an immense, pyramid-like structure rose in the distance, her gaze was first drawn to a dark red fog that covered the floor and reached as high as her knees. The sulfur-smelling fog was so thick that she couldn't see her feet. The air, though almost painfully hot, seemed breathable.

They were inside a circular room so immense that it could have contained a small city. The distant walls and ceiling glowed like impossibly large swaths of molten steel. Far above, massive murals depicted demons in flight, as well as perched atop outlandish, lava-filled landscapes. Tasia had stepped inside beautiful cathedrals and was surprised that the alien ship made her think of them. The strange murals, with their hues of red and orange and their reproductions of the demons and their home planet, reminded her of stained-glass windows—though hundreds of times larger.

"The demons come here to pray," she said quietly, a shiver sweeping through her. "They pray to themselves."

Jerico turned on his power detector, but its needle didn't move. Several Seekers followed his lead, but none of the instruments seemed to work.

"Don't bother," Tasia said, trying to stay calm, looking for threats. "They've been disabled."

As Guardians asked about the power detectors, Zeus turned back toward the Orb. "Forget the damn things. The bombs will still work and that's what matters. But before we blow these devils straight back to hell, how many of us are missing?"

As a Guardian answered, Tasia felt fear rising up from deep within her, from a place that spawned her worst nightmares. She had brought them all to the blackest, most evil part of the universe. Civilizations had been extinguished and enslaved because of this place. Humanity has been shattered for just drifting into its shadow.

Trying to steady herself, she sought to gather her thoughts, then forced herself to do a quick estimate of their numbers. Including herself, there were fourteen Guardians present, and perhaps five times as many Seekers. Their force was pitifully small and would be quickly overwhelmed.

Tasia was about to speak when K'ail called out to her.

Ne'ith comes for you. She comes to rule your mind.

"And what about you?" Tasia whispered.

We fight for the Orb. Once we control it, you and I shall meet again.

Tasia ignored K'ail's next words. She turned to the men and women gathered around her. "We have to get in there," she said, pointing to the distant pyramid. "Whatever controls this ship ... and powers this ship ... will be in there. We need to hurry because—"

A woman screamed as a demon emerged from the Orb, smashing into a group of startled Seekers. The beast pounced on two men at once, tearing them apart as several Guardians sent bolts of energy into it. Shrieking, the demon died, but it had still managed to mortally wound a Guardian.

"Go!" Zeus shouted at Tasia. "I'll stay here! I'll fight them!"

Jerico shook his head. "But our bombs! How will you know when to drop back down to—"

"Just go!" Zeus interrupted, holding his staff with his good hand and pointing it at the Orb. "And let an old man die with honor."

A distant shriek drifted toward them, prompting a fresh, new terror to sweep through Tasia like wind filling a sail. Soon they would no longer be alone. "Don't die," she said, nodding to Zeus. "You can still live."

"Run, Tasia. Run like you've never run before."

Holding her staff with both hands, Tasia turned and started to sprint toward the pyramid. The air was so hot that sweat almost immediately dampened her from head to toe. Breathing was difficult, but she continued onward, aware that the ground was hard beneath her feet. Jerico ran beside her, encouraging her onward, his strides long and rhythmic. Several Seekers were even faster and hurried ahead. She yelled for them to set some explosives at the base of the pyramid, so that they might blast open a passageway.

Though Tasia tried to control her fear, to continue to believe in herself, the magnitude of the demon ship seemed to swallow her whole. She looked down at the staff in her hands. What good would it do against a thousand demons? Against Ne'ith?

Shrieks rose from ahead, piercing the hot air, seeming to reach into Tasia's mind. "No," she muttered, gasping for breath. "Not yet."

A nearby Guardian stumbled and fell, but quickly rose to

her feet. Jerico's rifle swung back and forth in his right hand as he sprinted ahead. His hair was damp with sweat and his backpack bounced up and down. A wide beam of light emerged from the pyramid.

"We can do this!" Jerico shouted, his legs parting the fog before him. "We can still win!"

Jerico's words and belief seemed to echo within Tasia. He was right. The demons weren't gods. They weren't invincible. "Fight until we win!" she shouted, her throat burning from the hot, sulfur-rich air. "Until we win!"

Far behind them, gunfire erupted. Tasia turned. She hadn't realized that two Seekers had stayed behind with Zeus, but she saw them confront several demons that emerged from the Orb. Zeus's staff flashed as he fired at his foes, downing one and then another. But three more demons emerged, wheeling away from each other so that they could attack him from different directions. He knocked one from the air, but the two others dove at him from opposite sides, engulfing him. A single rifle fired, and then was silenced.

Tears streamed down Tasia's face, mingling with her sweat and obscuring her eyes. She turned back to the pyramid and realized that some sort of immense archway spanned its lower half. A demon flew out of the archway, followed by another. Rifles cracked to the front and rear of her. More demons poured out of the pyramid—both from the archway and its hollow summit.

Tasia suddenly wished that Jerico wasn't beside her. The

thought of watching him die terrified her, and she pointed her staff at an approaching demon, fired at it, and watched it tumble down. Yet more and more demons engaged them, forcing them to slow. A Guardian near the pyramid was pulled upward by two demons, fought for above, and torn apart. Tasia fired her staff again and again, trying to create a shield around them.

"Knock them down!" she shouted, aware that the ship's demons weren't used to dodging attacks from the ground. They didn't change directions and dive. Instead they soared and drifted, making themselves easy targets. Though their numbers were vast, they fell with increasing frequency, their insides charred from the weapons that they'd created a century earlier.

"Fight me!" Tasia screamed at her foes, still running, her lungs seemingly on fire. Her staff pulsed in her grasp, sending bolt after bolt of energy into their attackers. Demons shrieked, thrashed, and plummeted. Jerico's rifle cracked repeatedly, and he managed to bring down a particularly large and slow beast. It crashed to the floor beside them, writhing and dying.

The archway was made of the same strange gray material that comprised the rest of the pyramid. Though demons still flew from it, they were more leery of the small band of mortals. Tasia hurried ahead, believing that victory was achievable. If they could get inside the structure and set their bombs, anything was possible. They'd likely die in the explosion, but at least they might cripple or destroy the ship.

"Don't stop running!" Jerico yelled beside her as several Guardians paused to fire at distant demons.

Tasia shot a bolt of energy into the pyramid, which loomed before her. She saw its interior, saw a path to victory, and then everything changed.

A massive, white demon, at least three times the size of any other beast, emerged from the archway. Tasia lowered her staff toward it, preparing to fire, but then strange, incoherent thoughts forced their way into her mind. The thoughts changed into shrieks that assailed her from the inside, exploding within her skull, driving her down. She fell to her knees, somehow holding onto her staff, trying to close her mind to the unseen assault.

Screaming, Tasia reached for Jerico, who took her hand in his. He called out to her, and though his words didn't make sense, she recognized his concern, his love. She found strength and hope and power in his gaze, and somehow everything that she saw within him seeped into her. For the briefest of moments, her mind cleared, and she fired her staff at the white demon, which she now knew was Ne'ith. Though none of her bolts struck home, she kept firing, driving Ne'ith away.

Tasia struggled to her feet. But before she could take a single step forward, the pyramid ahead of her seemed to rise, and the floor angled upward. Somehow, she realized that the ship was moving. All around her Guardians and Seekers fell. She reached for Jerico, missed his outstretched hand, then toppled onto her side. The angle of the floor increased, and men and women screamed as they began to slide away from the pyramid. Tasia slid with them, unable to stop herself.

"Jerico!" she shouted, desperately reaching for him, barely able to see in the red fog. She felt the barrel of his rifle and grabbed onto it as he called out to her. They slid faster now, over the hot, smooth floor. Above them, demons plunged toward helpless victims, pouncing on them, tearing them apart. Tasia no longer tried to stop herself from sliding but instead fired her staff, again and again, into the air above her.

Ne'ith attempted once more to force her way into Tasia's thoughts. Screaming, Tasia struggled to resist, feeling as if she were fighting to hold a door shut against someone much stronger, someone who was smashing against it over and over. If the door fully opened, she would die. And so she battled as she never had—pushing back, desperate to close this opening to her soul. A pain borne of heat and rage poured into her, scalding her mind. The doorway into her opened further. Ne'ith was winning. Unable to think or breathe, Tasia fought instinctively, struggling like her earliest ancestors had, battling to stay alive against an ancient, powerful force. Yet Ne'ith was too strong, too terrible a foe. The world around and within Tasia seemed to spin and sway and explode.

She didn't understand Jerico's cry of warning. She couldn't.

Still shouting, he struggled to pull his rifle from her, but she continued to grip its barrel—unaware of the white mass that approached her as she slid toward her doom.

CHAPTER 39

Somehow, even in her stunned condition, Valeriya recognized Aki's voice. Though she wanted to respond, she was barely conscious, and while her lips parted, no sound came forth. Blood dribbled down her face from a wound near the top of her head, stinging her eyes. Her broken left forearm throbbed, and the agony kept her from passing out. Moaning, she tried to make sense of her surroundings, realizing that she lay in a pile of cement blocks and debris. Clouds of dust hung in the air, obscuring everything.

Reaching up with her good arm, Valeriya felt the large bloody bump on her head. She winced, clenching her teeth against the pain. Aki called out to her again, and Valeriya recognized the urgency in her companion's pleas.

"I'm … fine," Valeriya whispered. The effort of speaking increased her dizziness, and she leaned back, only then seeing that debris covered her legs. She tried to move them but couldn't. Heavy concrete slabs pinned her to the ground.

Valeriya once again wondered what had happened. She remembered running for some reason, then recalled that a demon had been chasing them. It was about to catch them, but then everything had gone black. Had the electricity gone out? And why was she on the ground, buried under so much debris?

"Aki?" she asked, using her right hand to try to free herself. "Where … where are you?"

A demon shrieked, the sound of its cry so loud that Valeriya thought her head might explode. She twisted from side to side, alert enough to realize that the demon was nearby. The clouds of dust prevented her from seeing it, and understanding that she also must be nearly invisible to it, she stopped moving. Again the demon shrieked, and bricks clattered as they bounced down the pile of debris.

"Stay still, Val," Aki said in a quiet, controlled voice. "I'm coming for you."

Bricks tumbled onto her lap, and Valeriya put her good arm above her head, trying to protect it. She didn't know if Aki or the demon neared her. A presence was approaching, a shadow that seemed to drift toward her. Repressing the urge to scream, she struggled to remain quiet. The dust was settling, and a shape materialized, reaching for her. Panicking, she held her breath, terrified that the demon's talons were about to tear her to shreds.

"It's me," Aki whispered, then squeezed her shoulder.

"Where is—"

"Be quiet."

Valeriya could now see Aki's face. Dust covered her skin and hair. Stifling a cough, Valeriya looked around, able to see farther now. The pile of debris was much larger than she'd guessed, extending beyond her field of vision. Aki lifted a cracked cement block from her stomach and carefully set it aside. She reached for another block, but then froze in place.

The large black demon emerged from the dimness, not more than thirty feet away. Its left wing was bent and broken, dragging on the ground. Something was also wrong with its left leg. The explosion must have blown off its helmet. The beast labored ahead, its mouth open, its fangs red with human blood. At first, Valeriya thought it hadn't seen them, but its eyes locked on hers and it shrieked.

Aki, who had no weapon, picked up a fist-sized rock and threw it at the demon. "Get away from her!"

The demon shuffled forward, struggling over debris. It came to a fallen steel beam that rose to its waist and blocked its path. Shrieking again, it grasped the beam with both hands and tried to lift it. But the steel wouldn't budge. The demon started to limp around the obstacle, its shattered wing dragging uselessly.

Aki struggled to pull Valeriya from the rubble, but too much weight was still on her legs. When Aki yanked hard, Valeriya screamed, as pain exploded within her broken arm. Moaning, she tried to help Aki push over a cement slab that lay on her thigh. The slab slid away, but then the demon rounded the steel beam.

"Run!" Valeriya told Aki. "Just run!"

Aki picked up another stone and stepped toward the demon. Grunting, she threw the stone at the demon's face, but the projectile merely bounced off its jaw. The demon opened its mouth wide, and Aki's next stone broke the tip off one of its fangs. Shrieking, the demon struggled forward.

"Help!" Valeriya shouted, terrified of dying while trapped, of taking her last breath so far from the forest she loved. "Someone help us!"

The demon shrieked again, fell, and shuffled ahead. Aki threw stone after stone at it. When she finally struck its right eye, she shook her fist in triumph, but the beast merely blinked and moved forward.

As frightened as Valeriya was of dying, the thought of watching Aki suffer was worse. "Go!" she yelled. "Just go!"

"No!"

"Please!"

The demon was only ten feet away. It seemed to be weakening and paused with every half step.

"I'm going to kill you!" Aki screamed, now digging through the rubble. "You hear me, bat? You're going to die down here, not us!"

Valeriya realized that Aki must have been looking for a sharp stone or a piece of steel—something with which to stab the demon's eyes. With her good hand she reached into the debris beside her, desperate to find a nail or even a piece of glass. But she only turned over chunks of bricks. She struggled to breathe, to think, screaming as she twisted beneath the weight of the rubble that pinned her.

The demon took another step forward, and Valeriya reached for Aki, tugging on her arm. "Please … please go! You need to go!"

"I'm not leaving you!"

"But—"

"Shut up!"

Valeriya again tried to stand, nearly passing out from pain, but far too much weight pressed on her legs. Tears mixed with the blood on her face, creating red drops that fell to her chest. Still she struggled on, pushing more debris away from her, aware that Aki had stepped toward their attacker and now threw rock after rock at the demon. Aki swore at it, dangerously close to its outstretched talons.

Shifting her weight, twisting with all her strength, Valeriya fought against the rubble that seemed to entomb her. But her feet wouldn't move, no matter how hard she pulled at them.

The demon reached for Aki, who stumbled back.

"Run!" Valeriya shouted, sobbing. "Don't make me watch you die!"

"This bat won't touch you!"

"Please. I can do this. And you can live!"

"No!"

"Run! You can still run!"

Aki picked up another stone and hurled it into the demon's

face. It shrieked and groped for her, and she toppled backward, falling.

"Help us!" Valeriya cried out, still trying to wrench herself free.

Aki rolled away from the demon, barely avoiding its outstretched hands. The beast took another half step ahead. Aki reached behind her head and into her backpack, but Valeriya had packed it and knew it only contained water, food, and ammunition. Between them they'd only carried one grenade, and it was gone.

And so Aki swung her backpack at the demon, batting its talons away. She cursed it, damned it, and fought it, the backpack a blur in her hands until the demon yanked it from her grasp.

"No!" Valeriya shouted as the demon reached for Aki, who bent down, picked up a rock, and lunged forward, throwing herself at the demon's face. It reared backward, surprised by her attack. But the stone in her hand only struck the corner of its right eye, and its talons darted toward her.

Valeriya screamed.

And then the demon paused, looking down at Aki, letting her know it had won.

CHAPTER 40

The alien ship continued its ascent, and as Jerico slid on his back beside Tasia, he saw that the monstrous white demon was plunging toward them, its talons outstretched. Shouting, he wrenched his rifle away from Tasia's grasp, then shot at the demon's wide red eyes. His bullet struck its forehead, and even as he slid, he slammed the bolt handle of his weapon backward and forward, reloading it.

The demon tucked its wings toward its body and dove at him. Jerico took careful aim and fired again. But he was moving too fast to be accurate, and his second bullet ricocheted off the demon's jaw. Yet his two shots seemed to awaken Tasia, and she rolled onto her back and fired a bolt from her staff, penetrating the demon's left wing. It shrieked, wheeled away from them, and dove toward a distant group of Seekers who slid facedown, more focused on stopping their ascent than protecting themselves from dangers above.

"Look up!" Jerico shouted just before the white demon smashed into the men, crushing two with its vast bulk and ripping another apart.

Tasia fired her staff again and again at the demon, but it was too far away now, and bolts of energy sprayed past the beast. Still, she managed to keep it away from the two of them, barely turning in time to strike a smaller demon that plunged straight toward her. Suddenly lifeless, the demon tumbled through the thick hot air, thudding against the floor behind them. It bounced, then started to slide down not more than ten feet away from Jerico. To his left and right, demons dove toward helpless men and women. Though a few of them fought back, most of the remaining Seekers and Guardians were panicking, trying to stop their descent rather than warding off their attackers. The sliding humans were easy prey for the demons, who fell on them as if hawks hunting mice. Men and women were lifted into the air, torn apart, and dropped to the floor. Several more demons were killed, but hundreds of the beasts had poured from the pyramid to become involved in the struggle.

Jerico glanced at the wall that they slid toward. Curving and massive, it supported the domed ceiling that might have been five hundred feet above them. Demons darted in every direction, converging in mid-flight to fight over Seekers' remains. Others carried off wounded Guardians, who flailed helplessly at the taloned hands that clutched them. So many demons shrieked that the emptiness reverberated with their cries.

"It's going to crush us!" Jerico shouted at Tasia. The dead demon had slid into them, pushing them faster ahead. When they struck the wall, its weight would pulverize them. As she kept firing her staff, he reached for her hand, dragging her toward the beast's feet. He grabbed one of its legs and tried to pull them around it, glancing at the approaching wall, suddenly desperate.

"Jerico!" Tasia screamed, briefly turning to him before wounding a large black demon that had landed near them and was tearing into a Guardian.

He pulled her against him. They were now between the dead beast's feet. In a matter of seconds they would strike the wall. "Get on its other side!" he shouted. "Right now!"

Struggling, Tasia managed to move around the demon, climbing up on one of its wings. Jerico followed her, amazed that she continued to fight, to fire at the hordes of demons above.

"Hold on!" he yelled, right before they reached the wall.

The impact was terrific, and despite his grip on the demon's wing, Jerico was flung forward into the alien steel. He managed to protect his head, however, and his right side took almost all the impact. Somehow Tasia kept her grip on the demon, screaming as she came to an abrupt, violent halt. Human bodies slid through the knee-high fog to slam against the wall on either side of them.

"We can't stay here!" Tasia shouted, fighting once more.

The sight of so many approaching demons filled Jerico with

terror. He knew they were coming for her, that they'd hurt her in unimaginable ways. Whatever risk he had to take to save her, he had to act now. Reaching into his backpack, he yanked out the two hand grenades he carried. But instead of throwing them at a demon, he pulled their pins and tossed them, one after another, ahead of him, so that they landed where the wall and the sloped floor met. The twin explosions knocked Tasia and him backward, off the demon's corpse. But shrapnel didn't hit them, and they struggled to their feet.

"Follow me," Jerico muttered, slightly dazed, stepping ahead toward where the grenades had struck. Smoke and fog lingered, partially obscuring the two of them from their pursuers. His right side aching, Jerico hurried onward, aware that Tasia was firing her staff behind him. A demon tumbled, thudding against the floor. She shouted in defiance.

To Jerico's wonder and relief, he saw that the two grenades had punched a jagged hole in the structure, right where the wall and the floor met. The opening wasn't much wider than he was, and he yelled at Tasia to jump through it. She stumbled ahead of him, fired twice at the nearest demon, and then slid into the hole, dragging her staff behind. Jerico didn't even look to see what the demons were doing. He leapt forward, feet first, into the hole. Sharp, ruined metal cut into his shoulders and back, but he fell away from the demons, almost immediately landing on Tasia.

Above them, demons slammed into the hole, shrieking. They were much too big to squeeze through the gap, and so they grabbed at the metallic plating, trying to pull it backward.

Tasia struggled to her feet, as the floor beneath her was still sloped. The ceiling was barely higher than her head. She aimed her staff toward the hole, and fired again and again. Demons shrieked and died, falling away from the opening. Tasia kept firing, her bolts piercing the body of a dead demon.

"Let's move!" Jerico said, his hands shaking, his breath seeming to catch in his throat.

Tasia nodded, sweat pouring down her face. Jerico barely noticed the heat as he made his way forward, realizing that only the two of them had escaped. Whoever still lived above them would die soon, unless they could make it to the hole. He wondered what had become of Aki and Valeriya, thankful that he hadn't seen them on the ship. Maybe they hadn't dropped into it. Maybe they still lived.

The narrow corridor through which they traveled was far too small to have been built for demons. Jerico had to stoop slightly. Steam emanated from what appeared to be some sort of reddish rock face that mostly covered the metallic plating of the floor and walls. There didn't seem to be any visible source of light, and yet the passageway glowed with such intensity that it was easy for Jerico to see.

"It's like a lava tube," Tasia said quietly behind him. "But it's too small for them. Why would they even build it?"

"I don't know. But I'm glad it's small. Maybe they can't get down here."

Tasia stopped walking when the floor once again tilted

beneath their feet. But this time everything seemed to level out, as if the ship had ceased its climb. Jerico wasn't sure if he should be pleased or worried. He felt weak with relief that they were still alive, yet he knew the demons would soon come for them.

"They know we're down here," he said. "Where should we go?"

"Back on the island, in their base, I was in tubes like this one. They all led somewhere."

"Then let's keep moving. Maybe we'll find a control room or an engine room."

"We don't have much time," Tasia replied, shaking her head. "I can feel them gathering above us."

Nodding, Jerico walked ahead, wishing he could better calm himself. Although his life had been punctuated with battles and escapes, he'd usually felt somewhat in control. And yet now, when he needed his strength the most, he seemed powerless. The entire right side of his body throbbed, and he reeled from the knowledge that they were alone. There was no Stronghold nearby for them to hide in, no friends who might come to their rescue. They might have been the only survivors of the attacking force, and in all likelihood the demons would find them soon.

"We've come so far," he said quietly.

"We're still moving. We're not dead yet."

"I don't want to lose you here. Not like this. Not to them."

"I know."

The passageway curved to their right. The red rock that

covered so much of the metallic plating disappeared, and was replaced by what looked to be large, glass-like screens. Strange white images glowed on the screens—perhaps diagrams or words. The pebble-sized images changed constantly and never seemed to repeat. Jerico didn't know if he was looking at instructions or gauges or a navigational system. He shook his head, wondering if the screens should be smashed or left alone.

"We have to keep going," Tasia whispered, almost to herself.

Jerico followed her forward, still holding his rifle. Something exploded behind them. "Maybe someone's still alive," he said. "Maybe they've found the engine room."

"It's not that way."

"How do you know?"

"Because ... something's ahead of us. I don't know what. But it's something powerful. Kind of like an Orb, but much, much bigger."

The passageway continued, as did the glowing screens. Jerico wondered if there were cameras within the screens, if the demons knew exactly where they were. He was about to ask Tasia what she thought when they came to an intersection. One corridor led straight, but one went left and another right.

Tasia sighed, pausing to lean against a screen. She grimaced, then rubbed her brow. Jerico saw her lips move, and knew she was communicating with one of the demons. A tear ran down her cheek. Then another.

"What?" he asked. "What's happening?"

She shook her head. "They have Zeus. And they're ... hurting him."

"We shouldn't—"

"He's screaming, Jerico. Somehow I can hear him screaming."

"Don't listen. Shut your mind."

"K'ail says we're all that's left. And they're coming for us."

Jerico nodded, thinking about his loved ones. He remembered their faces, not as they died, but as they lived. "We might be all that's left," he said. "But we're not all alone."

"What do you mean?"

He touched the names on her sleeve. "Can't you feel them? They're with us. They've always been with us."

She bit her lower lip as he wiped away one of her tears. "And we'll always be with them."

"I'm scared," he admitted, looking to his left and then his right. "But I want to be strong. I want to be like you."

"I'm scared too."

"So ... which way should we go?"

She pointed her staff ahead of them. "Something's there. Something I don't understand. It's like ... it's like a million minds."

"A million minds?"

"Or a million thoughts."

"And we should go to it?"

Tasia nodded. She then started forward, holding her staff with both hands. Jerico followed her, aware of distant shrieks, of vibrations beneath his feet. For now the small passageway protected them. But surely it would lead to bigger places. And then the demons would come at them.

Suddenly Tasia began to run. Jerico didn't understand why she rushed forward, but she whispered to someone and he hurried to catch her.

CHAPTER 41

Aki's leap had carried her toward the big demon's face, but the stone in her hand had only cracked against the corner of its right eye. When the beast had smashed its forearm into her belly, it drove her backward, knocking the wind out of her.

She now lay on her back, struggling to breathe, in too much pain to defend herself. Rising to her knees, she tried to stand, but the demon's good foot slammed into her ribs, flinging her toward Valeriya. She fell on top of the rubble that covered Valeriya's legs and, as her companion screamed for help, Aki gasped for breath, nearly overcome by agony. Fighting against the blackness that threatened to engulf her, she weakly tossed her stone at the approaching demon. The stone struck her adversary's forehead but fell impotently, clattering against other debris.

The demon lowered its massive head until its fangs neared Aki's face, shrieking in triumph.

"Don't look," she whispered to Valeriya, then closed her eyes, vowing not to scream, no matter how vast the pain. Valeriya embraced her from behind, and tears fell to her face. All she could do now, at the very end, was squeeze Valeriya's hands. She was tired of fighting, of defending herself. No longer could she climb that mountain.

Aki brought Valeriya's fingers to her lips, kissing them, shuddering. She felt as if she were a pebble tumbling down a stream, carried by the strongest of currents—rolling over and over, dropping into even deeper waters. Still, she continued kissing Valeriya's fingers with her eyes closed, wanting to feel her companion until the very end.

The demon's hands encircled Aki's neck, and she felt an unbearable pressure as the beast squeezed hard. Its talons cut into her flesh, and though pain seemed to rip her in two, she clenched her teeth, suppressing a scream. Reaching up, she groped for her attacker's eyes, trying to claw them out. But all she felt was agony and despair. She couldn't breathe. Couldn't think. Blackness poured into her, suffocating everything but her will to live, to fight. Convulsing, she blindly gouged at the demon with her fingers, breaking off nails, struggling in the darkness.

Then the demon shrieked again. But this time its cry wasn't made in triumph, but suffering. A bolt of energy had darted into its shoulder, penetrating its natural armor, then its soft tissue and bones. The demon reared back, releasing Aki. Another bolt struck it. And then another.

Aki opened her eyes in time to see the demon fall sideways and tumble away from her. A man holding a staff stood at the bottom of the pile of rubble. It took Aki a moment to recognize him. "Trax?" she whispered, disbelieving everything she saw.

The man below collapsed, the staff falling from his hands. Aki turned around, embracing Valeriya. They held each other tight, shaking, tears on their cheeks. Valeriya said something, but her words didn't register with Aki. Only now could she breathe properly, and she glanced at the tops of her shoulders, which were cut, but not too deeply. The demon had been toying with her. Only the tips of its talons had penetrated her skin. She shuddered, ran her aching fingers through her hair, and slowly sat up, still in disbelief that they were alive.

"Trax needs our help," Valeriya said quietly behind her.

Aki nodded. She then turned and began to throw more of the rubble away from Valeriya's legs. Some of the bigger concrete slabs were jammed together, and she understood why it had been so hard to move them. But now that she could study their layout, she was able to pry them apart and place them aside. Valeriya helped as best as she could, but her left arm was obviously broken, and she often winced as she moved it.

It took several minutes to uncover Valeriya. Though her friend's legs were bruised and battered, Aki realized to her profound relief that they hadn't been crushed. With Aki's help, Valeriya was able to stand. Unsteady on their feet, they made their way to Trax. He had fallen near the corridor's wall and lay on his back. When he saw them approach, he smiled.

"I do believe ... I was almost too late," he said quietly, his face pained.

Valeriya dropped to her knees beside him, reaching for his hand. "You weren't too late. You saved us."

His shirt and pants were drenched with blood. Aki kneeled and unbuttoned his shirt, surprised to see a small round hole below his right collarbone. The wound didn't look to have come from a demon, and as she applied pressure to it, she shook her head. "I don't understand. What happened?"

Sighing, he closed, then opened his eyes. "At the children's hospital ... fate found me."

"Fate?"

"I had come to save them," he replied weakly, as if speaking stole his strength. "I had a staff. And I ... stepped toward that beast. Then some frightened soul ... shot me by mistake. A child maybe. Some sweet child. But die ... I did not. So when I saw the demon chase you ... I tried to follow."

Valeriya started to rise. "We need to get you help. I'll find a doctor."

He reached for her. "Wait, dear. Just wait."

"Why?"

"Let the doctors ... save those who can still be saved." He coughed, and blood dripped from the corner of his mouth. "It's too late for me."

Aki tore off a piece of her shirt and gently wiped the blood from his face. She cleaned him as best as she could. "You saved us. But you could have saved yourself."

"Maybe. But why ... save one person ... when I could save two?"

Her vision blurring from sudden tears, Aki nodded. Trax was struggling to breathe, and she understood that the bullet must have pierced his lung. "You should be on your submarine," she said quietly. "Listening to your music and watching your whales."

"I'll miss ... my whales."

Valeriya stroked his brow with her good hand, her touch tender and loving. "How can we help? What can we do?"

He looked to her, then to Aki. "I just ... want to remember."

"Remember what?" Aki asked.

"What it felt like ... to be young."

One of Valeriya's tears fell to his forehead. "Tell us what it was like," she said quietly. "What do you remember?"

He grimaced, struggling to breathe. "Valeriya. Such a pretty name. Like some ... ancient goddess."

"Your childhood," Valeriya said, still stroking his brow. "What was it like?"

"The sea ... always felt warm. And there ... was no end to it."

Aki wiped more blood from his lips. An ache rose up from deep within her, from where the most wretched and profound of all miseries arose. "Please ... go on," she said. "Talk about ... the sea."

"The waves ... carried us. Like ships."

Somewhere distant, an explosion rumbled. Aki ignored it, reaching for Trax's hand, squeezing it, letting him know that he wasn't alone, even as she felt herself breaking into a thousand pieces.

"My brothers … are all gone," he whispered, his voice growing weaker. "But I … I go to them now."

Valeriya leaned down and kissed his forehead, her tears falling to his face. "You'll swim with them again. In those same waves."

"That would be … lovely."

"Look for them," Valeriya said, holding him tight. "They're waiting for you. I can hear them calling to you."

"Just lovely."

Valeriya kissed him again. "I see them. They're reaching out to you. You're with them now. You're swimming together."

The faintest of smiles crossed his face. The tension seemed to flow out of him—like water over rocks.

And Aki wondered if he saw his brothers then, if waves once again carried them forward together—boys on their magical ships, forever young and free.

CHAPTER 42

Tasia hurried through the corridor, which continued to be covered in large glass-like screens. She couldn't see through them, nor did they show any reflections. Instead they glowed with thousands, if not millions, of small, ever-changing symbols.

As Tasia moved ahead, she felt as if she'd entered some sort of bloodstream. Yet this stream looked to carry information. No symbol ever appeared twice, and she didn't understand how any language could have a seemingly infinite amount of characters. Adding to her confusion, the glowing glass looked so different than anything she'd ever associated with demons. It contained no hint of lava or heat. Neither did it seem to honor demons in any way, shape, or form. The demons thought themselves to be gods, but this place didn't appear to have been made by gods. It hinted of something else altogether.

The temperature in the corridor had cooled considerably. No

longer did Tasia sweat. Even the air seemed easier to breathe. Again and again she asked herself why the demons would build a corridor that was too small for them to enter. If there were a way to open or enlarge it, their pursuers would have done so by now. Unless, of course, they wanted Jerico and her to rush into a place of their choosing.

Suddenly K'ail's words materialized within Tasia's mind. Drawing a deep breath, she slowed her pace and let them unfold.

You understand so little of the universe.

"Then explain it to me."

My days of explaining life to you are over. Soon you will suffer and then die. Like my old adversary, Zeus.

"He was—"

Blinded. I took his eyes, Tasia. Then I took so much more.

"Stop."

He—

"I said stop!"

We found the explosives he carried—so trite and insignificant. You think something you can carry in your hands could bring down this ship? What fools you all are. You might as well blow on the walls beside you.

She shook her head. "I don't believe you. You're frightened. Ne'ith tried to get inside my head, but she couldn't. And you're afraid. I can feel your fear."

Our ship crosses the universe. It bends time and space. And yet you think—

"Then why are we still alive? Why can't you reach us down here?"

We shall soon—

Tasia blocked out his words. She forced away thoughts of Zeus, turning to Jerico. "They didn't make this place."

"Then who did?"

"I don't know. But they don't come down here. They can't. They see themselves as gods, and maybe they think some tasks are beneath them. Because gods fly. Gods rule. They don't work in engine rooms."

Jerico shook his head. "I don't think this place is an engine room."

"Neither do I."

"Then how do we find it?"

"The demons live up there, in that open space, in that pyramid. So we need to stay down here."

"Even if you're right," he replied, limping slightly, "we still don't have much time. They'll figure out a way to kill us. It won't take long."

She nodded, clutching her staff. As she hurried ahead, she thought about her many conversations with K'ail. She remembered how he'd said that gods had the right to conquer, kill, and enslave.

Around them, the glass-like corridor began to pulsate with energy, its countless symbols changing with ever-increasing speed. Tasia wiped sweat from her brow, feeling strangely empowered. She moved with a sense of purpose, following her instincts when intersections appeared before them. K'ail continued to try to communicate with her, but she ignored his words.

Something around them was changing. Somehow, they seemed to be passing from one world into the next. And even when the corridor appeared to end, when a blinking glass wall confronted her, Tasia knew it was a mirage of some sort. She stepped through it, holding her staff ready. She felt herself drop for the briefest of moments, as if she'd stepped into a miniature Orb.

Immediately her surroundings changed. She was in an immense glass-like room. Aliens stood before her. Yet these creatures weren't the demons of her nightmares; rather, they were small humanoid beings. One turned to her, raising some sort of device, aiming it at her. Without thought, she squeezed her staff and a bolt of energy darted toward and through the alien. It fell back, a smoldering hole in its chest.

Jerico was about to fire his rifle, but Tasia grabbed its barrel and thrust it toward the floor.

None of the other aliens had moved. They were only about half Tasia's height. Naked and sexless, they were somewhat shaped like humans, yet were thin and gray, with oversized heads. The aliens didn't have hair or ears. Their faces were dominated by large black eyes, flat noses, and lipless mouths. They all had been facing the glowing walls beside them, but they had turned toward the intruders. Only then did Tasia realize that their naked bodies seemed to be covered in scars—

long, ancient wounds that had never healed properly. The aliens were also tethered to the walls with some sort of metallic cables that fastened about their right ankles. And yet the alien Tasia had killed wasn't scarred or chained.

When she'd first dropped into the room, Tasia hadn't realized how far it extended. But she now saw that it went on and on. Hundreds of the diminutive humanoids stood at its walls, all facing her. The walls themselves blinked with millions of symbols. A nearby alien glanced at the closest wall, and the symbols before it glowed and changed.

"This is a control room," Tasia whispered, turning to Jerico. "And they're … controlling these instruments with their thoughts."

Jerico reached into her backpack and pulled out one of the two bombs that she carried. "Then let's blow it up."

Tasia nodded, then removed the second device. As Jerico hurried to the center of the room, she wondered why the humanoids, if they were prisoners and controlled the ship, couldn't somehow escape. Maybe she was wrong, she realized. Maybe it wasn't a control room at all, but something much less important.

"Wait," she called out to Jerico as he affixed his bomb to a section of glass that none of the aliens could reach.

"Why?" he asked. "If this is a control room, and we destroy it, maybe the ship will fall."

"Maybe's not good enough. We have to be sure."

"How can we be sure, Tasia? We can't read any of this stuff.

We don't even know where we are. But at least we can set these off and—"

"And we'll die here," she interrupted, holding the bomb in her left hand. "There's no Orb nearby. No way for us to escape."

He shook his head. "But what should we do? All we know is that we can blow this place up. If we go any farther, the demons might find us. But if we put the bombs here, we could set them to go off in a few minutes. We could run and maybe find an Orb."

"I just don't—" Tasia stopped short when a nearby alien touched her leg. Surprised, she looked down, noticing that the humanoid had two or three times as many scars as those near it. Some of the wounds were very old. Others appeared to have been much more recently inflicted.

The alien turned to the wall beside it and symbols began to change. Tasia still couldn't make sense of them, but they appeared to drift together, then explode apart. The transition repeated itself over and over, faster and faster.

"What?" Tasia asked. "What are you showing me?"

The alien's oversized black eyes blinked. Again the images coalesced, then scattered. Yet now the same pattern repeated itself not only in front of the alien, but on all the walls around them. The entire room flashed and darkened to the synchronicity of the condensing and expanding images.

"It's trying to tell us something," Tasia said, then glanced at Jerico. "But what?"

His hands fell away from the bomb that he'd been arming. He started to speak, then stopped. Then he nodded to himself, turning to Tasia. "You were a prisoner once. If you'd been imprisoned for a hundred years and your species had been wiped out, what would you want?"

"Freedom."

"And revenge?"

"I'd want freedom the most."

To Tasia's surprise, Jerico smiled. "So cut it free."

She brought her hands together, nodding. Without further thought, she aimed her staff at where the metal cable that restrained the humanoid was connected to the glass. Squeezing gently on her weapon, she fired a small burst of energy into the cable, which immediately snapped.

The alien's face showed no change of expression. Yet the images near it changed once again, swirling together. Tasia was about to step toward Jerico when the humanoid reached for the bomb in her hand. She started to pull it away but resisted the impulse. The alien stepped closer to her, almost eye-level to the bomb. It blinked repeatedly, cocking its head slightly to the right. Then it started walking toward Jerico. Each alien it passed cupped its hands together, forming a circle with its touching fingers. The circle was then lifted up, above each alien's head. Tasia didn't understand what she was seeing, but the aliens moved in near unison. The freed humanoid turned around and looked at Tasia, its large eyes blinking again.

"I think it wants you to follow it," Jerico said, pulling his bomb from the wall.

Stepping ahead, Tasia moved behind the alien. Once again,

she studied its many scars. She recognized those scars—a similar one was in the middle of her hand, left there from Ur'sol's talon. She understood then that the humanoid race had been conquered and enslaved. They helped operate the demons' ship. They'd been defeated, yet guessing from the evidence of their countless scars, they still resisted.

Tasia put her bomb in her backpack. She then reached out to Jerico. He did the same and his hand felt warm in her grasp. Around them, the diminutive aliens continued to hold their hands aloft, their touching fingertips making almost perfect circles. The images on the walls changed as well, morphing into thousands of identical, hollow circles that resembled golden rings. Tasia couldn't comprehend what she was seeing but shook her head in wonder. The aliens, it seemed, were of one mind, one direction.

The humanoid reached the end of the rectangular room. It turned around, raised its hands over its head, and made a circle with its touching fingers. The wall flickered before it, and Tasia realized that it was another miniature Orb.

"Where's it taking us?" Jerico asked.

Tasia studied the aliens behind her. Suddenly she understood what they were prepared to do. And so she set down her staff and then raised her hands above her head, forming a circle with her fingers, trying to honor them, if possible.

"Like you said, they want their freedom," she replied, studying the expressionless faces before her, still holding her circle aloft. "And they're going to show us where to put our bombs."

CHAPTER 43

The train platform was eerily silent. Supporting Valeriya, who could barely walk, Aki looked around in wonder. Every demon in Kyoto seemed to have either died during the fight near the Orb, or dropped into it. Several thousand humans— mostly Hiders who had remained in the city—crowded the platform, their eyes fixed on the alien ship far above them. Fires smoldered. Piles of human corpses rose near ruined machine-gun and laser-rifle emplacements. And scores of dead demons served as viewing stations for the men, women, and children bold enough to climb them.

Aki had already been reunited with her family, and to her profound relief, they were all fine and well. They'd hidden in a secret room deep within the Stronghold and hadn't been exposed to the fighting. Now they were back underground, caring for the injured. Her mother was stitching up wounds, while her father assisted surgeons. Even her younger siblings helped—acting as runners, bringing equipment and supplies where needed.

From time to time Aki glanced at the nearby Orb, longing to see Tasia and Jerico emerge from it. Then her gaze drifted back to the alien ship, which was now even higher above them, and looked only about twice as large as a full moon. She impatiently waited for the ship to explode. If it didn't, everyone on Earth would soon die.

If Tasia failed, humanity would cease to exist.

"I wish we could help them," Aki said quietly.

Valeriya, whose broken arm was in a sling, winced as she shifted her weight from one leg to the other.

Aki's brow furrowed. "You should sit."

"No."

"No?"

"I want to be standing when they blow it up."

"And if they don't?"

"Then I want to die standing."

Aki sighed, her gaze drifting to Slate, who had been shot dead and lay near the Orb, next to Ishaam's body. Both the scientist and the Seeker had betrayed their own people. To her surprise, Aki didn't hate them but pitied them. To do what they did, the demons must have wielded great power over them.

"I hope Trax is with his brothers," Valeriya said, turning to Aki. "I hope they're on those waves."

"And what about you? If you die today, where will you want to go? In your … afterlife?"

"To Paris. With you. I'd still want to go to Paris."

Aki tried to smile. "You wouldn't rather go fishing? Really?"

"That can come later. Remember, my grandfather taught me how to be patient. So you can show me Paris. Then we'll do other things."

"That's good. And maybe you can teach me how to be patient."

The wind rose, ruffling the hair of the living and the dead. Valeriya looked at the demon ship, then at Aki. "Why didn't you run?" she asked. "Why didn't you leave me?"

Aki's pulse quickened at the memory of the fight. She'd never come so close to death. "I'd miss … braiding your hair. And watching you try to ride a bike. Who could entertain me like you could?"

"No, Aki. Tell me the real reason. Tell me why you didn't run."

"Because you don't run from someone you love. You stand beside them. You fight and fight and fight, and if the end comes—at least you'll die together."

"We could die right now. At any instant."

"I know. And I'm not ready. I don't want us to end."

Valeriya leaned toward her, kissing her lips. Aki wrapped her arms around her companion, drawing her even closer. Whatever emotions Aki had experienced during their first kiss, they felt a thousand times stronger now. It seemed as if her insides were flooding with love and hope, sadness and fear. Such powerful feelings compelled her to kiss Valeriya with an urgency and a longing that she'd never known.

Finally, they separated.

An explosion rang out in the distance, and Aki flinched, fearing the end. When nothing happened, she looked up at the distant ship. "I'd give anything to help them," she said, shaking her head. "But if we stepped into the Orb right now, we could end up anywhere. She's not here to guide us."

"She'll be back."

"Why?" Aki asked. "Why do you say that?"

"Because I believe in her."

Try as she might, Aki didn't share Valeriya's optimism. Although she had faith in Tasia, the demon ship was too vast, too powerful. Surely there was no way that a small group of Guardians and Seekers could bring it down.

"If people begin to die around us," Aki whispered, "kiss me again."

"Why?"

"Because I want your lips to be the last thing I feel."

Valeriya started to reply, but then simply nodded. She looked away as tears fell to her cheeks.

And Aki knew then that Valeriya was just as frightened as she was. No one around them was laughing or smiling. Instead people held hands, embraced, or prayed. Nobody really seemed to believe that the demons' ship would fall from the sky. The sun was more likely to crack in half.

"At least I got to love you," Aki said, crying openly, no longer trying to stop her tears.

Valeriya nodded, pulling her close. Aki closed her eyes. They held each other, tears racing down their cheeks.

A strange stillness seemed to dominate the landscape, as if the world and all its creatures were in a trance. Everything was suspended in a temporary, precarious balance between light and dark, life and death.

But everything was about to change.

CHAPTER 44

The scarred humanoid disappeared into the flickering wall. Tasia stepped forward. She felt the briefest and most manageable of drops, and she almost immediately appeared inside a narrow, vacant corridor. Jerico materialized behind her. More flickering glass-like panels glowed around them, depicting countless symbols that constantly changed.

Once again, the alien started forward. The passageway soon became so small that Tasia had to stoop to follow, holding her staff low. Somewhere in the distance, another explosion rang out, and she wondered if a few Seekers or Guardians were still alive and had detonated their bombs. Yet the demons' ship didn't even tremble, seemingly invulnerable to whatever attacks or events were taking place.

The corridor branched into other passageways. At every intersection, the humanoid didn't change its pace but simply turned left or right or walked straight ahead. Soon Tasia felt as if they were in some sort of magical maze. As symbols flashed around her, she continued onward, passing through two more translucent walls and experiencing short drops.

She was about to ask Jerico how he felt when K'ail's words materialized before her. She let them enter her mind, fearing what he might say.

We know where you have been and where you are going. Involving our slaves was a mistake. Now they too will suffer. Some already have.

"They won't die as slaves," Tasia whispered. "They'll die free."

We conquered their civilization two thousand years ago. For generations they have been born into captivity. They know nothing of freedom.

"Then why do they have scars? Why do they still fight you?"

A rock that tumbles down a mountain has scars. The presence of such wounds means nothing.

Tasia followed the humanoid as it reached another intersection and turned left. "Soon I'll walk outside," she whispered. "And I won't ever have to look up—just like my father hoped. Because every last demon will be dead."

We rule—

"And as you die, I hope you finally understand that you were never gods. You were as mortal as us. You were just too arrogant to believe in anything bigger than yourselves."

You shall kneel before—

"Goodbye, K'ail."

Do not shut your mind to me! Not—

Tasia ignored his words, drawing a deep breath and continuing on.

"What did he say?" Jerico asked.

"Nothing new. Just hollow words."

As Jerico took her hand, Tasia began to pray, asking that they find the strength to do what must be done. She prayed to a god she'd never met or seen but felt was real. She also asked her father to help show her the way. He'd always believed in her, and now, in what were likely her last moments, she hoped he understood how grateful she was.

"Thanks," she said quietly, squeezing Jerico's hand.

"For what?"

"For showing me what's possible."

"We showed each other."

She sensed an immense power not far ahead. It was as if a million staffs had been bundled together and had coalesced into a force with the strength of a star. She'd never felt anything so potent. Her pulse quickened. Sweat gathered on her brow. Something so mighty would not be unguarded.

"We're close," she said, then bit her lower lip.

"To what?"

"The end."

He started to reply, but the words of countless demons sought to enter cracks within her mind. Ne'ith might have tried as well, but somehow Tasia was able to force their thoughts away, struggling to stay strong, to continue to believe. Her pace faltered, but Jerico helped her forward. The source of power ahead overwhelmed her. Nothing like it existed on Earth. The surge of the oceans and the fury of every storm that ever blew amounted to nothing compared to what lay before them. Its might was infinite.

The humanoid turned right, walking faster now. Still stooping, Tasia and Jerico hurried ahead, struggling to keep up. She tried not to doubt herself, but the growing presence of the demons' power astounded her. Any species capable of harnessing such a force boasted abilities beyond her comprehension. Maybe they were gods. Maybe K'ail had been right all along.

Her legs weak, her emotions unchecked, Tasia continued on. The terror she'd tried to repress rose up within her, threatening to overwhelm her every thought. Demons continued to call to her, eager to enter her mind. Still she resisted. The floor seemed to sway, the walls to close in on her. But she moved ahead, clutching her staff, seeking to draw strength from it.

The humanoid came to another translucent wall, which they dropped through. They materialized into a different glass-like corridor, walked ahead, and saw something glowing in the distance. The diminutive alien slowed its pace as they approached what looked to be a nearly transparent spherical porthole. Yet beyond this shoulder-high obstacle, whatever it was, lay a vast, shimmering chamber the likes of which Tasia never had seen.

The room seemed endlessly long, with a curved ceiling

that might have been five hundred feet above the floor. In the center of the space, near the floor and stretching as far as she could see, was a horizontal cylinder of energy. The enormous, glowing energy conduit was supported every twenty or so feet by vertical rings of some sort of steel that were mounted to the floor.

"It's like … a giant Orb," Jerico whispered.

Tasia nodded, realizing only then that dozens of white demons occupied the chamber. They looked so small compared to the glowing energy conduit. Some of the demons flew above it. Others stood before it. A single black demon was positioned near the center of the room.

K'ail. He was waiting for her.

And yet, the distant demons didn't seem to know from where she and Jerico might emerge. Tasia moved as close as possible to the spherical, nearly transparent opening, looking out. The chamber's walls and ceiling appeared to be dotted with thousands of similarly gleaming hatches, and she wondered if each hatch represented the end of a corridor. Maybe the complex of corridors was like a maze, and the corridors emerged into the room from countless points. In that case, the demons wouldn't know from which hatch they'd come, and there weren't nearly enough demons to watch every position.

Tasia and Jerico knelt before the glimmering hatch, studying everything before them. The energy conduit was at least two hundred feet away from them. Six or seven demons stood or hovered almost directly in front of them, including K'ail.

"They're protecting it," Jerico whispered. "And they wouldn't bother to protect it if we couldn't destroy it."

Nodding, Tasia reached into her backpack and withdrew her bomb. She handed it to Jerico. "I think you're right," she said quietly, her hands trembling. "And it's a giant Orb. All those steel rings seem to support it, so if we destroy them, maybe we can destroy it."

"Do you think we can drop through it, right before we blow it up?"

"Maybe. But it's so … big. So insanely big. Maybe it'll just grind us up into a billion atoms. Maybe it was only designed to bring the ship from one place in the universe to another."

Jerico carefully set down his rifle and then wiped sweat from his brow. "We have to destroy it. Whether we live or die, we have to destroy it first."

"I know."

"You lead the way. Clear a path for us with your staff." He studied her bomb, flipped a switch, and then pushed several buttons, which illuminated and changed small digital numbers. He repeated the process for the other device. "Once I throw these, we'll have five seconds to jump into the Orb. Then they'll go off."

Tasia wiped sweat from her brow, wishing that her raging heart would settle down, that she didn't feel like everything was moving so impossibly fast. "You'll throw them at one of those supports, when we're about to jump into the Orb?"

"That's right."

"Just a five-second delay?"

"Any longer and they could get them out of there."

She ran her free hand through her damp hair, then squeezed his arm. Her heart pounded even faster, as if someone were beating a giant drum within her. It felt as if she couldn't breathe, couldn't stay standing. She needed to cling to something, to hold tight, as if hurricane-force winds were about to blow her away.

"In that book you read," she said, "about the old man and the giant fish … tell me again how he found the strength to catch it."

Jerico started to speak and then stopped. "His name was Santiago. And he didn't … he just didn't allow himself to fail. The shark, the ocean, his old age—none of them could beat him."

Nodding, Tasia took a deep breath, then turned to the humanoid. The diminutive alien lifted its hands above its head, once again forming a circle with its touching fingertips.

Tasia turned back to Jerico. "I love you," she said, leaning closer to him, kissing his lips. "And that's what I'm going to think about when we jump into that Orb. And if it's my last thought … at least it'll be the perfect one."

He closed his eyes, nodded, and then once again looked at her. "It won't be your last thought."

"How can you say that?"

"Because I believe in you. And so do those demons. That's why they're all waiting out there, protecting their ship from you."

She lifted her hands up above her head once again, forming a circle with her trembling fingers, trying to thank the humanoid for its sacrifice, its gift. Because whatever happened next to Jerico and her, the small alien and all if its kind would suffer or die.

"It's time," she whispered, leaning forward.

With each hand he picked up a bomb, cradling them. "We'll find a way," he promised, nodding. "We've always found a way."

CHAPTER 45

K'ail stood near the center of the room, protecting the power that he and his kind had long taken for granted. Around him, more than fifty white female gods flew and rested. Their thoughts and accusations assailed him.

He tried to ignore their rage. When Tasia was soon killed, there would be a reckoning. She'd come too far, damaged too much. K'ail knew his punishment would be severe and was tempted to step into the nearby glowing energy conduit—which the gods called the Pathway—and drop back to Earth. Though he hated that cold, dying planet, at least within its frigid air he could kill once again. He could delight in the pain and suffering of mortals, and when one finally killed him, he'd die with blood on his fangs, as a god should.

Yet despite these desires, K'ail didn't move. He wasn't sure if he was strong enough to endure the Pathway, which allowed his ship to travel from one galaxy to the next, to bend space and time. His hate for Tasia also kept him motionless. She had outsmarted him, used him, and even mocked him. Were it not for her, his standing among the gods would never have been higher. Instead she'd stolen his pride, his status, and his future. This girl who couldn't fly, who had no inklings of all that dwelled in the universe, had taken everything from him.

Before K'ail was judged, he wanted to bring her down, to hear her scream and see her torn apart. At least then he could die after her, knowing that her species soon would be destroyed. The dreams of humanity would be no more.

A massive white demon flew into K'ail's field of vision. He tried to ignore Ne'ith's words, but his will weakened, and her promises of what she'd do to him caused him to look away from her. For the first time in his existence, K'ail was fearful. So foreign and cold, the emotion coursed through him like poison, afflicting his mind and body. He suddenly felt the weight of his long and violent years. And neither the faces of his victims nor the memories of his victories brought him any comfort.

Ne'ith promised to disgrace him, mutilate him, and abandon him on Earth, where he'd spend the remainder of his days suffering within a cold, hostile land. While the rest of the gods resumed their conquest of the universe, he would die alone, marooned within the same hell that he'd always yearned to escape from.

Shaking his vast head, K'ail wished that he could travel back in time, that he had simply killed Tasia instead of trying to manipulate her. Her taunts reverberated in his mind, and he wondered if he might not be a god, but a mortal like any other creature. If a human could better him, how could he possibly be divine?

K'ail's world seemed to have begun a slow collapse, like a pile of sand assaulted by a rainstorm. Everything he had believed in, and fought for, trembled and disintegrated. Though the humans hadn't won and Tasia soon would be dead, she'd given rise to the fear within him. No longer did he have the urge to flap his giant wings and soar, as a god might, as he always had. Still, he would take to the air and fall upon her, tearing her apart. And then in one final fight he'd attack Ne'ith. She would kill him, of course, but at least he would die with honor, and his name would be remembered for as many good reasons as bad.

Imagining how he might strike Ne'ith, K'ail's mind wandered. He then thought about Tasia, wondering, as he had many times before, how she had managed to trick him. Maybe she'd been right all along. Maybe love, while a human creation, was a power that he'd never understood, that he'd underestimated.

K'ail asked himself if love was stronger than hate, than fear, than ambition. Maybe love took away all the pain.

CHAPTER 46

Tasia took one final glance at the humanoid. Then she turned to Jerico. He crouched, holding one bomb in each hand. Sweat glistened on his forehead. His chest rose and fell. She saw the names of his loved ones on his sleeve.

"We can have it all," she whispered to him, her heart thumping wildly, her body trembling.

He nodded. "So let's take it all."

Gripping her staff in both hands, she stepped forward through the shimmering portal. Immediately she was within the cavernous room, and without further thought started to run toward the glowing energy conduit. At first, none of the demons saw her, and so she simply ran toward what would be freedom or doom. Then a flying white demon shrieked, wheeling in her direction. She squeezed her staff, and a brilliant bolt of energy darted upward, slamming into the beast, knocking it back.

More demons circled toward them, none holding back.

Tasia fired her weapon again and again, and the silver staff pulsed in her grasp, maiming and killing its makers. They fell dying to writhe on the floor, reaching out to her even in their death throes. And yet she still ran, circumventing them, power flowing through her as never before.

The demons attacked her from all sides, dropping with rage and speed. She spun, light on her feet, protecting Jerico's back and then turning to cleave open a path before them. Her staff seemed to magnify her hate and rage a thousand times over, feeling alive within her grasp. Never had she, or any Guardian she'd ever seen, used a staff with such skill. Maybe it was her proximity to the Pathway, or to her own death or escape, but whatever the reason, Tasia fought without thought or fear. She didn't attempt to hide or to flee, but ran straight at her enemy, led by her instincts alone.

Waves of white demons seemed to fall upon her, and her staff fired so swiftly and often that it might as well have emitted a constant beam of death. The white demons had never faced a Guardian and didn't know how to dodge her attacks. They saw her diminutive size and thought they could crush her. Only K'ail held back, circling above, waiting for the right moment.

A dying demon slammed against Tasia, knocking her sideways. Its talons cut into her hip, and she cried out in pain but didn't fall. Jerico yelled something behind her, but his words made no sense. The Pathway was fewer than a hundred feet from them, and despite Tasia's wound, her feet carried her like never before. She ran, jumped, spun, evaded, and killed.

More demons fell—smoking, ruined carcasses even before they thumped against the floor.

The call of freedom, of victory, was the strongest feeling Tasia had ever experienced. It consumed her, and as she neared the Pathway, she felt a strength she'd never known. The demons that confronted her died, their insides charred and blackened, their final thoughts filled with nothing but surprise and horror.

The power of the Pathway seemed to merge with Tasia. She sensed it ripple through her, bursting out of every pore in her body. She screamed, feeling as if she were dying and being reborn, again and again, stronger with each rebirth. Her staff glowed, seeming to merge into her body—held in her grasp, but also in her blood, in her thoughts. She swung it in all directions, firing faster than appeared possible, her power darting through her to ignite and explode from the ancient weapon.

Shrieking, Ne'ith came for her, gripping the necks of two smaller demons. Using them as shields, Ne'ith dropped toward Tasia. And yet Tasia killed the lesser demons, turning them to near ash, lighting fires in Ne'ith's hands. Undaunted, Ne'ith surged toward her, but Tasia didn't turn, didn't flee. Instead a scream arose from deep within her, the scream born from a lifetime of hiding and fear. She ran at Ne'ith, her staff afire, bolts of energy slamming into the massive white demon, spinning her sideways.

Something knocked against Tasia's head, but she was barely aware of the blow. She stumbled forward, the Pathway almost within reach. Jerico shouted, and she saw the two bombs tumble past her, settling beneath one of the steel rings that supported the Pathway. Jerico grabbed her hand, keeping her from falling.

Then she leapt forward, toward the light.

But right before the Pathway enveloped her, K'ail dropped from above, smashing into them, driving them ahead into the blinding brightness. His mouth opened and his fangs neared Tasia's neck.

She didn't try to defend herself. Instead she thought about love. She remembered who she was.

And she dropped.

Somewhere above her, twin explosions seemed to rip the world asunder. She sensed heat and pain, noise and death.

Demons shrieked, wheeling away from a sudden eruption of light and fury.

Tasia heard their cries. She felt their agony as an inferno consumed them—the white-hot, infinite power that once created planets and stars. By the thousands demons died—all in one instant.

Then Tasia sensed K'ail as he dropped beside her, his fangs nearing her within a tomb of blackness and light. Everything appeared to come together, then to burst apart, and she screamed, dropping between worlds, between life and death. The universe seemed to buckle, crack, and burst forth from deep within itself. For an instant she sensed the divinity that the demons spoke of. But then it was gone, and she felt pain and fear and mortality. She was an atom, a dream, a memory. The vastness of the universe was too much for her mind.

Her soul shattered—again and again, a thousand times over.

And still she dropped—holding her staff, fighting to embrace all the love she'd ever felt, somehow knowing that only it could save her.

CHAPTER 47

Tasia dropped out of the receiving Orb, trying to corral her thoughts, to escape the massive presence that loomed over her. She stumbled backward, twisting and falling, barely aware of slamming into the ground.

K'ail materialized before her. He shook his massive head, as if trying to clear his mind.

But Tasia was quicker. She remembered who she was, conscious of her hope and love and belief.

K'ail shrieked, his good eye focusing on her, his body tensing, readying itself to spring.

"We won," she said, then squeezed her staff.

The bolt of light darted into and through K'ail's right shoulder, driving him back. He twisted, his mouth agape, as a pain he'd never known ripped through him. Tasia attacked him again, and this time her bolt struck him in the belly, scorching his insides. He tumbled away from her, but then righted himself and tried to crawl back to her.

Tasia stood up. Jerico moved beside her, and suddenly people appeared from everywhere, hurrying forward, weapons in hand. Tasia heard Aki's voice, but didn't respond. Instead she stepped away from K'ail, holding up her hand so that none of the Seekers present would fire at him.

For the last time, she opened her mind to his words.

You shall never ... get them back.

Tasia thought about her father and Calix, Fareed and Draven. "They never left me," she whispered so quietly that only K'ail would understand her.

And your planet ... is dying.

"It's being reborn. We're being reborn."

K'ail lifted up his head, glaring at her with his good eye. *You shall never rule the stars ... as we did. And—*

"And you're no god, K'ail. You never were."

I—

Tasia fired her staff into his open mouth, driving him away from her. He fell sideways, landing on the ruined bodies of Seekers, of those who had fought to defend the Orb.

Jerico reached for her, embracing her. She heard his words, but her connection to the demons' ship was still too strong to resist, and so she looked up. Far above, the ship remained perched in the sky. But black smoke poured from its sides, obscuring the distant sun. A violent explosion ripped through the front of the ship, causing giant flames to burst out of the cracks in its hull.

Tasia thought about the humanoids, aware that they were dying, but glad that they were finally free. She lifted her hands above her head, making a circle with her fingers. And then the demons' ship seemed to shudder as another explosion cascaded through it, booming like a distant thunderclap. The ship started to split in two, drifting sideways away from them, and then plunging from the sky, towards faraway mountains. Gathering speed, the ship began to break apart, fragmenting from the force of more detonations, arching across the emptiness, trailing flames and smoke.

When the blazing remains of the ship struck the distant mountains, the land beneath Tasia's feet trembled. An immense explosion seemed to sear her eyes and a wave of heat washed over her. A brilliant ball of fire enveloped the mountains as people around her cheered. The voice of a single demon reached out to her, but she ignored it, and then it was gone. The connection she had to the demon ship was severed forever. More explosions rumbled, sending building-size masses of debris shooting into the sky.

Jerico hugged her, lifting her off the ground. Tasia dropped her staff and wrapped her arms around him, pulling him closer, kissing his brow as he shouted in joy.

Aki and Valeriya came forward. Though both were wounded, Tasia was thrilled to see them alive. She welcomed them into the embrace, and the four companions jumped up and down, holding each other, their fingers and bodies intertwined. They shouted and hugged and celebrated, unaware of their injuries, of the memories that had once haunted them. The defeats and pains of their lives would never be forgotten, but were now a part of their histories, as integral to their triumphs as anything else.

Tasia glanced above, remembering her father, hoping he could see her. His everlasting wish was to walk beneath an open sky, and never again would she hide from the light. She'd feel its warmth, remember his words, and rejoice in the simple fact that so many of her loved ones and friends still lived. The War for Earth was over. Humanity had won.

More explosions ripped through the air, and people began to pick up weapons and run toward the burning debris, though it was miles away. Tasia knew they'd find nothing but flames. The demons were all dead. Her mind was finally free of the burdens wrought by their existence. She lifted the hands of her companions above them, and they danced around in a circle, laughing like the children around them, free for the first time in their lives.

Tasia stumbled on K'ail's outstretched arm, grateful that he had come into her life, that he'd inadvertently shown her the path to victory. If she had never been captured, she'd still be hiding, still be afraid of the future.

K'ail had given her the key.

After whispering her thanks to the dead demon, Tasia thought about her mother and brother, knowing that they were finally safe. She watched Aki and Valeriya kiss and wrapped her arms around them, not wanting them to break away from each other. Then she turned to Jerico, kissing him hard and long, feeling his hands on her face and rejoicing in the knowledge that never again would she be alone.

CHAPTER 48

A week later, Aki and Valeriya stood on the bank of the Seine River. In the distance, the Eiffel Tower rose proudly, though it tilted to the west and would fall one day. Much closer, a massive cathedral, with some of its stained-glass windows still intact, towered above trees and apartment buildings. The river flowed swiftly, creating eddies around a half-sunken sightseeing ship that had crashed into a bridge's pilings. Brown-winged birds wheeled about the vessel, diving to pluck minnows from the water.

Aki ran her hand through her dark purple hair, set her rifle against a table, and nodded to an old man. He rested on a stone bench that once had been covered with graffiti, but the sun had bleached nearly clean. In his gnarled hands, the old man held a guitar. He began to pluck at its strings, his fingers moving slowly, his mouth etched in a weathered smile.

Her left arm protected by a cast and a sling, Valeriya stepped toward Aki. She was wearing a blue silk dress. Her hair was elaborately braided, and a string of pearls encircled her neck. She also wore old-fashioned white gloves that nearly reached her elbows. Though makeup highlighted her face, she went barefoot, and her red toenails seemed to sparkle in the sun.

Aki wore a rose-colored dress that looked to have been created by the same designer. Her dress was sleeveless, fitted around her chest and waist but flared around her ankles. Black gloves covered her hands and forearms. A sapphire-encrusted necklace and matching earrings complemented her outfit. She also went barefoot, and her toenails were the same color as Valeriya's.

The companions moved together and began to dance, swaying to the rhythm of the old man's music. Their faces carried smiles, and neither one of them glanced up at the sky. That morning they'd dropped into Paris straight from Kyoto. Throughout the previous days, no one had seen a single demon. Tasia had said they were gone forever, and Aki believed her.

After a short stay in Paris, Aki and Valeriya would drop into Angkor, where they'd once again meet up with Tasia and Jerico. To everyone's surprise, the Orbs hadn't shut down. No one understood why or how, but people were happy to be able to still travel the world. Tasia had taught Aki and Valeriya how to control the destinations of their drops and Aki was pleased to never have to return to certain places.

The old man strummed the guitar with increasing speed, and Aki put her hands around Valeriya's waist and drew her closer. They twirled—smiling, completely lost in the moment.

"We'll fish tomorrow," Aki promised, feeling Valeriya's toes brush against hers. "You can cast one of your spoons out there and see what happens. I'll probably pass out from excitement."

"That'd be nice. Then I can fish in silence—the way it's supposed to be done."

"What do you know about anything?" Aki asked, grinning. "You still ride a bike like an octopus."

Valeriya laughed. "An octopus? Really?"

"On your best day."

"Well, my teacher wasn't worth much. Her face was pretty, but there was a lot of air between her ears."

Aki bumped into Valeriya, ruining the cadence of their dance. "You know what, Val? You can shoot straight. You can fish. But you're a simple girl from Russia, and it's a good thing for you I'm not too choosy."

The old man began a different song, which he accompanied with his raspy voice. The wind blew, ruffling their dresses and hair. Aki started to glance up, but stopped herself, her gaze once again falling to Valeriya's face.

"After Angkor," Aki asked, "where should we go next?"

Valeriya smiled, dancing with more passion, moving faster. "I want to see Neverland again. But it won't be easy to get to. There's no Orb nearby."

"Why Neverland?"

"Because my friends there need our help. And I want to let them know that we won, that they don't have to be afraid anymore. Then we can go back to Kyoto, back to our little place by the river."

"And make your swing and your zoo?"

"Just for injured animals. Once they're better, we'll let them go."

Aki glanced at the sky, enjoying the warmth of the sun, of freedom. "Do they have stores in Neverland, or just fish?"

"Stores that have never been picked over. Stores that you wouldn't believe. And you can bring your family. They'll love it."

"If you're lying about the shopping, I'll—"

"Try to kiss me on a bike?"

"That's right. That's exactly what I'll do."

"Then we'll go. And you'll see."

Valeriya's grin was infectious. Aki leaned closer to her, kissing her on the lips. Their sway of their bodies slowed, though the music quickened. They turned as one, unaware of the old man or the Eiffel Tower or the birds above the river. The entire world seemed to slumber around them, deep within a dreamless sleep.

Their lips parted, then met again.

The old man kept playing.

And Aki smiled—grateful for the warmth on her skin and in her heart.

At long last, she finally felt at home.

CHAPTER 49

Tasia followed Jerico as he walked barefoot down the beach. His footprints were deep and evenly spaced. He wore shorts but no shirt, and his long hair blew in the breeze. She'd rarely seen him without a rifle slung over his shoulder, and the sight of him without a weapon pleased her. From time to time he bent down, picked up a stick, and threw it ahead for Rex to fetch. Though Rex's front left leg had been injured by a demon and he wore a bandage, he was able to run forward and retrieve the stick. From time to time he barked, and no longer did Jerico command him to be quiet. In fact, he encouraged Rex to be as noisy as he wanted, often bending down to tousle the fur between his ears.

That morning Tasia and Jerico had dropped to the Galapagos Islands, and after meeting some of the local Hiders—who no longer cowered in their underground bunkers—they'd gone to walk the beach. Though she carried her staff, Tasia didn't look up at the sky. Instead she reveled in the beauty around her. Marine iguanas clung to symmetrical formations of hardened lava at the sea's edge. Small penguins basked in the sun and frolicked in the waves, chasing unseen fish. And her favorite sight—mother sea lions nursing their young, which lay beside them on the warm sand, yelping at their brothers and sisters. The nearby water was turquoise and still, and though she couldn't see them, she knew rays, sharks, and sea turtles drifted beneath the surface. In the distance, another volcanic island rose, scraping the bellies of ivory-colored clouds that contrasted against the blue sky.

Tasia thought about the past week, about how people had started to migrate to small cities and villages that could be rebuilt. She and Jerico already had dropped into Angkor to see her mother and brother, and soon would do so again. They'd also been to New York to visit her father's grave. And before long Jerico would show her where his family was buried in Beijing.

As a blue-footed bird plunged into the nearby water, Tasia reflected on the loss of her loved ones. While she still grieved for them, she'd always been most upset by the feeling that future moments with them had been stolen from her before they'd ever had the chance to occur. She had grieved for the future, not for the past. Memories should have been created and cherished, but so many never came to be.

And yet now, the future was so much brighter. Tasia would see her brother turn into a man, and her mother would watch her flourish as she was meant to. She also relished the thought of spending more time with Aki and Valeriya, of laughing with them as they continued to discover each other.

And Jerico. Tasia envisioned the bond between them strengthening, no longer partly fueled by desperation and fear, but by the promise of all the days ahead. Though challenges surely awaited them, their time together wouldn't be defined by conflict and conquest but the simple joys of their companionship.

Jerico turned to her, then reached for her hand. They walked together, sinking into the sand, feeling the warmth of the sun on their skin. He smiled at her, and she admired the strength and grace of his face.

"What?" he asked, still grinning.

"Where are you going to take me?"

"Today?"

"Today. Tomorrow. And all the tomorrows after that."

He glanced at the sea, then back to her. "I'm going to learn to fly a little plane. And I'll take you to the most beautiful places in the world—the Taj Mahal, the Great Wall of China, the cathedrals of Europe. They're what I want you to see. What I want to see."

"Why?"

"Because we should see the best of what once was. Where we came from and where we can go."

Rex barked, digging ferociously in the sand. Small crabs darted away from him. He chased one, then another.

"He's so happy," Tasia said. "It's good to see him so happy."

Jerico smiled, leaning down to pick up a small yellow shell. He turned the shell over and rubbed the sand from it. "This reminds me of you."

"How?"

"Well, I've always been sort of a collector. I've spent my whole life searching for shells and stories and beauty. And I've found so many wonderful things. But you're my best … most magical discovery. Nothing I've ever seen shines as brightly as you."

Her eyes watered and she smiled. Nodding, she squeezed, then kissed his hand and they walked together, neither looking up. Ahead, the sun-bleached bones of a whale's skeleton lay across a hardened lava field. They left the beach and stepped onto the lava, walking around red-clawed crabs, a resting sea lion, and groups of marine iguanas. The giant skeleton faced the sea, as if, with its last breath, the whale had tried to swim out into the waters that always had sheltered it.

Jerico bent down and unwound a tattered plastic bag that the wind had somehow wrapped around one of the whale's ribs. He pocketed the debris, then looked at her. "We have to start somewhere," he said. "Let's start today."

"With fixing the world?"

"With undoing what we've done."

Tasia moved toward him, careful not to step on the whale's remains. She took his hands in hers and drew him closer to her. "We don't need to be afraid anymore."

"Because of you. You won the war for us."

She shook her head. "No, that's not right. I was just a tiny part of what we did."

"You believed in yourself, in what could happen."

"I believed in love, in hope. I always will."

"And that's why you won."

She leaned toward him, kissing him. And within the wonders of that kiss, she felt as if she were rising up, above herself, above the beach. Though her eyes were closed, the sun seemed to fill up the world with warmth and light and wonder. The universe was safe. And the future was full of so much promise that she wanted to rush toward whatever lay ahead.

"We'll see those beautiful things," she said. "But really, all I want is you."

"And Rex. Don't forget him. He won't want to be left out."

Smiling, she kissed him again. "Let's run," she said, tugging on his hand.

"Where?"

"Everywhere."

They stepped away from the whale, returned to the sand, and then began to run down the beach—moving fast and free. Rex raced after them, biting at their heels, barking as if he wanted every creature on Earth to hear him.

Jerico and Tasia laughed, their feet blurring beneath them, leaving footprints that the waves would soon wash away. Faster they went, scattering a flock of birds, and then leaping up, as if they too might fly.

The world moved about them—wounded, but healing.

Still Tasia ran faster, empowered by their freedom, by the sound of Jerico's voice.

They had won.

And whatever stories were told of them, whatever legends might grow from their deeds, she would always remember this moment—running over the warm sand with the man she loved.

Rushing ahead, into the future, without ever looking up.

The End.

STAIRWAY TO YOUR SOUL

I should be a poet
To write of you.
And speak a thousand languages
To find the perfect words.

I should savor every sunrise
To see what made you.
And listen to the ocean
To remember whispers meant for me.

I should search the world for magic
To best understand you.
And feel the caress of a summer breeze
To rest with you as before.

I should love and wander and soar
To celebrate the wilderness that is you.
And smell each rose and orchid
To let you fill me once again.

Every gift of yourself that you have shared
I must open as if for the first time.
And when I finally rediscover you
I'll be reborn.

I'll be that poet,
That ocean,
That wilderness.

And I'll hold you tight until the end.

A LETTER
TO THE READER

I'd like to take a moment to offer you my profound gratitude. Countless worthy and wonderful novels exist, and I'm honored that you decided to read *The Demon Seekers*. I've thought about this series for many years and hope you enjoyed my story.

Never have I taken readers for granted, and I have always tried to interact with as many of my supporters as possible. If you wish to stay in touch with me, or perhaps to send me a note, please follow me on Instagram or Facebook. You can also reach me through my website at johnshors.com.

If you enjoyed *The Demon Seekers*, I'd be most grateful if you'd help me spread the word about Tasia and her companions. Authors depend on the goodwill of readers, who recommend books, write online reviews, and do so much more. In the past, I've tried to repay such goodwill by supporting children's charities around the world. I'll continue to do so.

I'm unsure what novels, if any, I'll write in the future. But if you enjoyed my storytelling, you might be interested in my earlier books. I've previously published seven novels, most of which are works of historical fiction. My favorites are *Unbound*, *Beneath a Marble Sky*, and *Temple of a Thousand Faces*.

Once again, I can't stress enough how truly grateful I am for your support. I wish you the best of luck as you move forward in life, and hope you enjoy much happiness, success, and peace.

ACKNOWLEDGMENTS

The Demon Seekers trilogy was a massive undertaking for me, written over the course of six years, in the midst of time spent with my family as well as the pursuit of other projects. And while writing this series was a solitary journey for me, I'm grateful for the support of my loved ones and friends. To all of you—thank you a thousand times over.

I was also blessed to receive the feedback of many young readers, who looked at the first book in the series and let me know their thoughts. In no particular order, I'd like to thank Breck Dunbar, Bill Chang, Ludo Green, Kaia Gerber, Melanie Thompson, Emeili Hui Peng Fowler, Will Halverson, Quinn McIntyre, Hayden Miller, Sophie Hanselmayer, Luca Barakat Craine, Leo Barakat Craine, Charlie Shors, Sam Shors, Oliver Shors, Shyamana Shors, and Khelan Shors. And to my children, Sophie and Jack, I'm grateful for you both and couldn't love you any more.

Finally, I'd like to thank readers, librarians, and booksellers for their steadfast support. My very best wishes to you all.

ABOUT THE
AUTHOR

John Shors is the internationally bestselling author of ten novels, which have been translated into nearly thirty languages. In addition to *The Demon Seekers* trilogy, he's written *Beneath a Marble Sky, Beside a Burning Sea, Dragon House, The Wishing Trees, Cross Currents, Temple of a Thousand Faces,* and *Unbound.* He has won multiple awards for his novels.

Boulder, Colorado is home to John and his family. In his free time, he enjoys traveling the world, reading, and fishing.

For more information on John, please visit **johnshors.com** or follow him via social media:

facebook.com/johnshors
instagram.com/johnshors

'THE DEMON SEEKERS' SERIES

Book One
Book Two
Book Three

Now available at bookstores everywhere.

ALSO BY
JOHN SHORS

UNBOUND

John Shors reimagined one of the world's greatest love stories—the romance that inspired the Taj Mahal—in his critically acclaimed, international bestseller *Beneath a Marble Sky*. Now, with *Unbound*, Shors recreates an ancient and celebrated Chinese legend about a pair of young lovers separated by war and the Great Wall.

The year is 1548, and the Chinese Empire faces an imminent Mongol invasion. All that prevents the violent end of a dynasty is the Great Wall. Yet even this famed fortification has weaknesses, and against his will, a talented Chinese craftsman is taken from his home and wife, so that he may labor alongside the wall's defenders.

Fan has been missing for a year when his wife, Meng, decides to do the impossible—to leave everyone and everything she knows in a daunting effort to find him. At a time when many women fear even stepping outside their homes, Meng disguises herself as a man and begins a perilous journey of deliverance.

As two armies gather at the Great Wall, the fates of Fan and Meng collide with a Mongol horseman seeking redemption, a Chinese concubine fighting injustice, and a ruthless general determined to destroy them all.

"*Unbound* is utterly captivating—an epic, historical page-turner with a beating heart. I loved it."
—Jamie Ford, *New York Times* bestselling author of *Hotel on the Corner of Bitter and Sweet*

"An intense, historical page-turner… a legendary tale."
—*The Shanghai Daily*

CPSIA information can be obtained
at www.ICGtesting.com
Printed in the USA
LVHW051505300120
645335LV00004B/665

9 780999 174463